NORTHERN THUNDER

ANDERSON HARP

NORTHERN THUNDER

A WILLIAM PARKER MISSION

ARCHWAY
PUBLISHING

All the characters in this book are fictitious, and any resemblance
to actual persons, living or dead, is purely coincidental. This
novel was first released as "A Northern Thunder", however, the
present edition reflects changes of characters, plot and story.

Archway Publishing books may be ordered
through booksellers or by contacting:

Archway Publishing
1663 Liberty Drive
Bloomington, IN 47403
www.archwaypublishing.com
1 (888) 242-5904

Map of Korea: Thom Hendrik
Author photo: Bob Hancock

ISBN: 978-1-4808-3011-0 (sc)
ISBN: 978-1-4808-3010-3 (e)

Library of Congress Control Number: 2016912444

Printed in United States.

Archway Publishing rev. date: 4/25/2017

To Lucille and Siler...

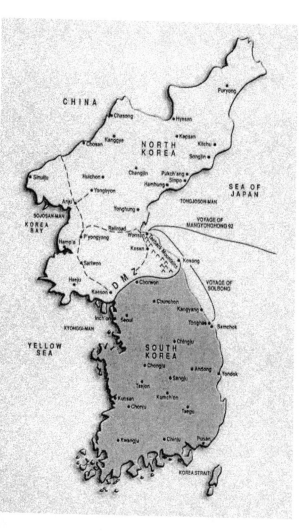

OCTOBER 6, 2011

"Is this seat 8A?"

Dr. Myler Harbinger looked up to see a young Asian-American man standing in the aisle. "Yes, I guess it is," Harbinger said, glancing at the window seat beside him.

"Thank you," said the stranger, who looked like one of Harbinger's graduate students, no more than half the professor's age. "If you'd rather have the window, I don't mind."

Harbinger had no preference. He simply wished to remain undisturbed. "No, I'll stay here. Thank you."

Wrinkled and disheveled, with reading glasses on his gray, bushy head and an unlit pipe in his mouth, Harbinger looked every inch the professor he was. He had hoped the flight from Washington, D.C., to San Francisco would provide him an opportunity to work on his most recent research project. He had treasured the promise of four hours of quiet time in the air, and he hoped his seat neighbor would end the small talk quickly. The muscles in his jaw flexed as he chewed on his favorite pipe, turning his attention back to the small pad he always carried. He had it placed on top of a worn leather satchel on the seat back tray, which was serving as his desk.

The young man took off his leather jacket, wiggled past the table and Harbinger's knees, sat, and began reading a newspaper.

Out of the corner of his eye, Harbinger noticed the newspaper's odd lettering. It was clearly from some other language.

"Excuse me, sir," said a flight attendant, "but you'll need to stow the table for take-off. May I take that briefcase for you?"

"Yes, thank you." Harbinger handed the satchel to her and, as she put it in the overhead bin, the tag hung out of the bin door:

Dr. Myler Harbinger, Ph.D.
121 Briar Street
Berkeley, California

"And may I take your coat?"

The young stranger hesitated briefly, then handed it to her. It would be much later that she remembered the oddity of the jacket. It had no tags in it, as if the owner had cut them out with some specific purpose in mind.

"And, Professor, you do know you cannot light that pipe?"

"Yes" he replied. "Professor? What gave it away?"

"Just a wild guess."

The man next to the professor also knew Dr. Myler Harbinger's occupation, but not from his luggage tag. He knew where Harbinger taught, how he dressed, what he liked and disliked. In fact, for several months, the man had researched every minute detail about the man sitting next to him, including the precise airplane seat assigned him on this flight. A Ph.D. in mathematics and the world's leading mind on the development of GPS—the Global Positioning System Satellite network—Dr. Harbinger stood as the Grace Hopper of his time. Like Hopper, the famed naval captain, genius, and inventor of the COBOL computer system, Myler Harbinger was a decade ahead of all his peers, except, perhaps, one.

"Where do you teach?" the young man asked once the flight attendant had left.

"I'm at the Engineering Department at Berkeley."

"Oh, a very fine school. And, engineering—I thought the computer eliminated our need for mathematics and engineering."

Harbinger kept his eyes on his pad of paper and humphed in response.

"I work in cable television in South Korea," the man continued. "Without the satellite, we couldn't exist."

The comment hit strangely close to Harbinger's work. Suddenly, he felt uncomfortable.

"What brought you to Washington, Doctor? Or do you prefer Professor?"

"A meeting on satellites at NASA."

"Oh, really?" the stranger said as he leaned over, peering at the doctor's notes.

Harbinger, feeling the man's body enter his space, leaned back in his chair. "Excuse me," he said.

"Sorry," said the man, "I did not mean to cause you alarm. I was just curious. I find satellites most interesting. I cannot imagine a world without them. And the military—I would think it could be paralyzed if a satellite failed."

Harbinger did not mention that this secret conference had been, curiously enough, on that very subject. He did not mention the representatives from U.S. Space Command, nor their concern that space debris, whether natural or intended, could destroy a satellite—nor the effect that would have on the military and its aging, costly fleet of satellites.

It became quiet again and, not long after,

the stranger turned away, placed a pillow under his head, and fell asleep.

It was several hours before the flight attendant interrupted Harbinger. The other passenger was just emerging from a sound asleep.

Harbinger glanced at the man's pale white hand. There was a scar covering the top of the right hand. It was a clean, deep scar with a sharp, clear edge—probably a knife wound, as if the man had protected himself from a blow.

He also noticed the ring on his other hand—ostentatious gold – crafted Centuries ago during the Korean Silla Kingdom – and twisted in the shape of a dragon. To him, it looked out of place on the hand of a man who dressed so simply.

"Gentlemen," the stewardess said, "we have about an hour until we reach San Francisco. I apologize for the late meal. Would you care to have the chicken or the steak for dinner?"

"I believe I have a special meal ordered,"

said the professor. "Would you mind checking on that?"

"Certainly." She turned to Harbinger's seatmate. "And you, sir? What would you like?"

"Steak would be fine."

Harbinger's special request was a poor choice for his final meal.

| | | |

As the flight attendant cleared away their two trays, the young stranger struck up another conversation.

"Did you know the United States wastes more food in a week than the Democratic People's Republic of Korea consumes in a year?"

Harbinger had taught long enough at Berkeley to know how to interpret a comment like that. To the rest of the world, the Democratic People's Republic of Korea, or DPRK for short, was known simply as North Korea. South Korean businessmen did not refer to North Korea as the Democratic

People's Republic of Korea. Only someone from across the border of North Korea would refer to it that way.

"I've heard that North Korea has had a difficult time," Harbinger said.

The stranger nodded. "Thirty-eight miles from Seoul, children are dying from malnutrition. They lie there, gasping for breath, a short drive from one of the largest, best-fed cities in the Pacific Rim."

As Harbinger looked for a way to shift or stop the conversation, the pilot announced that the plane had been cleared for approach into San Francisco's International Airport. The professor was thankful for the interruption. This young man was more than a cable television businessman from South Korea, and the more Harbinger heard, the more he wanted the flight to end.

He looked at his watch. His wife had agreed to pick him up at the airport. She was always perfectly on time. The landing could come not soon enough.

Thirty minutes later, as the aircraft taxied

to the gate, Harbinger tried to turn his thoughts to the class he had to teach tomorrow.

The rush of people to the front of the aircraft caused a bottleneck in first class, and Harbinger did not notice his row-mate twisting the gold ring on his finger as he got up from his seat.

"Well, I hope your remaining journey is pleasant," Harbinger said, trying to show some civility. He gestured for the young man to go ahead of him.

"You, too, Doctor." As the man passed Harbinger, he patted the professor lightly on the shoulder.

Harbinger felt a small prick as he joined the crowd surging toward the exit. They seemed to be moving more quickly now; the North Korean was walking far ahead of Harbinger, who suddenly realized that he was holding up the passengers behind him. He tried to step forward but, as he did, pain struck his chest, as if a sledgehammer had knocked the breath out of his body, and he crumpled to the ground, his satchel plopping down beside him.

His fellow passengers found their anger turning to alarm as he fell, but none realized that Myler Harbinger, a world leader in micro-electronic technology, had a highly concentrated dose of sodium nitroprusside surging through his veins. His heart had frozen like an engine suddenly out of oil. The professor had been dead even before his body slumped to the aircraft floor.

Across the nearly deserted country road stood a defunct gas station, a large sign declaring the availability of "Diesel $.59/Gallon" and "Boiled Peanuts." The signs had bleached with time, and the price of the fuel gave some indication of the number of decades that had passed since it had last filled the tanks of its customers, but a small shack on the property still functioned as a store for locals.

"Where the hell is he?" the old man asked, wondering why the driver was taking so long to get directions.

In military parlance, the senior ranking officer was always the "old man." For this "old man," the scorching heat and humidity made everything unbearable—even sitting in the glossy black executive car with the air conditioning at full blast.

The other passenger leaned forward and said, "I don't think he's been to Vienna before." A faint British accent was evident in his words. Black sunglasses hid part of a scar running down his cheek.

They had stopped on the edge of Vienna, a small town in south Georgia not much larger than the one-block town square framed by the red brick courthouse. Locals had come up with a special pronunciation—VEYE-anna. Any comparison to the Austrian city ended with the identical spellings.

"I don't give a damn where he's been or not been before," Admiral Krowl told his companion. "I told the Marine Corps to have their best driver available—at least somebody who knows where to go." The gas station's screen door banged and a young Marine with lance corporal stripes jogged over to the car, hopped in, and shifted into drive.

Krowl leaned forward. "You know where to go now?"

"Yes, sir. Only seven more miles down on the left." The lance corporal's well-creased uniform was beginning to show signs of the heat. The October day felt like one in July. The passenger in the back was no help as well.

Rear Admiral Julius "Jig" Krowl could not stand waiting, whether in a car in rural Georgia or in a Pentagon briefing room. He also hated his nickname, but it had stuck. In his first week at the Naval Academy, "Julius" had been shortened by an old Marine mustanger who'd served in both World War II and Korea. "Julius? Bullshit," the captain had barked. "Henceforth, you will be "Plebe Jig." The Marine was referring to the old phonetic designation for the letter "J."

While he couldn't change his nickname, Krowl, a high-ranking military official for a long, long time, had grown accustomed to getting his way on everything else.

"I can't believe we have to resort to this," he grumbled. "Surely, Langley could give us a better option."

Beside him on the seat lay a thick folder

marked, "Top Secret: CIA." Over its center was a large seal marked "SCI," followed by a bright red warning that fines and imprisonment were the penalty for unauthorized use.

"If Langley had any other option," said the other companion in the vehicle, "we would have used it."

Krowl turned to him. "And if this doesn't work? Who will they go after?" Krowl was angry, not so much about the proposed idea, but that the CIA might rob him of the credit. As soon as he was sure this plan was a winner, Scott would be shoved to the background.

| | | |

James Scott had heard admirals spout off before, and, frankly, couldn't have cared less. A career officer with the Agency, he'd learned a long time ago that the mission was primary. He had met the admiral only the day before, but Scott took pride in his ability to size up people quickly, and he sensed Krowl was a man to keep a close eye on.

When he answered Krowl, his words were

slow and deliberate. "From our discussions in the EC yesterday, you know this is the best choice we have. We bloody well need him, and we need him badly."

The EC, or Executive Center, was little known—even by many military insiders. In the Pentagon, no sanctum was more secret.

During their meeting the day before, even James Scott had been impressed. He'd seen many secret facilities during his years in intelligence, but this one was unique. The EC was the Secretary of Defense's private war room. Soundproofing on all sides prevented any eavesdropping. An eye-scanning device had a limited history of those few it would let in. The assault on that infamous September day had had no impact upon the center. It remained impregnable.

As Scott had entered the steel vault, he had been met by an armed sentry—a Marine armed with a 9-mm Beretta in a shoulder holster—behind a small, green-tinted Plexiglas opening. The lines of his green utility clothing betrayed a bulletproof vest beneath.

He identified himself crisply to the Marine.

"I need to see additional photo verification."

"You have the eye scan."

"Yes, sir . . . but this briefing has the highest classification—Top Secret, Need to Know Only, SCI." No superior would complain if the sentry refused to allow into the top-secret facility someone who lacked all the proper identification. To enter, even the most senior executive at Defense had to comply with all requirements.

Scott pulled out his identification card. The sentry inserted it into a scanner.

"Now, sir, please place your right hand here."

Scott put his hand onto a small black box. A red light flashed as the machine hummed, and he heard a click as the system registered its approval.

"You're clear, sir. You're to go to the conference room, third door on the left. Admiral Krowl is waiting for you."

"Thank you, Marine."

Scott had walked the short distance down the small hallway to another set of steel doors. As he stepped near the front of the third door and his foot touched a thick gray carpet pad, he heard another click.

Above the door was a lit sign in a small metal box: "TS . . . SCI . . . Conference in Session."

A voice came over a wall speaker. "Yes?"

"James Scott, CIA."

The second door clicked.

A short, graying, heavy-set man in an admiral's uniform stood just inside. His thin, round, gold-metal eyeglasses accentuated coal-black eyes and eyebrows.

"Scott, I'm Rear Admiral Julius Krowl, repping the Joint Chiefs. This is General Louis McCain of the Marine Corps and Mark Wolf of DIA." The Defense Intelligence Agency, or DIA, was one of the U.S. military's main providers of intelligence, much of it obtained from spy satellites. DIA was the eavesdropper capable of snooping electronically anywhere in the world. Telephone conversations, whether from land lines, cell phones, or satellite phones, fell within the electronic scope of DIA surveillance, as did e-mails.

McCain, a three-star general, commanded the Marine Forces Reserve, more commonly referred to as MARFORRES. Based in New Orleans, the entire reserve force of the Marine Corps was under his control. Though the Reserves were playing a greater role nowadays in front-line defense, it was unusual for a MARFORRES rep to be at such a meeting. Scott knew, however, why the reserve commander's attendance was appropriate.

The admiral pointed to a high-backed leather executive chair, one of four surrounding a small shiny, fine-grained, reddish-brown mahogany table. Scott sat down, taking in his surroundings—a small room with red striped drapes on three walls, there to further reduce sound and obscure any conversations. Sounds seemed to drop off at the end of each spoken sentence. On the fourth wall hung three screens surrounded by drapes. And above the screens were six clocks, one marked Seoul, another Honolulu, another Washington, another Beijing, and the last two London and Moscow.

"Mr. Scott," said Krowl, "Admiral Williams, Commander of USPACOM, is with us by satellite." USPACOM, short for U.S. Pacific Command, was responsible for all Defense Department matters in the Pacific.

On one of the screens appeared a four-star Navy admiral with graying, close-cropped hair and a well-tanned face. "Hello, gentlemen," said Admiral Williams. Based in Hawaii, he was the lead commander in any crisis that might occur in that part of the world. His was an enviable job. Admirals throughout the Navy fought for the chance to be Commander, USPACOM. With hot spots such as China, North Korea, Pakistan, Vietnam, India, Cambodia, and the Spratly Islands within his purview, Admiral Williams was guaranteed plenty of CNN exposure. Only Central Command provided commanders more media attention. With enormous areas of ocean lying within the Pacific Command, the post always had gone to an admiral.

"Gentlemen," Krowl said curtly, "there are to be no notes. This is Need-to-Know Only." He didn't care about Wolf or Scott, and considered McCain no threat. "Admiral Williams, naturally you're exempted, sir."

Krowl had turned to Scott. "Now, Mr. Scott, what is so urgent that we needed to get together?"

"Admiral, the Yongbyon project has gained new life. After the Taepo Dong 2 failure, they changed their team, acquiring someone who we believe can put it all together for the first time, and he has gone straight to the multi-stage next generation. It will have a range of ten thousand-plus nautical miles and carry a five-hundred-plus load."

"*Shit*," Williams muttered.

"He's also working on a sixth-generation weapon."

Silence hit the room. Everyone knew the potential impact of a soon-to-be operational missile with a range that crossed the Pacific. Virtually every city in the continental United States would be within its reach. Several sixth-generation nuclear weapons could be carried by a five-hundred-kilogram load-capacity missile.

And that was how Scott had found himself here, with Admiral Krowl, in this small town, looking for the one man who could pull off the mission at hand.

As everyone in the courtroom stood, Judge Anderson Roamer, a barrel-chested bull of a man with dark, thick, horn-rimmed glasses, took the bench, sitting well above the floor of the cavernous old courtroom. The courthouse, built with the detailed craftsmanship of the 1930s, now had large, hand-sized strips of paint peeling off the walls and ceilings.

After shuffling some papers, Judge Roamer looked down at the two attorneys.

He pushed his glasses up with a finger, stained brown from years of smoking. "We have heard from the defense. Is the State ready for closing argument?"

Will Parker stood up. "The State is ready, Your Honor."

"Go ahead, Mr. Parker."

"Folks," said Will to the jury, "we just met two days ago, so let me reintroduce myself—I'm William Parker."

As he spoke, a door squeaked open in the rear of the courtroom. Everyone glanced toward the two dark-suited men who entered. The older one sat in the last row of benches—a balding head, heavy, dark eyebrows, and bright gold glasses that framed a pair of dark eyes. The other man, who had a military-style haircut, wore dark sunglasses even inside the courtroom.

Will turned back to the jury. He looked each juror in the eye through thin glasses that framed his own sky-blue eyes and created the impression of a teacher. This, in contrast to his demeanor, which seemed more like that of a neighbor talking over a fence. His blonde-brown hair had a high part, and his tall, athletic frame dominated the jury box. A small scar over his left eye did more to accent his face than to distract. Will had a calm presence, speaking with a voice more of a judge than a prosecutor, more of a general than a sergeant.

"I was born in this town. Except for school, the Marine Corps, and the Gulf, I have stayed in this town. Like each of you, I care for this town and the people who live their lives here." His voice was quiet but sincere. He smiled, and as he did, a small dimple appeared on his cheek.

Will turned to the table across from the jury box and picked up a small, square black object with a short, slender black wire attached. The wire, like an antenna, extended an inch from the object. He slipped it into his pocket, turned back to the jury, and looked directly at one juror.

"This case has been about the illegal transport and offer for sale of an illegal substance—ten kilos of cocaine, to be exact," said Will. "Using recorded conversations, we have proven that this defendant, David Ikins, possessed cocaine when he secretly flew into the Dooley County airport in the early morning hours of July 3rd—on a twin-engine Cessna

401 seen in a coastal airport in Colombia, South America, the day before. And we have shown that the defendant flew the drugs here, to our country, to our home, for the purpose of selling them to Ham Aultman."

Will turned toward a thin man in the seats beyond the trial area. Ham Aultman, dark and ill-shaven, sank into his seat as the courtroom's attention shifted to him. His tie crumpled up the collar of his off-white shirt like a laundry bag pulled too tight. Oversized clothes notwithstanding, Ham had apparently done his best to clean up for court.

"Ham Aultman is a convicted felon . . . a thief . . . a drug dealer. Not someone I especially like, but in this particular instance, he is the state informant who made this case. Before the defendant landed, Aultman had been caught in a drug bust. As soon as he was booked on that charge, Aultman, to gain leniency, bailed on the Ikins scheme and agreed to wear a wire. In reality, he was merely a mule for the ten kilos. He didn't have the financing or the nerve for such a big load, so he squealed on his delivery man—the next one up the ladder. The U.S. Attorney in Macon saved Aultman several decades in prison in return for his cooperation in the much bigger Ikins case before you."

Ikins, with long dark hair tied in a ponytail, glared at Will, who returned the look. The sharp, custom-tailored attorney sitting on Ikins's side stared forward, trying to ignore Will's glare and the jury's attention.

"And," continued Will, "Mr. Writesworth has done an excellent job as defense counsel in showing each of us that Aultman is, in all likelihood, a dislikeable, unbelievable person. But this is not about your believing Ham Aultman or his word under oath."

With that, Will turned back to his table, walked over to the low black box, and flipped a red switch. A clear, audible voice emerged— his own, from a few minutes earlier. "This case has been about the illegal transport and offer for sale of an illegal substance—ten kilos of cocaine, to be exact." Several of the jurors smiled.

Will flipped off the play button. "This case is about the reliability and credibility of modern electronics. If you doubt the reliability or credibility of our recordings, then you need to return your verdict for the defendant. Otherwise, you need to find for the State." Will stopped at the corner of his table and turned back to the jury. "Thank you."

Judge Roamer straightened in his chair, and the jurors shifted their attention to the bench.

"Ladies and gentlemen," said the judge, "I have the responsibility to give you instructions on the law, or as we call it, the charge of the Court. Before doing that, though, I must ask the marshal to gather the evidence, and I will need to talk briefly to the attorneys. Since it's nearing lunch hour, I'm going to call a recess at this time and we'll reconvene at one-thirty. Please do not discuss this case with anyone, or even with each other, until I tell you to do so.

"Marshal, you may take custody of the defendant. We are in recess until one-thirty." Judge Roamer cracked his gavel, and the jury left. He turned to the lawyers. "Gentlemen, I need your proposed instructions of law before lunch. Any questions?"

"No, Your Honor," the two attorneys said in near unison.

"I'll see you back here at one-fifteen." And, with that, Roamer slid his chair back and quickly left the courtroom. The marshal touched the defendant on his shoulder. Ikins stood and walked to the side door.

"Clark," Will said to the young court reporter sitting beside the judge's bench, "I'm going up to my office." Clark Ashby was a tanned, freckled redhead with a petite but well-shaped body—a runner who took pride in her ability to outrun most of her competitors. Some thought she had taken up running with a specific purpose in mind. District Attorney Parker was known for his success in marathons. Looking into Will's eyes, she did not disguise her thoughts.

"If that's an invitation, I'll be happy to join you."

As he smiled, the sly dimple again showed

on his face. "Well, if I ever want to review a trial transcript in detail, I'll do it with only one court reporter."

"I was hoping for more than a transcript . . ."

"I'll tell you what," said Will, brushing back the hair from his forehead, "I'll chill a bottle of champagne and move some of the appellate briefs off my desk." He enjoyed the banter.

"Will . . ." Clark paused. She enjoyed this, too.

He turned at the door. "Yes?"

She laughed but said nothing. She might just come by his office—to see if the champagne was there or the desk had been cleared. He knew she didn't expect either to be true. Perhaps a cold Coke, though.

Will all but hopped up the two flights of stairs to his office. Always proud of keeping in shape, he had just won his second marathon—a much longer distance than the races he won in college. The Marine Corps had instilled in him the pride of accomplishing any challenge he gave himself, and running the 26.2 miles in a marathon had become *the* challenge.

After many years of successfully prosecuting criminal cases, Will still wanted challenges. He had seen the dregs of society—and sent many of them to jail—but others constantly took their place. The process had become monotonous, repetitious. He would see the same criminals sentenced, serve part of their time, then commit the next crime while on release. A constant cycle of catch, try, and release, then catch again. The game had become boring. Will knew the criminal code better than anyone in the state, but he would never find a way to truly win it.

The closest thing he had to a real victory was his reputation for successful convictions. Drug dealers had begun to avoid Vienna. Most would skirt the town and Dooley County altogether just to avoid him. But newcomers still broke the law in Dooley County. The county had U.S. Interstate 75, a direct connector from Florida to the north, so the pipeline continued to flow. There was even a rumor from DEA that one cartel had offered a reward for the man who took out Parker.

Running had become Will's new form of competition. His first marathon, for which he'd trained two years, had pushed him to the edge, the way prosecuting criminals no longer did. He had always achieved a first-class score on his Marine fitness tests, but the marathon tested his ability to endure the pain and challenge of a two-hour-plus race. After ten miles, the salt would hit his eyes; fifteen miles and he would see runners stop, withering in pain. The best marathoners tended to be thin, wiry, small men, but Will, an exception, was larger and more muscular. It was his inner strength, he believed, that often surprised his competitors at the twenty-mile mark, where he passed many of them.

As he passed through the front door of his office, his secretary was standing up.

"What's going on?" Will asked.

Connie Graham, who'd worked for Will for several years now, had seen him threatened by some of the worst criminals in Georgia.

As a district attorney, he had prosecuted and put more than twenty on death row. Will was not easily excited and, after a dozen of these threats, neither was Connie. But her face had a different look now.

"There are two very strange men waiting for you in your office."

"What do you mean by *strange*?"

"Definitely not from Vienna—or Georgia, for that matter. One has a different accent. The heavier one acts like he's doing his best just trying to be nice. He asked for a cup of coffee and then basically ordered me to put two scoops of sugar in it. I thought they were some of your Marine buddies."

"What do they want?"

"They asked to meet with you privately for a minute, so I put them in your office."

"Thanks," said Will. "Send the Ikins jury instructions down to Judge Roamer and don't disturb me unless he calls."

As Will stepped through the door marked "District Attorney—Private," the two men turned around. The older one had been looking at a wall photograph of Will, taken with his ANGLICO unit in Iraq. ANGLICO, short for Air Naval Gunfire Liaison Company, was a small, elite Marine unit assigned the job of calling in instructions for specific naval gunfire targets. Often, Will's team, a small patrol of six Marines, would travel well beyond the front lines, deep into the enemy's territory. Usually, they were dropped there, under cover of darkness, by Marine helicopters, or else they parachuted in from AC-130 aircraft.

"Colonel Parker?"

"Yes." Will immediately knew the men were not here on a criminal matter. In his civilian world, he was rarely, if ever, addressed as Colonel.

"I'm Admiral Krowl and this is Mr. Scott."

As the introduction was being made, the dark, younger man slid past Will, closed the door, and turned the lock. Will's curiosity went up another notch.

"What can I do for you?"

Scott pulled out a brown folder with a striped, bright red cover marked "Top Secret."

Krowl pulled up his chair.

"Before I answer that, Mr. Scott needs to ask you a few questions. This won't take a lot of time, but the matter is quite sensitive. I hope you won't mind."

Will tried to place the name "Krowl." When he went through SEAL training in San Diego, he had heard about a former Navy SEAL Admiral named Krowl who was not well regarded. Will had been surprised to hear SEALs disparage an Admiral and fellow SEAL, which was why the name must have stuck in his mind.

"Forgive me for these simple questions,"

Scott said as he opened up the folder. "You are Colonel William Parker, United States Marine Corps Reserve, Social Security Number 140-44-4802?"

Will noticed Scott's slight British accent. "Yes."

"You're forty-two."

"Yes."

Scott raised his eyebrows. Will knew why: he was one of the youngest colonels in the Marine Reserves.

"Do you have your Common Access Card with you, Colonel?"

Will pulled out his CAC identification card and handed it to Scott.

Scott reached next to his chair and took from the floor a black briefcase, which he opened, revealing a slim, metallic-looking computer inside. Scott opened the computer, pushed a button, typed in a code, and then passed Will's identification card through a slot on the machine. Will had been issued the new identification card—a card with a holographic seal of the United States and, more importantly, an encoded chip that held every essential detail about him as a Marine.

"Colonel, you attended college as an undergraduate at the School of International Service at American University in Washington, D.C.?"

"Yes."

"You speak Spanish and Russian fluently and graduated with honors with a degree in international service?"

"Yes."

"And at the Defense Language School you picked up Mandarin and Arabic."

"Correct." Will knew that this assortment of language skills made him one of less than half a dozen who were on active duty and had the same capability.

"You were raised in Georgia."

"Yes."

"Both parents lost in an airplane crash."

"Yes."

In 1988, for their wedding anniversary, Will's parents had gone to London for a week. The 747 Lockerbie explosion gave Will nightmares for years, and he'd developed the lifelong habit of showing little emotion.

It was interesting, he thought, that the record only showed them as victims of an airplane crash.

"During your freshman year, you roomed at McDowell Hall, a freshman dormitory on campus?

"Yes."

"You lived on the second floor?"

"Yes . . ." Will thought he knew his resumé well, but these seemingly insignificant facts had him puzzled. Who would track this kind of information, and why on earth would it matter?

"You served with the 1st Marine Division, with an initial primary military occupational specialty of 0802—artillery officer?"

"Yes."

"You served as a forward observer with Fox Battery 2/11 ?"

He nodded his head.

"And then attached to 1st Force Recon and then 1st ANGLICO?"

"Yes."

"You served as an Arctic survival instructor at the Advanced Mountain Warfare Training School in Bridgeport, California?"

"Yes."

As to Bridgeport, they were light on their information. Will had been the Marine Corps's expert on cold weather survival and warfare. During the years following Vietnam, this was a rare specialty. Well into the 1980s, the Marine Corps focused on jungle warfare, as did all the services. But one general at 1st Marine Division had recognized that the Marine Corps needed to have expertise in other environments. The Korean War veteran had remembered the hundreds of casualties from the cold of the peninsula and was determined that young Marines would be well-prepared for all types of climates.

"Did you undergo training also at Fort Greeley in Alaska?"

"Yes."

A young captain at the time, Will was chosen to be the Marine expert on cold weather environments because of his reputation as an outdoorsman capable of survival in any circumstance. Pulled out of the 1st Marine Division, he'd been sent, almost alone, to the Arctic survival course at Fort Greeley, Alaska, for several months of deep-winter training.

At Fort Greeley, Will had learned to live off the land in temperatures reaching fifty, sixty, and sometimes seventy degrees below zero. Surviving in ice caves stuffed with pine boughs, he would disappear for days at a time, living off the resources of the land. His training took him deep into the Arctic Circle.

An expert skier, and an experienced mountaineer, Will knew how to get around in a cold, mountain environment.

"At 1st Force you were a platoon commander and at 1st ANGLICO you were a Fire Power Control Team Leader?"

"Only for a brief time."

"Long enough that you were awarded two purple hearts and a Legion of Merit with V."

The last comment touched a nerve, and Will felt his face flush. The original decoration

ANDERSON HARP

had been downgraded after a run-in with a General at a combat operations center.

"Would you agree with the following characterization? Your record reflects a highly resourceful Marine who prefers lone wolf or small-unit type of operations."

"Yes, sir." Will considered the last comment his badge of honor. "So, why are you here?"

"Mr. Scott works for a branch of the U.S. Government. At present, that is all you need to know. As to why we are here, let me ask you one other question." Krowl paused intentionally to create suspense and to gauge the impact on Will. "Do you remember a man named Peter Nampo?"

This was the last name Will ever expected to hear, particularly from a U.S. Navy Admiral. Peter Nampo had had no connection to Will's legal career, or, for that matter, his Marine career. It was also a name he'd have preferred never to hear again.

"I *knew* Peter Nampo." As an American University freshman, Will had been assigned

Nampo as a roommate in McDowell Hall. Peter Nampo was the son of a Japanese executive who had made a fortune in cigarettes. Nampo's father's family was *ch'ongryong*. The *ch'ongryong*, a large and growing people of Japan, were historic descendants of Korea, many of whom kept their original family ties. Many had gone on to great financial success in Japan.

Nampo was there to learn life in America. He was to become an engineer, but the father wanted him to experience a year or more in America and, with American University being in the capital, it seemed best. He was to learn capitalism.

Peter Nampo, however, was no capitalist. For whatever reason, Nampo hated his millionaire father, and he elected to show it by be rebelling in a fairly overt manner, constantly criticizing America and the American way of life.

It didn't take Will long to realize that he and Nampo were like oil and water. Before the freshman year was half done, Nampo had moved out of the room and and then disappeared. The move may have come just in time, too. Will later learned that Nampo, increasingly active in his subversive efforts, had been under FBI investigation and about to be deported.

"Engineering nerd" was another apt description of Nampo. He had spent countless hours working with computers, sometimes well into the early morning hours, and he had a bright scientific mind. He was obsessive and fanatical about his work, and constantly nervous.

"Finally, Colonel," said Krowl, "my most important question by far. In fact, I would not be overstating it to say that your answer to the next question could have an impact on world events. Could you pick Peter Nampo out of a crowd from a distance, say, of three-hundred to five-hundred meters, using a telescopic camera?"

Will thought for a moment, picturing Nampo. Surely, the CIA or some other intelligence agency could find Peter Nampo and, if need be, get closer to him than three-hundred meters. Couldn't they?

Will nodded. "Given the right opportunity . . .yes, I could pick Nampo out of a crowd." He thought of the one characteristic of Peter Nampo that would not have changed after all these years—one subtle quirk you might notice only after living with the man.

Admiral Krowl continued to stare directly into Will's eyes. "Well, then, Colonel, I have a proposal for you . . . a most unusual proposal."

From his four years of active Marine Corps duty and fifteen years with the Reserves, Will knew one thing––Admirals don't come to Marine reservists in rural Georgia and make them proposals of any kind.

The telephone rang before he could respond. "Yes?" Will said into the receiver.

It was Connie. "Boss, the judge is on the line. He wants to talk to you . . . about hunting, I think."

"Tell him I'll need to call him back."

Connie hesitated, obviously shocked that Will would put off Judge Roamer, or, for that matter, any judge, so brusquely.

"Is there a problem?" she whispered over the line.

"Everything's fine. Just hold all my

calls . . . and call Gary Matthews and tell him I need to talk to him about a Court of Claims case this afternoon." For many years prior to becoming a civil attorney, Gary Matthews had been Will's fellow prosecutor. He was someone Will could trust—always.

"What Court of Claims case?"

"Connie."

"Okay, okay. Oh, and Clark is on her cell. She wants to talk to you now."

"Tell Clark I'll get back to her."

He turned back to the Admiral as he hung up the telephone. "Admiral, we will not be disturbed again. About this proposal. . ." He leaned back in his chair and placed both hands into his coat pockets.

"Colonel Parker, if you accept this proposal, there will be many further details given to you at a later date."

"Yes, sir." Despite himself, Will Parker felt the thrum of excitement in his veins. The thrill of a hunt entering in his blood.

"The United States Government needs you to go deep into a very hostile environment and take a photograph of Peter Nampo. He has been cooperating with a certain unnamed enemy in the development of certain dangerous technology. Despite our best efforts, we've not been able to identify him with absolute accuracy. And, particularly in the present environment, we must be able to clearly determine what he looks like."

More things made sense to Will now. Even in the brief months he knew him, Peter Nampo refused to be photographed. At the time, Will thought it an absurdity, but perhaps Nampo knew more about his possible future than Will appreciated.

"Colonel, you are a reservist. Even as an active-duty Marine, you could not be ordered to undertake such a mission. At the very least, the effort will require several months of training and preparation."

Will thought that, even with several *years* of training, this mission's success sounded uncertain. A "very hostile environment?" A mission the Marines and CIA themselves couldn't take on? The U.S. had assets aplenty in both China and Russia. One could buy virtually anything in those countries for the right price.

No, this had to be a rogue nation with limited access and limited ties. Iran? Syria?

"The U.S. Government is willing to train you," Krowl continued, "insert you into the country with a highly capable team, and . . ."

Will noticed a hesitation on Krowl's part.

". . . allow you to claim a reward under the RFJ."

Scott leaned forward, his hand over his jaw, masking his reaction.

"RFJ?" Will asked.

"The State Department's Reward for Justice Program."

"The one that offers rewards for terrorists?"

"Yes. If sent under orders, you could not claim a reward. Under our proposal, you could." The RFJ program had existed for years, but after 9/11, the State Department had enlarged the list and substantially added funding. Several targets on the list had bounties of twenty-five million dollars on their heads.

This mission must be totally off the wall, Will thought.

Scott was more astonished than Will. Money was nothing new to the CIA. More warlords and allies had been bought and sold by the Agency than the public ever needed to know, and while it was clear that this particular man was absolutely needed, Scott was still not sure what Krowl was thinking.

"And?" He spoke the word softly. He knew that a pause and silence could sometimes be a powerful tool in getting others to talk. Krowl took the bait.

"Nampo is one of the targets with a twenty-five-million-dollar reward on his head. He is deemed a grave potential terrorist threat. He is not a disclosed, listed person, but we warrant to you that he is on a private, approved list."

Will shifted in his seat. "You're talking about a mission requiring much preparation. I'd have to resign as district attorney. I'm an elected official, and a leave of absence is not doable," Will said. "Also, if the mission is as secret as you suggest, I may not even be able to return to this town, or this way of life. People would say I might disappear again, at a moment's notice, and leave their case hanging—leave *them* hanging. My credibility would be shot. I won't be able to tell anyone in this town what I'm doing or why. I'm sure of that. Never mind the danger involved."

Krowl sat back, letting his silence have the same effect on Will.

"I take it this mission is of the highest national urgency and that you must have an answer immediately," Will said.

"That's correct. In fact, we must have this mission completed by thirty-one January."

Will nodded. "I'll do this, but I require absolute, total control over how the mission is accomplished. And you will supply me whatever and whomever I need."

Krowl nodded. Apparently, this demand had been expected.

Scott turned to Will as if on cue. "We'll have an aircraft waiting to pick you up at the

Cordele airport next Friday at twenty-three hundred hours." Cordele, another small town, lay less than seven miles down the road and was the only nearby community with an airfield.

Less than an hour before, District Attorney Will Parker had been in the final stages of a major criminal trial. Now, he would be stepping into another world. It didn't matter when they sent the airplane. With a visit by two strangers to his office and his resignation to the governor shortly thereafter, Vienna would have plenty to talk about for years to come. A private jet landing at the local airport at midnight should finish the stories off nicely.

A knock sounded on the office door, and Will opened it to find Connie. "Will," she said, "the jury's back and they're waiting for you."

"Thanks, Connie. Tell the deputy I'll be there in half a minute."

Will turned back to his two guests. "I take it I'll get a full briefing this weekend?"

"And I take it that you have accepted our

offer." Krowl stuck his hand out and Will grabbed it. The grip was like a vice for both men, but ever so subtly, Will's hand consumed Krowl's grip.

"Yes, sir. As they say in law school, we have reached a meeting of the minds, consideration has passed, and we have a contract."

"Yes," Krowl said, "indeed." He didn't look Will in the eyes when he spoke. He looked over Will's shoulder at the other man in the room.

Will turned toward the hallway and bounded down the stairs to the courtroom. At the back door, Judge Roamer was smoking a cigarette, his black robe open and unzipped. He wore a white shirt, blue jeans with an oversized western buckle, and pitch-black alligator boots.

"Judge, you look like you'd rather be on the farm today than trying this case." No matter the response, Will knew he was right.

Roamer was a man Will had great respect for. A linebacker at Georgia on one of the early teams Vince Dooley coached, Andy

Roamer slept under red and black sheets at night—a Georgia bulldog whose loyalty ran deep. He was a man who looked you in the eye and gave you an iron grip of a handshake.

"You know it," he said, "and I understand you had a visit from some DEA agents."

It didn't take the town long to put a spin on this, Will thought. But he actually liked the idea.

"Yes, sir, but please don't tell anyone. The U.S. attorney general wants me to help prosecute a major drug case against a Colombia drug cartel. It probably means I'll have to resign." Will liked the "don't tell anyone" touch. As much as he liked Anderson Roamer, he knew the news would be all over town in less than an hour. The judge would call his wife while his secretary listened through the cracked door. It was the nature of small towns, the opportunity to share gossip a special treat for a resident of a sleepy place like Vienna.

Roamer looked at him for a moment.

"Well, I don't want to lose you, but I can't think of anyone better to do a job like that."

"I told 'em I'd think about it. And I appreciate that comment."

Roamer turned and pushed the half-smoked cigarette into the sand of an old, dented ash can full of half-smoked cigarettes he'd put there during trial breaks. "Well, let's get this case finished." He zipped up the robe and strode into the courtroom as the deputy sheriff jumped up from his seat.

"All rise, the court is now in session," the deputy bellowed.

Will sat down at the prosecutor's table. Probably for the first time in his career, he failed to listen as the judge read the charges against the defendant.

As he sat on the stiff wooden chair, Will thought instead about his dangerous new mission, trying to identify Peter Nampo in a country that afforded little opportunity for U.S. spies to get near enough to take a photograph. And what made Peter Nampo so dangerous?

Will was sure of one thing—the money wasn't important to him. This mission would be a huge personal challenge—one that tested every part of his ability to think and survive.

"I want the test."

I   I   I

As the black car pulled away from the courthouse, Krowl reached for a small black object in the wooden compartment between him and Scott. He dialed a number and pressed a small red button that scrambled the signal. The Leprechaun SINCGARS radio sent the voice over an encrypted, narrow band that jumbled the conversation into digital bits that could only be put back together by another similar SINCGARS band receiver. It would be impossible for anyone to tap into this conversation.

"Chief, this is Admiral Krowl. Patch me into the J-3 secured line."

The chief petty officer, as communications expert, sat in the Admiral's G-V Gulf Stream jet parked at the airfield in Albany, some thirty miles away. "Yes, sir, I'll connect you through now."

Krowl heard two clicks. "Joint Staff, J-3 Vice Director's Office, Captain Kyle speaking."

"Kyle, this is Admiral Krowl. Connect me on a secure net to General Kitcher at U.S. Strategic Command."

"Yes, sir."

After a moment, a deep voice came on the line. Air Force General Michael Kitcher was the commander in chief of the U.S. Strategic Command. He was responsible not only for placing Defense Department satellites into orbit, but also for operating them. By the end of the last decade, the United States had placed more than 490 satellites into space. Kitcher's command responsibilities were growing daily—a Congressional report estimated that in the year 2010, a total of 1,700 commercial satellites would be aloft. More than 8,500 objects were being monitored in space. The intelligence and military satellites were continually at greater risk due to increased traffic. The sky was rapidly becoming filled with a host of satellites—some the public was aware of, and some not.

"Admiral Krowl, what's the word?" said Kitcher.

"General, I have authority to commence Operation Nemesis. Can you have USA82X in place by the December-January time frame?"

Certain U.S. military satellites were coded by the letters "USA" followed by a number. Occasionally, the satellite was given a name like "Dark Cloud."

The satellite USA82X had no such name. Few knew of its existence and fewer, even at JFCC Space Command, knew its purpose. It had been secretly sent into space two years earlier as a piggyback atop a more conventional satellite. They had announced that the Titan rocket was putting another weather satellite into orbit when, in reality, it was setting up two. Once in space, the USA82X had quietly maneuvered to a higher orbit.

"We will easily have it on station during that time frame," Kitcher said, "but final testing has not occurred. U.S. Strategic Command cannot warrant this bird until it has been fully tested, and that will take another year."

"I can assure you that JCS is aware of the limitations of this equipment. However, if we don't move by the December time frame, North Korea's launch capabilities will be beyond our control."

"We will have USA82X on station during your requested time frame." Kitcher clearly did not appreciate the admiral's strong-arming, but the mere mention of North Korea served to remind him of the grave threat involved. A terrorist bomb in Time Square might kill a hundred. A nuclear weapon from North Korea would tilt the world off of its axis.

As he turned off the SINCGARS radio, Krowl looked at Scott, a smile on his face.

"It's all coming together." Krowl lit another cigarette and took a long draw.

"I'm not sure how you're going to get him in," said Scott, "or how you're going to get him out. It was never our plan to do an insertion."

"Scott, you just described your mission. Just get it done."

"Oh, and an RFJ reward for twenty-five million dollars? That was a nice touch. Exactly how is J-3 going to fund that? And how are they going to do it without Congress finding out?"

"Scotty, old boy, they didn't make me an Admiral for nothing. I imagine your boys at the Agency have a few unmarked dollars—if they're ever needed."

As a Navy SEAL, Krowl was known as a man who got his way at all costs. His men in Vietnam called him "Mr. Fame and Pain"—*his* fame derived from *their* pain. His SEAL unit had the highest casualty rate of any similar unit, but Krowl had decided, even then, that priority number one was climbing the promotion ladder. As he moved through his subsequent promotions, Krowl learned how to keep his grading superiors content, often at the price of his subordinates. Soon, the junior officers learned and carried out the fine art of getting transferred so as to avoid working under Krowl. As many knew, an officer transferring in less than thirty days would not have a graded fitness report completed by his superior. It would be a small gap in a career officer's record and one easily overlooked at promotion time. Better to have such a gap than to be crucified by Krowl.

"You just get Parker prepared and I'll take care of the rest," said Krowl. "Do you have your team available?"

"Yes. But a December launch? The clock is ticking. I won't know for some time if he'll even have a chance."

The Admiral waved away his doubts. "You just get your goddamn team together and get him to that valley on time."

KOSAN, NORTH KOREA
ONE WEEK LATER

Several years before the first trucks started to arrive, the people's committee had chosen the valley just south of the village of Kosan, both for its location and secrecy. Kim Il Sung, the dictator and founder of North Korea, and the supreme commander of the People's Armed Forces, personally approved the selection. Kosan lay south of the eastern port city of Wonsan and met all the criteria for the project. Less than thirty miles from the coast, it was in a valley surrounded by the Taebaek Mountains. Security for the underground facility, though near the border with South Korea, could be easily maintained.

The Taebaek Mountains stretched along most of the eastern coast of North and South Korea. Sharp, jagged mountains were cut by the winds and rains of time, and their 12,000-foot peaks jutted up from the coastline, causing deep valleys inland to the west. Dark forests of pines and evergreens covered some of the western hillsides and valleys. By prohibiting any commercial development, the communist regime allowed the region on the North Korea side of the border to become pristine forest with increasing populations of wildlife. Roe deer and bear began returning to the mountains. Even tigers, nearly eliminated during the World War II years of Japanese dominance, were occasionally seen.

The roads to and from Wonsan were free of vehicles, except for the convoys of North Korea military units approaching or leaving the DMZ an hour to the south. Only the infrequent farmer, usually on bicycle, traveled these roads. It was the perfect setting for a top-secret military base—as close as possible to South Korea, Japan, and U.S. forces in the DMZ.

The Kumgang peaks stood out in the Taebaek Mountain ranges. A series of knife-like points, they had inspired visiting emperors from China and Korea for centuries. Older Koreans remembered a time prior to the Korean War when they had commonly traveled to Kumgang to hike the peaks, wander the forests, search for mushrooms, and stop by the waterfalls of the mountain streams and the Pukhamyang River that flowed north to south across the border and down to Seoul. Chumming was, as the Koreans called it, the Diamond Mountain, both sharp-edged and beautiful, and a great irritation to those in the South who had to abandon it to the isolationist communist government in the North.

On and off for centuries, Japanese armies had dominated the Korean peninsula, ruthlessly murdering, raping, and destroying any living thing that showed a hint of resistance. North Korea's hatred of Seoul was only amplified by South Korea's alliances with Japan and the

United States. Russia had aided in the training of young North Korean leaders. The father of the North Korean government and the North's absolute dictator for several decades, Kim Il Sung, had been militarily trained at Moscow's finest academies. And with this training, he had developed his ironclad rule of Stalinistic communism.

Kim Il Sung's gulags, as brutal as Stalin's, held nearly a quarter-million men, women, and children labeled as political criminals. In camps along the Chinese border to the northeast, children lived in the gulags of unimaginable horror.

When Peter Nampo first appeared in the North Korean capital of Pyongyang, Kim Il Sung himself instructed the National Defense Committee to give his project priority. It was rumored that, even on his deathbed, Kim Il Sung instructed his son and successor Kim Jong Il to do everything possible to obtain "the bomb;" this mean that Peter Nampo was regarded as a national treasure to be protected at all costs. But jealousy had intervened.

Other scientists had convinced Pyongyang to not trust the engineer, who had spent time in America. Only the failure of other missile efforts had convinced the government to give Nampo the opportunity he sought.

Nampo appreciated his place in the nation's pecking order. In a country short of fuel and food—in fact, unable to meet virtually all needs of daily life—he received great respect and full support. Here, the last haven of absolute Stalinist communism, his work was seen as helping the grand cause—stopping the spread of imperialism and the influence of the United States.

"Comrade Dr. Nampo, the helicopter has been delayed briefly in Wonsan. It should be here shortly."

A uniformed officer of the North Korean Red Guard addressed four eerily similar and identically dressed men as they stood near a helicopter landing pad in the valley just south of Kosan. He spoke to them as a group, but used the singular when addressing them. Captain Chan Sang, a short, thin man in his late twenties, was very thorough, which Nampo appreciated. Because Sang was a worrier, Nampo knew that any Sang mistake would be one of ignorance or misinformation, not of attitude or effort. Sang had that fear of failure that forced him to overcompensate for being less than bright, and because of his worries, Sang constantly and compulsively checked every detail again and again.

Nampo thought of the fat, lazy students at places like Berkeley and MIT. They relied upon their intellect to justify their decadent lifestyles. They would fail miserably under President Kim Il Sung's ideology of *Juche*— the art of self-reliance. Nampo had gained early respect for Kim Il Sung as a true ideologist, committed to the cause. *Juche*, as the leader saw it, was the path to a people's government of pure communism, a state of self-reliance that depended upon no other, especially the imperialist west. If starvation and hunger were the temporary price of victory, then so be it.

The key word here was "temporary." Kim

Il Sung believed the bomb would bring his nation permanent, long-term relief, ending the starvation that had paralyzed the country for years. It was the great leader's dedication at all costs to the cause that brought Nampo to North Korea, and it was Nampo's plan that brought his genius to the attention of the family of dictators. But in 1994, the omnipotent leader died suddenly, and Nampo, unsure whether his efforts were in jeopardy, had fallen into a weeks-long depression. Finally, when the son called him to the capital of Pyongyang after the last missile failure, Nampo was ecstatic. Like the Supreme Leader, Kim Jong Il realized that the future of the North Korean people rested largely on the shoulders of Dr. Peter Nampo. Nampo had been named "Director," a title that held near-absolute authority.

"Captain, it's coming," shouted one of the guardsmen as a blunt-shaped Soviet-built helicopter approached the valley from the north.

| | | |

As the helicopter passed over the village of Kosan and the small farm plots to the east, the helicopter's chief passenger spotted a small, well-camouflaged landing pad and a group of men standing near a vehicle where the road twisted around it. This vital installation would look quite harmless to a satellite in orbit around the Earth.

Comrade General Won Su of China had earned his stripes in the war to resist U.S. aggression and to aid Korea. He had gained great friendships, but lost many friends. As a young captain at the Chosin Reservoir, Won had fought the best of the U.S. Marines. Surrounding Marine units with overwhelming numbers, his unit and others had caused the imperialists to retreat. But Won also knew the other story—a story the propaganda machine did not mention. The Americans had fought well at Chosin. Against overwhelming odds, the hardened, determined 7th Marine Regiment had battled, inch by inch, to regain an escape route out of the mountains and back to the coast. The 1st Marine Division was a most worthy enemy. Eleven times the number of Chinese died as had Americans that day. Su was old now, barely able to walk but still a respected General and advisor. He had been called from retirement because the Chinese military leadership thought his mind the best to analyze North Korea's latest activity.

The helicopter began its final bank to the landing pad, and the passengers felt the slight rise of the nose as the back wheels lightly touched down. Won looked out to the side of the craft as a group of men, one in uniform and the others in plain khaki work clothes, bent over, protecting their eyes from the rotor blast. The weight of the bird settled down on its wheels, and the aircraft came to a stop.

Won glanced over to his seatmate, Comrade Colonel Tae Nam-Ki of the Democratic People's Republic, serving as his liaison officer for this visit to North Korea. The colonel was most helpful and respectful to Won. Every North Korean of a certain age knew that General Won had fought to preserve North Korea from the imperialist onslaught.

Nam-Ki had been only a child during the war, but he knew Won's history as well as anyone.

North Korea is our greatest challenge, the general thought as the helicopter's rotors slowed to a stop. *How do we channel this enthusiasm and effort to the common good?*

China's long-term strategy had been an unquestioned success. Russia was only a minimal threat. North Korea served as a conduit, supplying Chinese technology to nations such as Syria, Iran, Vietnam, and Pakistan without China losing status or stature with the United States or the world community.

But North Korea teetered on the brink of economic collapse. And, known to few, internal revolution. That was why Comrade General Won had been sent to visit with Dr. Nampo.

Won had observed first-hand the country's starvation and lack of infrastructure, and he thought privately that Kim Il Sung's relentless commitment to Stalinism and *Juche* had caused more harm than good. *How can*

ANDERSON HARP

*these people continue to endure without the
basics needed for human survival?* Outside
Pyongyang, Won had seen the gaunt look
of hunger in the children, eyes bulging
from their sockets, their skin stretched over
the bony outlines of their faces. He had
witnessed adults moving slowly, like dim,
fading lightbulbs. *How could they watch their
children become emaciated and die without
questioning* Juche? *But if, in order to survive,
they opened their gates to South Korea, would
China lose the buffer to imperialism that its
ally, North Korea, provided? Was a buffer
even needed anymore?*

Won's China had changed.

*I imagine the Americans would be troubled,
though,* Won thought, *if Mexico suddenly
became a radical Stalinist nation. Yet the U.S.
seems not to understand our concerns about
North Korea becoming an open capitalist
market. How can North Korea preserve the
communistic state, remain our ally, and still
bring in badly needed capital?* Won had

far more on his mind than merely a visit to another clandestine military installation.

"Comrade General, it is our greatest pleasure to welcome you to the People's Kosan Project." The young captain had managed to open the door to the helicopter and execute a sharp salute at the same time. As General Won returned the salute, the group of men at the edge of the helicopter pad stepped forward. The four men, all dressed in Mao-styled jackets with matching khaki pants and black combat boots, looked almost exactly alike in age, size, and shape.

"And which one of these fine men is the famous Dr. Nampo?"

"Comrade General, whenever we are outside, beneath the sky of the spying imperialist, Dr. Nampo makes no effort to distinguish himself from his group of colleagues." The captain made this unusual comment as if it were common knowledge, and the general took no offense. He shook the hands of each of the four men, unable to discern which one was actually Nampo.

"If you will come this way, General."
Captain Sang pointed to the vehicles below
the helicopter pad and helped the general
down the steps to four vehicles waiting in line
with their drivers. Sang assisted the general
into the first vehicle, a Soviet-made jeep,
and as he settled into the backseat with Tae
Nam-Ki, Won saw the four nearly identical
men climb into the second and third jeeps.
As the vehicles sped away, Won noticed that
the road, though topped with gravel, was
unusually smooth. *The gravel must be for
appearance's sake*, he thought as the vehicles
sped down the valley. *Surely, there must be a
substructure of cement.*

"Captain," he said, "is this road well-built?"

"Yes, sir. Twenty miles of gray cement
topped with gravel," said Captain Sang. "It
can handle all our support vehicles, but looks
like a rural road. We have thermal blankets
that shield the truck engines' discharge and
make them virtually undetectable."

What a curious nation, Won thought.
Highly capable. A dangerous enemy.

Across from the road, beyond a small, green-carpeted rice field, a man hoed a thin, sparse garden, his worn, tired clothing draped over his frail frame. The man was hunched over, his curved back welded into place by years of constant, nagging malnutrition, caused by an emaciating diet of a single daily bowl of rice.

As the lead vehicle rounded a curve along a small mound, Won noticed the road entering a short subterranean tunnel. A tight group of trees shaded another mound above the tunnel, but as the automobile drove down the tunnel ramp, he saw light at the other end where the road climbed back up. The vehicles stopped at the base of the tunnel and, in a quick motion, the captain jumped from the car and opened the door.

"General and Colonel, please come this way quickly."

Helped by Nam-Ki, Won exited the car and, almost as quickly, the convoy of cars continued through the tunnel and back up to the surface.

Ingenious, Won thought as the vehicles pulled away. To the eye of a satellite, the convoy would have passed into a small group of trees and then continued on. The satellite would have been unable to detect the stop. Won chuckled as he thought of the U.S. spy satellite following the vehicles for another ten or so miles until they pulled into a covered barracks somewhere north of the DMZ.

The captain led the group into another tunnel running perpendicular to the drop-off point. As they entered the facility and passed through a large gray blast door, a crowd of soldiers and white-frocked scientists met the party. To his side, Won noticed the four Nampos follow him into the entranceway. One of the four turned toward another vault-sized door and entered a combination on the security pad. The door clicked faintly as it swung open. As Won hobbled through the door, he realized the depth of this missile project, the entranceway leading to an enormous metal-grate balcony, through which he saw three massive subterranean floors.

"General, welcome to my home and to the home of our missile," said the man, who stepped forward and held out his hand. "I am Comrade Peter Nampo."

The knock on the door startled Clark Ashby. It was an early Thursday evening, her roommate had gone home to Atlanta for the weekend, and court had wrapped up several hours earlier than usual. Judge Roamer, uncharacteristically, had told all employees to go home. He usually took great pride in giving the voters no chance to criticize his courtroom for quitting early. Perhaps he was celebrating the trial of the drug dealer last week, which had gone well. The jury had taken less than an hour to reach its verdict of guilty. Whatever the judge's reason, Clark didn't question it.

While driving home, she'd planned out the evening in detail: a long, hot bath, blue jeans, and a series of rented movies. Then came the knock on the door.

Clark crossed over her bedroom in bare feet, pausing briefly at her mirror to comb her hair. With little makeup on, she felt comfortable answering the door, figuring it was a pizza delivery at the wrong apartment. Just to be sure, however, she quickly dabbed some perfume on the nape of her neck. Clark laughed for prepping herself so for a pimply, purple-haired delivery boy.

Clark undid the deadbolt and door chain, and as she swung the door open, her heart stopped.

"Well, of all the people I expected to see tonight . . ."

In her her doorway—tall and handsome in a sharply-fitted black tux—stood Will Parker.

"Miss Clark, as I promised." From behind his back, he pulled two champagne glasses in one hand, and in the other, a chilled bottle of 1954 LaGrande Dame champagne.

"I didn't know you made housecalls."

"Only for you."

Not that it took much from Will Parker, but she was charmed.

"Please come in."

As she turned the lock, it occurred to Clark, *Am I locking the door to keep someone out or someone in?* She turned red at the thought and suppressed a laugh.

"Is it something I said?"

"Not yet."

Will walked over to the table near the television, set the glasses down, and in one quick motion, popped the cork by striking it on the table's edge. He poured champagne into the two glasses and crossed back over to the sofa, where Clark had seated herself. As he sat next to her, she shuddered. His deep blue eyes were piercing, especially at such close range.

Clark noticed the small scar over his left eyebrow and smelled the subtle cologne. He handed her the champagne, lifted her legs, and placed them over his lap.

Then he leaned over and kissed her.

In all the romantic novels she had read, Clark had seen the word "swooned" countless times. Now she knew what it meant.

"I have until midnight," Will said. "At that time, I'm leaving on a jet, and in all likelihood, you may never see me again."

She looked into his eyes, seeking some hint of wry humor but finding none. What could he mean? Rumors had been flying around town. Will Parker was known as a man who let few people in. Clark had, on occasion, been one of those few. Still, Will always had some secret part of him that the town always talked about but no one knew. Many thought it had to do with the loss of his parents long ago.

Clark simply nodded at his remark, then stood and grabbed his hand. "Well, then, come with me," she said.

Clark turned off the bedroom light, leaving only the flicker of the television to illuminate the room. "I think we can accomplish several things in that amount of time."

Will loosened the black tie and flung his coat on the chair near her bed.

"I hope so," he said.

THREE WEEKS EARLIER

The customs officer was nearing the end of his shift when a darkly dressed young man came before him.

"What's the nature of your visit to Boston and the United States, Mr., uh, Chang?" asked the officer.

"I'm in the cable television business in Korea," the man said. "I just finished a conference in Paris, and I'm here to meet the Boston Public Television people for some possible joint ventures." He smiled, using another of the techniques he'd learned in training. At the intelligence school in Moscow, his instructors had always recommended tailoring one's legend to subjects evoking local civic pride.

"Where are you staying, Mr. Chang?"

"I believe they have me at the Marriott at Copley Plaza."

"All right. I hope you enjoy your stay in Boston."

Despite the pleasant farewell, Chang—his real name was Rei—didn't like the way the Customs Officer Jones had looked at him. Despite his misgivings, he used a casual stride to leave the airport. In the arrivals area, he stopped at one of the many airport billboards advertising rental cars. It was important to not go too fast or too slow. Mingle, merge . . . and don't stand out.

After a few moments, he proceeded to the taxi line.

"Where are you going?" asked his cab driver.

"The Marriott at Copley Plaza," said Rei.

As the taxi dodged through the light traffic, he noticed the dome of the Massachusetts

Institute of Technology's main campus across the Charles River.

"Has it been this hot for long?" Rei asked.

"No, sir, but the last several days have been very hot, for Boston . . . very hot, indeed."

The taxi wheeled through Boston traffic for half an hour. It took much less time than Rei had anticipated to make the trip from the airport through the Boston Tunnel, up the Charles River, and into the Copley Plaza area.

"Here's the Marriott," said the driver. "That'll be $12.50."

Rei gave him a twenty. "Keep the rest."

Rei walked into the Marriott and headed directly to the main floor restaurant. He ordered a quick meal—tuna fish on wheat toast with coffee—and ate it in silence. Then he paid the bill, dropped a five-dollar tip on the table, and took the elevator to the fifth floor. He intended to stay at the hotel for the shortest period of time possible.

On the fifth floor, he walked to the end of a hallway and quickly stepped into a stairwell. There, he opened up his bag and pulled out a short-sleeved white shirt. After he changed his clothes, he placed two mechanical pencils in his shirt pocket and removed from the bag a plain pair of black, horn-rimmed glasses with non-prescription lenses. Glasses did more to disguise the memory of a face than anything else—another trick he had learned in Moscow.

Rei disposed of the bag in an air duct and headed down two flights of stairs. On the third floor, he came out of the stairwell and took the elevator down.

As he stepped into the main lobby crowd, Rei noticed the escalator to the second floor exhibit hall. Walking quickly through the hall, he found a desk with two young women near a sign on a tripod. The sign, in bold blue letters, read "MIT ALST Conference."

"Is this the registration desk for the MIT conference on advances in light satellite technology?"

"Yes, sir. Would you like to register?"

"No, thank you," said Rei. "I'm Charles Won with United Press International, and I'm here to cover Dr. Walter's presentation. Do you know what time he's going to speak?"

The young lady stood up when she heard UPI's name mentioned. Whether it was because of the remote chance of getting one's name in the paper or because the reporters were considered lesser celebrities, Rei tended to find easy cooperation in America when posing as a news correspondent.

And it was the perfect dodge. Americans might know their television correspondents, but virtually no one could recognize a newspaper writer.

"He's to speak at one o'clock. Can I help you with anything? We would be happy to get you a seat up front."

"That's all right. Thanks." There would be no need for her favor. Rei planned to be well south of the city by one o'clock.

It was nearing noon when Rei walked across the bridge heading toward the MIT campus. The Charles River was covered with small, single person sailboats and rowing shells. The sails had varying striped colors of blue, red, and yellow on the white field of the sail, and the vessels darted back and forth over the wide river.

One small sailboat turned into the wind, its fluttering sail pausing in the change-over of the tack. The flutter caught Rei's eye. It reminded him of a similar small sailboat on a lake not too far south of Moscow—and of her.

Rei had been assigned to the Soviet intelligence school with three other agent trainees, one of them a woman, from the Democratic People's Republic of Korea's Intelligence Service. Several years later, he learned of her defection to the West. Rei had been incredulous.

In part, he had taken this latest intelligence mission because it would require numerous trips to the United States. At every airport, Rei had glanced through every crowd, at every face. His standing orders were clear. If given the slightest opportunity, whatever the cost, he was to find the female defector and kill her. He hated her, not only for her betrayal, but because it had held him back for years. They all knew how close she was to him. How could they not suspect Rei as well? It took years of working meaningless small jobs to build back their trust. He despised her for that lost time.

Rei crossed over the bridge and dashed across the street to the campus. Second building. Advanced Engineering.

As he approached the stairs, Dr. Lin Walter opened the door.

Dr. Walter was not the typical genius. Well-dressed, young—thirty at most—he had soared over every academic hurdle he had ever faced. Admitted to MIT at the age of fifteen, he'd obtained his Ph.D. in engineering at twenty-two.

"Excuse me," said Rei, stopping Dr. Walter, "but I'm looking for an MIT conference at a hotel near here. Could you tell me where the Marriott is?"

Lin Walter raised his eyebrows, then smiled.

"Not only can I tell you where it is, I can personally take you. I'm going to the Marriott to give a talk at one of the conferences there."

"Oh, thank you. I'm not from here and would greatly appreciate your help."

"Follow me."

Dr. Walter took off like a racehorse, a fit, well-conditioned man on a mission. Together, they crossed over the campus, following the identical trail Rei had taken. Rei knew exactly at what point he needed to strike. As they came to the street that paralleled the Charles River, Rei saw the professor preparing to cut across the traffic instead of walking the thirty meters down to the pedestrian walkway. Out of the corner of his eye, he spotted several bicyclists at the crosswalk and knew this would provide him a small advantage.

When Walter paused for the traffic, Rei moved up quickly to his side, turned the gold ring on his finger, and carefully flipped the small cap.

"Doctor, you're too fast for me. Please go ahead and I'll find it myself."

"Are you sure?"

"Yes, I'm sure."

"See that second tall building? That's the

Marriott. You shouldn't have any trouble at all finding it."

"Thank you."

As Lin Walter shook the stranger's hand, he felt a slight prick and yanked his hand back. The palm, at the base of his ring finger, had a dot of red blood. "Damn."

Rei withdrew as Walter, still in a hurry, turned and darted for a brief gap in the traffic.

A taxi honked and slammed on its brakes as the young professor fell to his knees in the second lane of traffic; despite its driver's best efforts, the vehicle struck Walter with tremendous force, apparently killing him instantly.

Rei turned from the street and walked slowly back toward the campus, leaving behind a crowd of students and citizens to tend to Dr. Walter.

The half-moon illuminated much of the old Army Air Corps facility. In the dull light, shadows from the hangar darkened the line of small Cessnas and an old Piper twin-engines tied down to the tarmac. Clumps of grass grew up through the broken asphalt. With its long curved roof, the rust-brown hangar was shaped like a large Quonset hut, and was pitch black inside its cavernous doors. Above the opening, etched in weathered paint, were the words "Cordele Aviation."

In the shadow of the old hangar, tucked next to its wall, Will and Clark sat, shaded and hidden, in an older, low-to-the-ground Mercedes sports coupe.

Clark knew that prosecuting high-level drug dealers had serious risks, but she didn't fully understand why the U.S. government thought the situation so serious as to fly an airplane to Cordele and pick up its prized passenger in the middle of the night. The events of the last few days only increased her curiosity, but Clark had learned a long time ago not to ask too many questions. She realized the risks didn't matter—not to Will Parker, anyway. She didn't think she loved him yet, but, given time, she very easily could.

"I may not be coming back to Vienna for many months," said Will. He pulled out a brown manila envelope and handed it to her. "This envelope has the keys to my condo and to this car. You can use them both as much as you like. I left you the title and deed, and signed both over to you. If you don't hear from me after six months, they're all yours."

The last comment startled Clark. It didn't sound as if he expected to return at all.

"Are you—"

"Also," he continued, "it's important to keep this in a safe place and tell no one you have it." Will handed her another envelope—a standard, white, letter-sized envelope. As she took it, she felt an object, small and square, inside. "It may amount to nothing, but just keep it safe. My future may depend on that envelope."

Will took in Clark's beauty in the dim moonlight. For years, local lawyers had mooned over her, but Will had always been too busy to pay much attention. She had sensed that, it seemed, and his unintended lack of interest had only intrigued her. Leaving her would be his greatest regret, he knew. And seeing her again his greatest incentive to survive and return to Vienna.

A low jet hum came from outside the car. Will rolled the window down and, almost instantly, the runway lights came on.

"How did that happen?" Clark wondered aloud.

"The field has a special system. When the pilot keys the mike to a certain frequency, it switches the lights on for a while. It's fairly common in rural fields without active towers."

Even with the lights on, Will could barely

make out a long, sleek jet as it turned for its final approach and landing. Will was surprised at how dark the aircraft looked; it seemed to have less navigation lighting than most aircraft. He heard the wheels screech as the plane touched down but he remained amazed by the quiet of the two-engine jet.

Will reached over and turned the Mercedes ignition, but he didn't turn on the lights. A long, black jet taxied up to the hangar entrance and stopped. The jet engines continued to hum as Will recognized the shape of a new, unmarked Gulf Stream V jet.

The spy business must have its perks, Will thought, watching as the aircraft door opened, revealing a figure standing in the doorway. As the aircraft stairs moved to make contact with the ground, it became clear from the man's shape that it was Will's newfound friend, Mr. Scott.

"Clark, be careful."

She leaned into him as he kissed her, long and deep. Then he touched her lips lightly with his fingers and exited the car.

Will followed Scott through the small curved door into the jet, carrying a small bag over one shoulder. Dressed in a starched white shirt, neatly creased khaki slacks, black loafers, and a blue sport coat, he looked like a successful businessman leaving on his annual vacation.

"Colonel, may I take your bag?" A young woman in a white shirt with black and gold-striped epaulets took Will's bag, which bore the well-worn imprint of the "Cordele Health Club."

Will saw on both sides of the center aisle a mahogany-paneled kitchen with gold-plated sinks, faucets, and a small refrigerator door. At the end of this short space, he could see dark wood panels broken only by the opening of a small door. Apparently, one could close off the cockpit and kitchen from the remainder of the aircraft.

Will stepped through the electronics cabin and another door into a large open room with several oversized, tanned leather chairs on both sides of the aisle. It looked as if the private jet of an oil-rich Middle Eastern prince.

"Have a seat, Colonel, so we can get this bloody show on the road."

As he sank down in the deep chair across from Scott, Will heard the front hatch close and felt the turn of the aircraft onto the active runway. A bit of acceleration and, seconds later, the nose of the aircraft tilted sharply upward, pitching into the black sky. Will's head sunk back into the chair, his eyes focused on the front wooden panel that formed the bulkhead between him and the electronics compartment. In the bulkhead wall were three small television screens. The top screen displayed a highly detailed map with the shape of a small airplane just above the word "Cordele." The second television was blank, but the third displayed a muted CNN correspondent.

"Well, Colonel, are you ready for this?" Scott swiveled his chair toward Will. Almost in perfect sync with his comments, the aircraft tilted down to a level position.

"I believe I am."

"What questions do you have?" Scott reached over and closed the door to the forward compartments.

"Here's what I've deduced. Peter Nampo has developed a high degree of computer, electronic, or engineering capability. He is in North Korea, using his talents to help that government, and thus has become a threat to the United States. Somehow, North Korea has hidden or camouflaged him to the point where we can't find or identify him."

"Right on all fronts," Scott affirmed. "Taking this job, handling this mission—flag rank may be in your future."

Will Parker didn't play that game. "Not at all," he said with a smile. Officers like Admiral Krowl played the bureaucratic game, regardless of who became pawns, in their quest for advancement. Despite his experience and record, Will had never applied to the General Selection Board. Many an undistinguished colonel would mail to Marine headquarters elaborate, thick books summarizing their successes, designed to persuade an impartial jury. But the jury wasn't impartial, and verdicts were typically reached weeks before the Selection Board met. Will had heard and believed that the Marine commandant was always consulted, and the Board always knew his preference. The king always had the last word. Will refused to play the game.

No, he hadn't agreed to this mission to gain the opportunity to become a Reserve Corps general.

Scott pursed his lips and nodded, as if to say, to each his own.

"You're responsible for supporting this mission?" Will asked, changing the topic. "You're the operation's sponsor?"

"Yes, I am."

"I want to do the training at Quantico."

"In point of fact, Colonel, your best bet for survival would be to keep this mission under wraps—to stay under wraps yourself—as long as possible. Quantico is open to everyone and has an obscene amount of traffic."

There were certain benefits to being

accessible, and Will wanted them. He was not prepared to put his entire fate in the hands of the CIA.

"I appreciate your concern, Mr. Scott, but I want a familiar training environment."

Like virtually every Marine officer, Will had begun his training at Quantico. He went through several weeks of Officer Candidates School there, and returned for several months of basic officer training. He was familiar with every running trail, every hill, every swamp.

"Also, I assume there will be a cold-weather cycle before making an insert in North Korea during the winter. I want to do that at MCMWTC in Bridgeport, California."

The Marine Corps Mountain Warfare Training Center was a small Marine outpost in the high Sierras near the Nevada and California borders. At one time, it had only a maintenance crew of ten Marines, but it had enlarged over the years into a modern, battalion-sized training center. It remained both remote and unknown, something Scott should approve of.

"I need to be patched into the op center at Langley," Scott said through an intercom. Will heard a door open in the rear of the aircraft, and a short, muscular, blond-haired man appeared through the cabin. Dressed in the same style white shirt and black slacks as the female crewmember, he gave every appearance of being a corporate jet crew member at home at any airport in the world.

Will, however, thought to himself, *This one is probably a senior Air Force enlisted man on attached duty to the CIA. A communications tech sergeant, maybe.*

The airman placed headphones on in the small electronics compartment, after which the telephone on the wall next to Scott rang in a subdued, buzzing sound.

Scott picked up the phone. "We need to switch operations training site A to Quantico," he said. "See if we can get the top floor of the dormitory at the FBI Academy sealed off. And begin planning on operations site B being moved to the Marine base at Bridgeport, California."

Quite accommodating, thought Will. Much more so than he'd anticipated.

"Okay, Colonel, I am quite certain that you have other suggestions for your training regimen. I look forward to hearing them."

"Comrade Doctor, thank you for both the tour and your hospitality." General Won, stepping forward from beside Tae Nam-Ki, grabbed Nampo's hand and wrapped his other arm around the small doctor's shoulders in a bear hug.

Unaccustomed to such physical contact, Nampo pulled away.

Won stayed close as he spoke. "Remember, Comrade Doctor, Sun Tzu's rule: 'To subdue the enemy without fighting is the acme of skill.'"

Nampo understood the message: China would extend its hand to its communist neighbor, but North Korea should never forget Beijing. And whatever Nampo convinced

Pyongyang his system was capable of, North Korea had best not push it too far.

"Your advice and counsel are greatly appreciated, General. Perhaps you will be able to return for our advanced testing."

"Both my government and I look forward to it."

A young aide came up to General Won and Colonel Nam-Ki and clicked his heels in attention, signaling it was time to go. Minutes later, Won and his companion boarded another vehicle in the tunnel, once again invisible to satellite surveillance as they left the installation.

A young North Korean captain approached Nampo from behind and came to stiff attention. Nampo turned, and the captain held out a sealed yellow folder with writing on the outside.

"Comrade Doctor, this just came in from Pyongyang."

"What is it?" Nampo knew the captain was the duty communications officer, and would have read the folder's contents while deciphering it.

"They want you in the capital as soon as possible."

"Transfer by the usual method?"

"Yes, sir."

"And when will the vehicle be dispatched?"

"It has been already. You have approximately twenty minutes."

Nampo scowled. A trip to Pyongyang, especially one with such short notice, would take him away from his work.

"Let me go to my quarters and change. Call Lin Po immediately and have him meet me here in fifteen minutes." Po was one of the assigned doubles. Generally, the trip to the capital was made as inconspicuously as possible. Security would allow Nampo to travel this time with only one double, and Po was a trained security officer capable of handling any situation.

"Yes, sir." The captain turned and hurried off while Nampo double-timed it for his quarters. Per security protocols, if he were not at the tunnel when the vehicle passed through, it would leave him behind. And missing this meeting would not be acceptable.

Nampo went directly to the closet, where his well-worn North Korean sergeant's uniform hung. As he quickly dressed, he barely noticed the woman enter the room and lie on the bed.

"Where are you going?"

"To the capital. They want to see me."

"But tonight?"

He turned and, with the full force of his body, backhanded the woman across the face. She pulled herself into a ball and began to sob.

"We have one purpose here. You know that."

Nampo turned away, buttoning the last button on the tunic. He grabbed a military hat from a table near the door and walked out of the room.

A troop truck had started down the entrance ramp into the tunnel by the time he arrived. At the same moment, a man nearly identical to Nampo emerged from the facility.

At the tail of the truck, a sergeant stood up. "Men, move forward," he told the troops already in the vehicle. "Make room."

Each grabbed his small pack and rifle and slid forward on the truck's wooden bench.

"Make room quickly." He turned to the two men in similar uniforms. "Get up. Do you have your rifles?"

As Nampo climbed up onto the truck, a security guard ran out of the tunnel with two AK-47 rifles.

Nampo grabbed the weapon as he sat down across from his double, Lin Po. However unpleasant these trips were for him, they would appear to others as another small squad-size troop movement made from the countryside to the city.

The truck took nearly an hour to complete its journey to Wonsan. The military dared not use the helicopter landing zone in the valley so as to not attract further attention to the site. Rather, the doctor had to endure the long bumpy journey to the city of Wonsan, where a larger troop-transport helicopter would meet them.

As the truck drove into the suburbs of Wonsan, Nampo smelled the acrid, overwhelming odor of the city's pollution. He had forgotten how sheltered his facility was from daily North Korean life. The truck pulled onto the Wonsan airfield near a large Soviet-made Mi-17 HIP helicopter. Its turbine was winding up so loud the sergeant had to shout out his instructions. Even so, he could barely be heard. Russian helicopters were well known as unstoppable, rugged, and tough, but also uncomfortable and noisy. The HIP, a larger brother of the Mi-8, was a flying tank, described as a 149-mph, medium-lift helicopter.

"Get up. Get hopping. Move it," said the sergeant. He jumped out onto the ground and helped each of the soldiers, including the two guests, to quickly unload. Each raced to the rear of the helicopter.

Nampo entered the loud, humming aircraft and took a seat near the front, where the crew chief signaled him to sit. Po sat next to him. Near the half-open door, Nampo felt the warm blowing air from the blades. The ship rocked as the blades danced it around on the tarmac.

The men filed in after Nampo and alternated their seats from one side to the other. Nampo noticed that each placed the barrel of his weapon down, ensuring that if an absent round were fired, it would go down through the deck and not up toward the jet turbines. With this, he turned his AK-47 to the floor and gestured to Po to do the same.

The helicopter lunged forward in a hopping fashion as the blades bit into the air and finally lifted. Nampo felt the blades shift from lift to forward movement. As the helicopter moved upward, the deck tilted as the aircraft banked in a 360-degree climbing turn out over Wonsan, the small town's port, and the Sea of Japan. Nampo saw the small fishing boats below in Wonsan's harbor and several military boats between them and the open sea.

As they climbed higher, Nampo saw the twisting outline of the coast to the south. Just below Wonsan, a large, odd-shaped object appeared in the waters off the small port of Changjon. Not much more than a pier, Changjon had moored a larger passenger cruise-liner with lights on in the middle of the day, strung like a Christmas tree from the front of the main masts to the rear. It was a strange sight for the North.

Nampo immediately knew what this ship was; a scowl crossed his face. Despite his protests, Pyongyang had allowed a South Korean tour boat to bring to Changjon a limited number of South Korean tourists to visit the Taebaek Mountains. A South Korean mega-conglomerate, Hyundai Corporation, had secretly consummated the deal, paying Pyongyang hundreds of millions in blackmail bounty. Even North Korea's leaders were feeling the shortage of goods and supplies and much enjoyed the infusion of cash.

It was only after many protests that Nampo was able to ensure that the tour groups would stay on the coastline, taking a bus from the pier at Chamgjon directly to the Diamond

Mountains. He did not want anyone to go anywhere near Kosan or his inland valley.

The helicopter banked one final time and leveled off at its altitude. As Nampo smelled the dull kerosene fumes from the jet engines, he turned over his shoulder and looked through the round Plexiglas window to see the sharp points of the Taebaeks lined up in a row, paralleling the coast. He soon spotted his small green valley, angled away from Wonsan and the coast.

The flight to the capital took well over an hour. Pyongyang, the largest city in a nation of twenty-two million, was known as the "hermit city." For more than fifteen hundred years, it had served as the capital of the peninsula of Korea, and for five decades, it was the secret city of Kim Il Sung, the father of the nation. It was rebuilt in his honor, according to his whims, with monies and designs provided by Moscow and Beijing. His son, Kim Jong Il, ruled for decades but now there were rumors that the next in line was being prepared.

At a small military airfield near the edge

of the city, the helicopter landed and taxied to the edge of an open, lit hangar. Inside it, Nampo noticed, was a troop truck similar to the one in Wonsan, and a large, box-shaped black car. The car, another Soviet product, was rarely seen in the countryside, but Nampo was familiar with it from the other trips he had made to the capital. As usual, Security's attention to detail was admirable. Under the protective cover of the hangar, a low-orbit spy satellite would see troops enter a building and a troop truck leave. Only with luck would the observers wait and catch a black car leaving from the other end some time later.

The troops bolted from the side door across a short space of tarmac to the interior of the hangar. Inside the building, Nampo and Po separated from the group and approached the Soviet car. A security officer snapped to attention, opening the rear door. Both Nampo and his look-alike climbed into the back of the vehicle. The broad heavy security officer slid into the front passenger seat.

"We are to go directly to NCDB, Comrade Dr. Nampo."

Nampo was surprised by this news. In previous visits to the capital, Nampo could expect a stay at one of the distinguished visitors' quarters. It was the sole perk from these tiring and boring trips. Although dedicated to the cause, he didn't choose to forego all personal benefits.

"Why the urgency?"

"Comrade Doctor, I was not informed why." The officer paused, wondering whether to say more, having learned the hard way over the years to say less. "I do know this is a special meeting. There are several in attendance." He paused again, fearing he had said too much, and left the sentence hanging in midair.

The silence in the car was disturbing. As they drove into the city, Nampo observed an open but corroding capital. The buildings were in disrepair. With few lights on, he could see the wood around the frames of windows, dark and twisted, the glass broken in many places. This part of the city was dark, with only an occasional flash of light that broke through the curtain-drawn windows. Candles or lanterns flickered in small, cold apartments.

Nampo took pleasure in his thoughts and observations. It's not that he cared about this misery as much as he knew it represented opportunity. He would be the shining light the city lacked—the hero of a nation.

Rain fell on the capital's streets as they headed toward the tall downtown building of the NCDB. The Nuclear and Chemical Defense Bureau was instrumental in Nampo's operation. It controlled funding and had oversight responsibility. This trip, although sudden, afforded a useful opportunity. Nampo was interested in how the other aspects of the operation were advancing.

The chunky Soviet car pulled into the rear of the building under a covered portico. Nampo and Po entered the building through large metal and glass doors pulled open by two stiff guards dressed in brown-buttoned uniforms with red stripes. The red star stood out on their collars and hats.

"I am always unsure which of you is Dr. Nampo," said the elderly Sin Tae-sam, senior vice president of the state, meeting them at the door. One or two military generals might have had greater stature, but he remained one of the most powerful men in all of the Democratic People's Republic of Korea.

"I am Comrade Nampo." Nampo stepped forward to grab the old man's hand, and Lin Po stepped backwards and off to the side. Inside the NCDB building, the ruse would be suspended. Po had done his job. Now he could slip away to a side hallway, try to grab a cigarette, and wait until Nampo went on the move again.

"Doctor, we have many important things to discuss."

"I look forward to it."

"Come with me." He turned and walked down a short stairway, across a wide hall to two dark mahogany doors guarded by two similarly dressed soldiers. The soldiers were backed up by two large, heavy, muscular men, preventing anyone—at risk of death—from passing without permission.

Nampo walked into the long, surprisingly narrow conference room. A wooden table covered with green felt stretched the length of the room. Nampo immediately recognized the remainder of the NCDB committee: three generals, men of power all, and another vice president, Choe Hakson, known as a direct advisor to the dictator.

On Nampo's right were two of the engineers in charge of the nuclear reprocessing facility at Yongbyon. They had the job of ensuring there was sufficient weapons-grade plutonium available for small nuclear warheads, but their tasks lay well down the line, so they looked relaxed.

To their side, Nampo recognized what he called the navigation unit—the intelligence officers assigned that task. In the shadows of the rear, on the left, was another man, not dressed like any of the others. Based on his dark, cosmopolitan look, he appeared to be a

European—someone from Paris or possibly New York. A black leather jacket with black trousers might appear normal in New York, but in this communist city, his dress stood out. Nampo noticed a glimmer of gold as the man's hand moved.

"Dr. Nampo," said Vice-President Sin, "have a seat in this central chair of great importance."

Nampo pulled the large leather chair away from the table and sat down. In the center of the green felt table stood several silver trays with bottles of water and bowls of fruit. Nampo, realizing he had not eaten for most of the day, grabbed an apple. Even for him, the tart, succulent, sweet taste of the apple was a rarity, and he ate with relish.

"So, Dr. Nampo, where are we?"

Nampo put down the apple and quickly set forth an updated timetable; in turn, Sin provided the recently obtained coordinates Nampo had long awaited. At the discussion's end, the elder chairman pulled his chair back.

"We are appreciative of the efforts of

everyone. This project will save our nation and its great cause."

As the men stood and began to depart, Nampo again noticed the dark figure in the back of the room.

"Oh, Dr. Nampo, please stay one moment."

Only the chairman, Nampo, and the man in the shadows remained. The chairman waved his hand in a small signal to the guards—more than an order to close the doors. If the supreme leader himself asked to be admitted, he would not be.

"Dr. Nampo, per our last discussion, we have now retired Professor Harbinger at Berkley, Walter at MIT, and Brooklins at Cal Poly."

Retired, Nampo thought. *Why bother to use such euphemisms here?* Of course, North Korea was a country of euphemisms.

"Did you bring an additional list?" said Sin.

"Yes," said Nampo. "But this list will be. . .fragile." Now even he was using euphemisms. The plan felt too dangerous to discuss out loud, but it was necessary.

The figure in the rear of the room shifted his weight in his chair.

"Who, Doctor?" said Sin.

"Wiretrack at Oxford, Feizer at Chicago, and. . .Boriskof at the Ioffe Physico-Technico Institute in St. Petersburg. And possibly one other at Japan's Riken Institute."

"We will take this into consideration," said Sin.

"Thank you, Comrade," said Nampo.

List acquired, the man in the shadows stood and exited through another door.

"What is a reasonable expectation for the first launch date?" asked Sin.

"Thirty-one December," said Nampo, "but we must be assured of a valid GEO orbit location."

"The target must be specific." Nampo mumbled to himself. Space was a big place and it was not part of his mission to select the right part of the sky. Others were responsible for that.

As he swung open the shutter doors, Tom Pope chuckled at the realization that his closet perfectly matched his life as a senior FBI agent. From right to left, virtually identical Brooks Brothers suits lined up in military row. Below, pairs of spit-polished dress shoes were neatly assembled, facing forward. A set of conservative, blue-striped, burgundy-striped, and dark blue print ties hung to the left.

"What's so funny?" asked his wife Debra.

"Nothing . . . . Just realizing how boring I am. Where are my blue jeans?"

Debra raised her eyebrows. Even on weekends, when he cut the grass at their Arlington, Virginia home, Tom Pope wore khaki trousers with a crease. The blue-jean question could mean only one thing to her.

"I think they're in the back end of my closet," she said.

He stopped his search, closed the doors, and crossed over to her larger closet. There, behind a line of dresses in plastic storage bags, hung the worn and frayed blue jeans—the typical outfit of a hardworking, blue-collar employee.

As he pulled the jeans and shirt off the closet rail, Debra snuck up behind her husband and gave him a hug. He turned and felt her warm, shapely body underneath her pajamas.

"What's this? You realize it's a Monday morning, don't you?"

"Yeah."

He smiled, glancing at the clock and realizing there was not enough time for anything more than a hug. The children would be bouncing into the room any minute now.

"What's going on today?" she asked hesitantly.

He smiled. "Don't worry, it's not undercover."

Debra hadn't known if her marriage would last. When Tom worked undercover in the

FBI's organized-crime section, living with danger every day, she'd asked him to move out—not because she didn't love him deeply, but because she simply couldn't take it when, at nine or ten o'clock at night, he still hadn't come home. Every time he was late or didn't show at all, it scared her to death. She was the mother of two young children, ages six and eight, and the idea of widowhood terrified her.

And she was not allowed to call him at the Bureau. The men and women of the agency quickly identified the wives who called, and knew those agents were destined to limited careers. A nagging wife, combined with the demands of the job, propelled most husbands and wives out of the field and into administration, performing background checks or other monotonous tasks.

Tom knew Debra was not a caller—and loved her all the more for it. Particularly because she didn't call, he would always tell her what was going on—sometimes more than he should. Tom felt he owed her.

"I'm just meeting a source. She called last week and asked to meet. No danger."

She breathed a sigh of relief. "Do you have to go far?"

"No—Alexandria."

"So, supper on time?"

"Believe it or not, I think so." He'd made it a point, years ago, never to answer "yes" to that question. As soon as he did, he was guaranteed to be late.

Tom strapped on his Glock .40 caliber in a shoulder holster, hiding it with his jean jacket, and plopped on a dark blue baseball cap bearing the name "C&C Construction Co." He hadn't shaved that morning. It was all a part of a conscious look.

He walked out the door of his small house before the kids woke up. A neighbor standing by his car stopped and looked twice at the Pope house. For a moment, he must have thought a thief was leaving the scene of a crime, because no one who lived there dressed like that.

"Hey, Mike."

"Oh, hey, Tom."

Tom made a point of waving, knowing his clothes would catch his neighbor's attention. He chuckled again, realizing the outfit he chose to disguise his true occupation stuck out like a sore thumb in his neighborhood.

A short time after parking his white, government-issue Chevrolet at a parking lot near the Arlington subway station and hopping the Metro, Tom stopped into the Starbucks near the town center. As he ordered a cup of coffee, Tom realized his clothing was probably too plain for Alexandria. King Street was jammed with monogrammed, white-shirted young Turks in their khaki pants. The occasional tourist couple walked the street in shorts, overloaded with shopping bags. Several young girls, carrying backpacks and sitting in the coffee shop talking into their coffee cups, glanced at Tom. That was a bad sign. He was trying not to stand out. At a quarter to ten, it was too late to run back and change into the khakis and golf shirt combo his wife called his "grass-cutting clothes."

He had only met the female source twice before, but Tom had quickly come to appreciate her reliability. On the first "meet," she had given him information that shocked the CIA. Very few reliable contacts passed along accurate information from or about North Korea.

She must work in New York, at the DPRK's U.N. representative's office, Tom thought. *But how does she get away? And, more importantly, why?* Tom, one of a very few FBI agents who had a high-level source of information in another government—and the only one within *that* particular government— didn't want to ask too many questions. He didn't know why she had picked him, but it had worked out well—not only was her information valuable, but it had also helped move Tom up several notches in the Bureau hierarchy.

She must have come to me because of the liaison trip to Moscow in '95, he often thought. Tom had been part of a small American team invited to Moscow to establish an anti-terrorist liaison with Russian intelligence. They all thought it ironic that after the Soviets ran out of money in 1989, fewer airplanes were hijacked, fewer bombs went off in London and Northern Ireland, and fewer Americans were killed and injured around the world. Now Russia wanted to work with the U.S. Even Moscow had its terrorists and wanted to join the worldwide effort to share information. Eventually, al Qaeda money replaced Soviet money, and the cycle of terrorism started all over again.

On the liaison trip, Tom had met several hundred people from several embassies in Moscow. It was his only international exposure—at least the only exposure he could think of.

Now, Tom's main concern was protecting his own source. CIA types had made it clear they wanted her name because they wanted to establish a direct relationship with her. If he shared "Joan" with the Agency, he knew her death as an informant was practically guaranteed. There could be only one handler. Period.

Someone even followed him the second time he tried to meet her. Imagine, the CIA following an FBI agent. He'd been steamed about it for months, but it only hardened his resolve to protect his source.

He looked again at his Timex, gulped down his coffee, and headed out the door. The plan was simple. He would stop, greet her, and then join her for a walk down King Street as if they were a couple, casually talking. He'd appear to be a construction worker taking a break. They would never meet for longer than this.

The wind gusted up just as he crossed the final street in front of the bricked city square. As he pulled down his beaten old hat, Tom saw a short woman in a black raincoat cross the street parallel to his path. He stopped, turned to meet her, and gave her a hug.

"Hello, it's good to see you," she said with a smile. Her perfect English disguised her North Korean heritage well.

"You, as well," said Tom. "How's the

family?" He had no idea if she had one, and he didn't want to. She had her reasons for playing informant, but what she was doing was dangerous stuff, and he couldn't risk getting too close.

At least it wasn't money, he thought. Tom respected her in that regard. She never mentioned money. In fact, she never asked for anything. But something had caused her to betray her government—likely, the contrast she'd discovered between life in the U.S. and in her native country. Anyone given the chance to travel outside the DPRK quickly realized that.

And she was bright and savvy—courageous, too. It was because of Tom's respect for her courage that he'd assigned her the FBI identifier "Joan," as in Joan of Arc.

"Everyone's fine. And how's your family?"

"Oh, very good. Cathy and young George are doing great." She knew there was no Cathy or George.

They started walking down King Street toward the river, keeping up the small talk.

Tom stopped on the curve, waiting for traffic to cross, and carefully glanced around. No one stood out. He felt his shoulders loosen slightly with relief.

His relationship with Joan was one of respect, and in a strange way, a friendship.

Never get too close, he reminded himself.

"Less than a month ago," Joan said quietly, "a Dr. Harbinger died of a sudden heart attack on a Delta flight into San Francisco. Within a week after that, a professor at MIT died—struck by a car. He was thirty-five, but died of a heart attack *before* the car hit him."

Joan had connected two seemingly unrelated events. Tom wanted to ask more: who else, when, where, how, and, most importantly, why? But he knew better. She would tell him everything she knew, or at least everything she was willing to say.

At the bottom of King Street, near the river, she stopped, turned, quickly gave him a hug, and left. Before Tom knew it, she had disappeared into a crowd of tourists.

Tom caught the subway back to Arlington

and drove home, where he changed and shaved before going in to FBI headquarters. He felt comfortable back in his blue charcoal-striped suit and black loafers. As he walked out the door wearing his unofficial Bureau uniform, Debra gave him a second kiss goodbye.

"See you for supper," she reminded him.

| | | |

On the third floor, Tom passed through security to the door marked "Anti-Terrorist Unit." Several agents looked up, curious. He had marked the day off for a visit to the dentist, but they all knew better. He wouldn't miss a day of work even if he had a mouthful of toothaches. They all suspected he'd been out to meet his contact.

Tom addressed the room. "I need everything on a Dr. Harbinger in San Francisco, who died of a heart attack on a Delta flight last month. Ditto an MIT professor who was struck by a car a week later. Also fatal."

Everyone in the room stood at attention, waiting for further instructions. This clearly had something to do with Tom's North Korean source.

"Also, I need to talk to Bob Mentor at the Agency as soon as possible."

"Got it," said Tom's assistant. "But you know he always asks me, 'What's it about?'"

"Tell him I talked to Joan."

"I bet he'll be over here before lunch," said the assistant with smile.

Tom nodded, his thoughts elsewhere.

DPRK operatives killing American scientists in the United States. What the hell was going on?

The red seat-belt light blinked again as the Gulf Stream turned in a final bank over Washington, lining up with the main runway into Andrews.

Will glanced at his watch and pushed the indigo illumination button. The cabin was dark. The dial showed ten minutes after one.

"What's the plan, Mr. Scott?" asked Will.

"We go straight to the Pentagon. They're waiting for us."

"Who's 'they?'"

"Believe it or not, I don't know . . . . Of course, Krowl will be there."

"Krowl," not "Admiral," "Admiral Krowl," or something more respectful. Interesting. . . .

The jet landed and quickly taxied to a large, oversized hangar that dwarfed the others nearby. Will knew of this hangar, its sides well lit, layers of concertina wire covering the tops of the fences, airmen patrolling the building with M-16s over their shoulders.

"Air Force One hangar," said Scott.

The Gulf Stream taxied like a racecar past the large hangar, down a line of smaller buildings, and into a hangar at the end of the row. Will noticed a black government executive car parked well within the shadows of the hangar. The government license plate and several antennas would make the automobile stand out elsewhere, but in Washington, it was one of many.

Scott led the way down the stairs and to the black automobile. The driver, a heavy middle-aged man in a plain dark suit, held the rear door open. Both men hopped into the back as the driver took Will's small bag. In the middle of the rear seat were two neatly placed newspapers—a *Washington Post* atop a *USA Today*.

Nice touch.

After a short, quiet ride, Will spied lights illuminating the low profile of the Pentagon.

"Have you been here before, Colonel?"

"Only once," Will answered. He had been there briefly, well before the events of that infamous September.

"We've made arrangements for you to stay at Fort Meyer after the initial briefing."

The small army base, tucked behind Arlington Cemetery, allowed for security but was also close to the Pentagon. Will knew Fort Meyer well because it was a neighbor to the Marines' Henderson Hall. Both Fort Meyer and Henderson Hall topped the natural bluff overlooking the Potomac River basin.

As the vehicle entered a tunnel leading into the bowels of the Pentagon, Will felt a sudden sense of apprehension and excitement.

Scott didn't wait for the driver to open the door, instead swinging it open as soon as the car braked. "Follow me. You can leave your bag in the car."

Will was briefly blinded by the bright lights of the tunnel. He followed Scott through a side tunnel and past a guard, who briefly examined Scott's identification card.

"He's with me," said Scott.

The guard gave Will a clip-on pass that said "Visitor—Escort Required."

The smell, like the faint odor of smoke and well-waxed linoleum, struck chords in Will's memory as he entered. They moved into a corridor and down another stairway, passing several other hallways as they went. The side hallways were silent and dark—only an occasional light. Door after door had tumblers on them, like vaults in a bank. That much had not changed.

Scott set the pace as the two men charged down the hallways and up several flights of stairs, finally ascending a dark, oak-lined stairway with marble steps, which opened into a broad hallway—the "Eisenhower Corridor," according to bold letters printed above. As they sped through, Will passed glass boxes containing photographs and letters of Ike Eisenhower—one as president of the United States, one as president of Columbia

University, and so on. Each hallway box delved into an earlier time in Eisenhower's life. As he passed the last box, Will found photographs of an Army lieutenant with the innocent young eyes of a boy from Kansas.

Another stairway led farther into the depths of the Pentagon. As they headed to the higher floors, they passed oil paintings, models of ships, and portraits of admirals and generals. On the top floor, the offices became simpler, their doors made of black or gray metal. It was in this part of the building that the far less visible work of the Pentagon was conducted.

Finally, Scott stopped in front of a plain gray door marked "Restricted."

To Will's surprise, it did not have a keypad or tumbler. Inside, Will found a narrow corridor lined with a gray, carpet-like material on the walls, ceilings, and floors. As they proceeded down the hallway, Scott remained behind him until they arrived at a small cubicle at the end. Scott then sidestepped Will, punching in a series of numbers and looking down into a microscope-like device. The door opened and, after passing through additional security, an armed guard, and another hallway, they stood in front of a set of steel gray doors with a lit sign above marked "TS . . . SCI . . . Conference in Session." After another click, the door opened to reveal Krowl.

"Well, I see you made it, Colonel." It was too late in the day, or too early, for Krowl's smug, irritating voice.

"Yes, sir."

"Scott, you know Mark Wolf of the DIA?"

"Yes." Scott and a nondescript, middle-aged man exchanged handshakes.

"Let's begin." Krowl pointed to four chairs—tall, sleek, executive-style—around a small table facing a wall with a screen. The clocks above the screen ticked away.

"Colonel Parker, earlier this week, you asked what this was all about," said Krowl. "Mr. Wolf, let's start with you."

"Thank you, Admiral." Wolf swung his chair around and pulled a computer keyboard out from below the lip of the desk. A small slim computer screen, built into the desk surface, popped up. As he typed into the computer, he said, "Gentlemen, this brief is Top Secret—Need to Know Only." The words appeared on the screen above an FBI warning about severe penalties for violations.

"We know Peter Nampo is one of the world's leading scientists on nano-engineering and nuclear engineering," said Wolf. "Since obtaining a Ph.D. in engineering from Russia's Ioffe Physico-Technico Institute, Nampo has been intent on leading North Korea in its development of a multi-stage rocket, its nuclear weapons program and, we believe, its satellite interdiction program. He's on the world's cutting edge of micro-engineering in electronics. He's effectively their Werner Von Braun."

God, he's come a long way.

A photo on the monitor showed a pencil-thin rocket during a launch.

"Each of the developed rockets has extended the range of North Korea's program, but the country always appeared years away from intercontinental missiles."

"Until now," Krowl said.

"Yes, sir. But payload capacity was also a problem. While our rockets might carry ten thousand pounds into space, theirs could only carry a few hundred pounds or so."

"And not into the higher orbits," Krowl interjected.

"We believe they are now nearing the completion of a multi-stage rocket that can reach any orbit."

A drawing of a larger, thicker rocket appeared. It was still shorter and thinner than U.S. rockets, but clearly multi-staged.

"Although cargo restrictions will still probably put the payload at 300-500 pounds at most, this one will have a range of up to 13,000 kilometers and be able to reach any orbit."

"And that makes Dr. Nampo a very important man," Scott said from the backside of the table.

"So with Nampo," Will said, "they can put up small satellites? Even miniature weapons?"

"They hope to, sir."

"And you wish to do what?"

Krowl leaned forward. "Colonel, in today's world, if we can identify what a nation is doing, then prove it on the international stage, we can build a coalition that will slow, if not stop, a program like this one. But in this instance, we must first prove unequivocally that Peter Nampo is the head of the program." With that comment, a satellite photograph of a small valley appeared on the screen. Will immediately realized this was not simply a spy satellite photo, but rather a live video feed. As Wolf continued to tap computer keys, the video zoomed in on the valley, then a road, and then a square shape near the hills.

The deep emerald green of the valley and its square-shaped rice paddies made for a striking tableau. The black peaks surrounding it on both sides gave the valley a sense of being sheltered.

"This square on the side of the valley is

a helicopter pad," said Wolf. "Several weeks ago, we were able to observe something most interesting."

The screen's image changed again to a videotape of the same valley. Out of the bottom right-hand corner, Will noticed some movement, just as the focus changed onto and enlarged the object. A Soviet-built helicopter.

The video followed the helicopter as it passed low over the valley and then turned to land in the loading zone. The camera focus switched to a small group of men and two vehicles, then zoomed in to where Will could see a man in a general's uniform, along with another man, exit the helicopter and greet the group. They all departed in two vehicles.

"We have gathered a couple of things from this video. First, the VIP who flew in on the helicopter is a General Won from China. Second, one of those men on the ground is *believed* to be Peter Nampo."

"What's he doing there in the valley?" asked Will.

"Not in the valley, exactly," said Wolf.

"The vehicles left the pad, drove another thirty kilometers, and then pulled into a covered hangar near a DMZ base."

"And?" asked Will.

"No significant bases, sights, or anything are within that thirty-kilometer stretch. Why drive it? You have a helicopter and another helipad there. Why not use them?"

"Couldn't they simply be concerned about having VIP helo ops too close to the South Korean border?" Scott asked.

"Perhaps, but that's not their typical MO."

Will found it interesting that Wolf used a criminal term. Another reminder of how far he'd come from *modus operandi* and his criminal trials of a week ago.

"So, question one is where Nampo and the Chinese general went," said Will. "Question two is why."

"Actually," said Krowl, "our first priority is to absolutely confirm that one of those people *is* Dr. Peter Nampo. Your job is to do precisely that."

In a low voice, Scott said, "Let me explain

the stakes here. If this missile is able to deliver nuclear weapons—no matter how small—into GEO orbit, it can disrupt and destroy major satellite systems—GPSs, communication systems, intelligence systems, you name it. According to some estimates, we are more than a hundred-billion dollars behind in updating our military equipment—tanks, jets, trucks, and so on. Most folks on the Hill, and quite a few in this building, believe we'll never catch up. They say the only thing that bridges the gap is our satellite-intelligence superiority. If another country didn't care about losing its own satellites in exchange for destroying ours . . ."

Krowl jumped in. "Our military and our society would be harmed almost as extensively as if we were the target of all-out nuclear war. Virtually every system we use in daily life depends in some way on a satellite."

"So what's our plan?" Will said.

Wolf flashed another image on the screen. "Simply put, sir, using a boat south of Wonsan, we insert you with a team of highly trained

Navy SEALs. You get in, confirm which one is Nampo, and take his photo with a digital surveillance camera. The photo is fed into a small, high-speed, hardened computer, then sent by AN/PSC-10 tactical satellite communications radio to one of our birds over the western Pacific. It's then transferred to a room like this and studied. If it passes muster, you'll be given the green light to get out of there and come home."

It sounded simple enough. But Will knew that "simple" and "military" in the same sentence constituted an oxymoron—two words that, in truth, should never be put together.

"The problem, sir," continued Wolf, "is that we can't risk having a U.S. Navy SEAL team discovered in North Korea."

"Mr. Scott?" prompted Krowl.

"We'll train each of the team members in both Russian and Korean," said Scott, "making the team appear, from dress, outfit, weaponry, and every other detail, to be Soviet Spetsnaz. If caught, you'll appear to be part of a highly trained, big-brother Soviet plot to keep track of its little friend's efforts to play in the big leagues."

Spetsnaz, the Soviet's elite insertion force, *might* conduct a mission like this, but it wasn't clear why. Will voiced the question.

"At the same time, we're going to have our people in Moscow leak a low-level story that the Russians are increasingly concerned about rogue nations' efforts to steal micro-electronics technology from the Ioffe Physico-Technico Institute in St. Petersburg."

Will nodded at the cover story, thinking, if the SEALs and he were captured in North Korea, the story wouldn't make much difference to them. They'd likely be dead.

"We'll change everything––your fingerprints, your teeth, et cetera––through dental work and other surgery, and everything will conform to Russian method and style."

Will appreciate the attention to detail but, again, he didn't like his chances of survival, even with the cosmetic transformation.

"Which Navy SEAL team and boat are we considering using, exactly?" Krowl asked.

"One of the Pearl Harbor-based SEAL teams and a Los Angeles-class submarine."

"Let me make a suggestion," Will told Scott, leaning back in his chair, angling it to face all of them directly. He knew these next comments would not make him a friend in the room. "Let's use a three-man recon team from Mobile."

"A reserve unit?" said Scott.

"Yes. More specifically, Gunnery Sergeant Kevin Moncrief, Staff Sergeant Enrico Hernandez, and Staff Sergeant Shane Stidham. I've worked with them all before."

"I don't know. . . ." said Krowl.

"Also, Admiral, I want to use an ASDS on SSGN728."

"A boomer to deliver a SEAL team?" asked Krowl.

Wolf, reeling from all the naval jargon, said, "Excuse me, gentlemen, but what are we talking about?"

Scott, turning to Wolf, said, "He's

suggesting using an Advanced SEAL Delivery System—a mini-sub attached to a Trident submarine. We've got a Trident program that allows some of our fleet to deliver teams and troops into light-intensity conflicts."

"Also, I want the gold crew of the *Florida*." Will was effectively saying he wanted to use his own people.

"I'm sorry, Colonel," said Krowl, "but that's a no-go. For all I know, 728 may be in the Atlantic, and the gold crew's schedule may not work at all."

Each Trident submarine has two identical crews—one tagged "blue" and one tagged "gold." The switch-off enabled the trillion-dollar boat to remain almost perpetually at sea.

This was the inevitable impasse that Will had been anticipating for several days—the demand to use his own team. He paused for a moment, then looked right at Krowl. "Thanks, sir, it's been interesting." He stood up, pushed his chair under the desk, and headed without hesitation for the door. He'd reached the sentry's station before Krowl reacted.

"Goddammit, go get him."

Scott reached Will as the door swung open.

"Marine, the gentleman will be returning to the meeting," Scott said with a subdued smile.

Will had played the hand and he won the first test with Krowl. He didn't create any additional drama; he simply walked back to the briefing room and sat in his chair.

"The Spetsnaz plan's fine," he said. "My recon team can dress and arm themselves as Spetsnaz, but I only want them to get me to the shoreline. Any travel on land, I'll do myself."

Will wanted his recon team as an insurance policy. With a briefer role, they were less likely to be deemed expendable. Also, he had another thought in mind.

"Okay, JCS will get SSGN728," grumbled Krowl.

"Yes, sir." Scott spoke more to affirm the decision than to make it happen. Krowl had all the power here.

"And we'll get one of the ASDSs at Pearl. What's next?" said Krowl.

Scott broke in, "Sir, we have a team ready for training at Quantico as we speak. Ten weeks there and then six weeks in mountain- and cold-weather training at Bridgeport, California. The first two weeks will be medical. Change dental work to be consistent with typical Moscow suburb work. Alter fingerprints. Then, a general fitness program with intel briefs and language training daily. Oh, and also Lasik surgery to correct any vision problems. No glasses where you're going," he told Will.

"Make it faster." Krowl decided he would dictate his own terms. "Much faster."

"We'll try." Scott looked at Will for agreement.

"Yes," said Will. Scott's thoroughness was impressive.

"Good hunting, Colonel." Krowl smiled as if he had gotten the last word in.

Will squeezed Krowl's hand and, as in Georgia, sensed that all was not right. "Until this is over," he said, "just call me Mr. Parker."

The memory of prior days hung in his mind as Rei, standing on the bridge, looked out over the lake. Small sailboats crisscrossed the green and blue water, and a cool breeze chilled his face.

Though it was a summer day in Moscow, Rei felt chilled. He pulled his collar up over his neck and glanced at his watch. The Seiko once stood out during trips to Moscow—he recalled glances, particularly in the subways—but Russia was changing. Many younger Russians had Seikos. Capitalism was creeping in.

The train to St. Petersburg would arrive around seven o'clock in the morning. His target, a professor at the Ioffe Physico-Technico Institute in St. Petersburg, was scheduled to give a lecture at the old Leningrad Polytechnic Institute's Laser Technology Center at 1 p.m. He would take the metro system from the Moscow station to the university campus and, later, a taxi to Pulkovo-2, the international airport, for his Aeroflot flight to Paris.

It was a simple plan, dependent on speed. Speed in leaving the country was always the best defense.

Isn't it ironic? I return to Russia, which trained me, to kill one of its preeminent scientists.

From the moment he had stepped out of the taxi to stop this time at a spot overlooking the lake, Rei had felt uncomfortable. *Never retrace old steps. Never walk the same path.* He remembered the old guidelines, yet here he was, violating each of them.

Perhaps I should move on.

He had three new targets, each a leader in his field. The one in Russia would be the most difficult, primarily because of the lack of reliable transportation. Russian trains were chronically late. Russian airplanes sometimes didn't fly. Russian taxis were hard to find.

My best hope is that the police are just as unreliable.

Perhaps, after this final list, he would ask his superiors for the opportunity to attend the people's military school. As he twisted the ring on his finger, he laughed, thinking how, in some future ceremony, he would give a new agent the ring. *Or*, he thought, *maybe I'll retire it.*

A taxi, its engine running, waited near the bridge. In perfect Russian, Rei barked his destination at the driver.

The train ride was typical for Russia. Always, the cars were either too hot or too cold. In this one, the stark smell of burnt cabbage filled the compartment. Where it came from, he had no idea, but the fat peasant woman and her elderly husband carrying a load in oversized plastic bags seemed the most likely suspects.

As the train pulled into the north St. Petersburg station, Rei grabbed his small, torn bag from the shelf above his seat. During a short visit to Moscow's traders market, he had bought it and some clothes—all of which had enabled him to blend in.

Rei walked from the train directly to a small coffee booth.

"A coffee," he quietly ordered in Russian. He drank the coffee slowly as he walked through a side exit onto the crowded street. Rei cut across two streets and down a small one before walking four blocks or so to a small grocery. The shelves were empty except for a few sparsely-placed canned goods. The bread shelves were full, and though he wasn't there for bread, he bought two loaves and placed them in the plastic bag he was carrying. At the right moment, he stopped and turned toward the store window.

Rei knew KGB training firsthand, and thus knew that KGB surveillance would have to keep him under a constant eye without entering the store. He looked across the street and saw no one. *So far, so good.*

He also bought a small pint of the cheapest

vodka. He crossed the street to the public toilet where, in a foul smelling stall, he took a large gulp of the vodka, swilled it around in his mouth, spit it out, and spilled a little on his brown, thread-thinned cloth coat. To anyone nearby, he'd smell like an authentic country Russian.

The metro took him to the edge of the St. Petersburg Technical University campus. Rei had studied the maps carefully. He was not comfortable with St. Petersburg, although, perhaps because he and Mi—another North Korean trainee at Moscow's KGB intelligence school—had taken a holiday here once. Rei was the son of an ironworker from Pyongyang. His father had helped build the new Pyongyang and, as a skilled worker in the big city, always had food. Mi, also from Pyongyang, had been less fortunate: the daughter of a Russian engineer married to a Pyongyang schoolteacher. They had been so far from home back then. They didn't see much of Moscow, living in a KGB flat near the train station. It had merely provided a brief break from training.

This summer day, Rei did not dare enter the Laser Technology Centre. He waited across the street at a metro entrance until he saw Imode Boriskof leave the Centre shortly after three in the afternoon.

Dr. Boriskof and two young associates headed across the street toward the same metro station. Rei would not risk a confrontation, but he had already formulated his plan as the three crossed. *I've got at least three hours before the flight to Paris.*

He pulled in behind the trio as they entered the metro. Rei guessed that the two students would eventually peel away from the professor as they headed north and he home.

As they all entered the subway car, Rei lowered his bags to the floor and reached into his pants pocket. There, in a white cloth, he had the gold ring—he'd been careful not to wear it on the train or even in Moscow. He felt the chill of its metal as he slipped it on his finger.

Rei picked up the bags and moved closer to the three and their conversation.

"We still have the problem with the progression." Boriskof's younger aide appeared to be making a point, although the doctor looked distracted.

"I have some ideas on that." The other aide seemed more experienced.

"Let me have them . . . Monday."

"Yes, sir."

As the subway car jolted through a turn, Rei was nearly on top of Boriskof. The old doctor's frayed collar was crumpled up in his brown, pinstriped coat. His black, paisley tie was tied in an oversized knot. Heeding his suspicions, Rei looked down to see the doctor's arthritic hands. He imagined the difficulties the professor must have had every morning tying that knot.

"Why don't you both come home with me for supper tonight?" said Boriskof.

Rei's heart froze.

"Thank you, Doctor. We would be most pleased," the older of the two associates spoke.

Rei weighed his options—wait or go? When the train came to a stop at the next station, virtually everyone except he and the scientists left the train.

Damn, damn, damn.

"Next stop, the Moscow station," the metro clerk yelled as he headed through the car. Boriskof looked at Rei and smiled, as if acknowledging the stupidity of a clerk yelling at them from only a few feet away.

Rei smiled back.

The train lurched to a stop, and a flood of people poured into the car. Rei quickly stepped to one side of Boriskof, placing himself between him and the door. The two younger men were on the other side.

Rei knew he would have but one very brief opportunity. If he stayed in St. Petersburg to await another chance, the risk that Boriskof's comrades would recognize him would be substantial.

As he neared Boriskof, pushed along by the influx of subway travelers, Rei detected the slight scent of vodka, and decided the good doctor was, indeed, a typical Russian. *It will make the drug work even faster.* At the same time, the doctor appeared to detect Rei's odor—a fellow vodka fan.

"Next stop." The young assistant and Boriskof braced themselves with the handles above their heads.

Swiftly, Rei flipped the ring over and grabbed the same handle. The doctor's hand jerked as the needle brushed his skin. He looked directly into Rei's eyes and reached up with his other hand to grab Rei's coat.

"He appears ill," Rei yelled to the associates. They both turned and grabbed the slumping professor, keeping him from falling to the floor. Others, on the outside, pressed in.

The car jolted to a halt and the doors to Rei's side slid open. Rei handed the professor's limp arm to one of the associates and stepped back.

"Someone help this poor man!" Rei yelled.

"Doctor Boriskof!" his older assistant screamed as he propped the old man up.

"I think it's his heart," Rei said, reminding himself not to leave the car too quickly.

The other, younger associate grabbed the emergency cord, jolting the train to a stop while still in the station.

"Good God, please get help!"

"I'll go." Rei left the car at a slow pace, then ran up a flight of stairs. At the top of the stairs, he saw an attendant, a gray-haired, fat-bellied man in a subway attendant uniform.

"A man just had a heart attack."

"Yes? Where?"

"Down on the platform."

Just then, a much younger man grabbed Rei from behind, a big hand on his shoulder. Rei turned.

"Sir, I'm with the police. What's the problem?"

Rei stiffened. "A man had a heart attack on Platform 1A."

"Yes, show me."

Rei ran down the stairs, dragging the officer behind and feigning concern. "There they are," he said.

The two associates had pulled Boriskof out of the car. Leaning his heavy body against a support beam on the platform, they pulled his shirt open, his white-haired chest showing. Then, one associate gently laid the body down as the other pushed down on his chest in a futile effort at CPR.

The officer took in the scene, pulled out a whistle, and began blowing it.

"This is Doctor Boriskof of the University," said one of the assistants.

"Yes, we are getting help," said the officer.

"He is a man of great importance."

"Yes," again he repeated, "and we are getting him help."

"Keep trying," Rei urged. As he did, the old man's eyes opened and he clutched at Rei's pant leg.

"You," the professor gasped, his blue eyes looking deep into Rei's.

"You," he gasped again, drool rolling down to his cheek and onto the collar of his frayed white shirt.

"Yes, I know you need help," Rei said.

"No. . .you." The dying man's grip held Rei's pants, as if it were the only way to hold onto life.

Rei knelt and put a hand on the professor's shoulder. "Take it easy. Help's on the way."

The professor gasped his final breath and went limp, his gray eyes, tinted with a white circle of cataracts, staring directly at Rei. Rei stood and stepped backward. Just then, as if orchestrated for his benefit, two white-jacketed paramedics brushed him aside and surrounded the old man.

Rei stepped away, subtly slipping the gold ring from his finger. He covered it with cloth inside his pocket. He could feel his heart thumping, a cold sweat on his forehead.

"I'll need to talk to everyone," the officer said, looking at him. "It's a matter of procedure."

The red brick building and its long, freshly painted gray porch reminded Will of a country club in his native South. At Fort Meyer, the VIP apartment of the bachelor officer's club was on the top floor of the three stories. As Will came back from his run, he loped up the stairs. The brass railing on the stairway, polished to a golden sheen, sparkled in the dawn light.

"How are you, sir?" A tall young black man stood up, stiff from leaning next to Will's door. He wore a plain black suit, and with his starched white shirt and dark tie appeared more in place at a funeral home. Yet the sharp, close haircut left little doubt about his occupation. Will noticed the bright Corfam shoes, shining like glass.

"What's up?"

"I'm Sergeant Carlson. I'm your assigned driver, sir."

"Okay, what's the plan, Sergeant Carlson?"

"Anytime you're ready, sir, I'm to drive you to Quantico."

"Good, give me ten minutes."

"Yes, sir." The sergeant leaned back against the hallway wall. As Will passed to open his door, he noticed the bulge and black butt of a Beretta 9mm under the lapel of the sergeant's suit jacket.

The door swung open too easily and banged against a dark, cherry wood desk to its side. The brass lamp with its green shade rattled as the door hit the desk. Reaching over to turn on the lamp, Will noticed the sergeant glancing over his shoulder into the living room of his quarters, enormous enough for two separate couches and a sitting area. Rich green and blue Persian rugs squared off the sitting area and another small dining table. Above the glass hung two oversized mahogany doors, inlaid with glass and brass knobs, and white lace curtains halfway parted, revealing a bedroom of similar elegance.

"Come on in, Sergeant," said Will.

"I'm fine, sir."

"No, come on in."

The sergeant sat on the first couch, on the edge of the seat, barely comfortable in the surroundings. He glanced over to the bedroom.

"Don't sleep much, sir?" The bed was clearly undisturbed.

"Got out of the habit years ago." For Will, getting out of the habit had begun with nightmares about the crash of his parents' Pan Am flight. Over time, sleep became a habit of an hour or two in a chair or on the couch.

"How about an orange juice?" Will said.

"Sir?"

"Or grapefruit or grape. You name it." Will walked behind the bar and flipped the light switch to reveal crystal glasses on several shelves in front of a mirrored backlight.

"Yes, sir, orange juice."

Will reached below the bar, opened a

mini-refrigerator full of canned drinks and little alcohol bottles, and tossed an OJ across the room to the sergeant before opening one up for himself.

"What branch?"

"Army, sir. Ranger."

"My grandfather was a Ranger. He was at Normandy." Will paused. "Let me get a quick shower and we'll get out of here."

"Sir, I'll get the car and bring it around to the side."

"The side by the general's quarters?"

"Yes, sir."

The VIP quarters were tucked away between tennis courts, several barracks, and a row of general's quarters that occupied a bluff looking out over Arlington Cemetery and the Washington basin. The Army's chief of staff occupied one of these mansions; when Will had jogged past the flag quarters before dawn, he'd noticed through the windows a white-jacketed servant turning on the lights. An enormous chandelier lit up the opulent dining room behind a broad bay window.

No wonder they have to be dragged into retirement, he thought. Left to their own devices, generals rarely, if ever, left the service before mandatory retirement age.

Ten minutes later, Will climbed into the back of the government vehicle, smiling as a platoon of young soldiers jogged by in formation. A few at the tail end glanced over toward him. From their glances, he knew they had to think him some important official—certainly more than a reservist colonel.

The trip south to the Marine base took less than an hour on the interstate. The sergeant seemed well prepared. Instead of driving through the main gate and base, he took another interstate exit farther south and cut across to the FBI facility. Abnormal mounds of grass and dirt stood out as they passed the aging ammunition dump, guarded by two young Marines standing at the gate, M-4 rifles slung over their shoulders.

The high-rise buildings and modern campus, comprising the main training facility for the FBI and its new field agents, seemed oddly out of place in the north Virginia woods. "Sir, are you familiar with the facility here?"

"Oh, yeah," said Will. TBS, or The Basic School, in the Marine Corps' simplistic vernacular, lay through the woods, a short distance from the FBI facility. Every Marine lieutenant trained there, learning patrolling, weapons tactics, leadership, and the art of war. Will had spent countless days on compass work and squad tactics, setting up ambushes for the "enemy." It had been a common sight on the roadway: a green, camouflaged patrol of Marines emerging from the woods.

The car stopped at the main entrance to the FBI Academy. As he swung the door open, Will stared up at a familiar face—Scott's.

"Hello, Colonel."

"Mr. Scott, I thought we dropped the rank."

"Hello, Mr. Parker."

"Ready to get to work?"

"Yes, let's play."

"Here's your security pass," Scott said, handing it to Will. "We've increased security substantially for your arrival. Though all the agent trainees have had extensive background checks and top-secret clearances, you'll still be segregated from the classes. Don't take it personally."

"Where to now?" asked Will.

"We have the training team waiting. This way." Scott turned and crossed the walkway to the main entrance.

It was a warm, not yet muggy morning in northern Virginia. Even rows of Bradford pear trees lined the campus. As he passed through the courtyard, Will noticed several agents in training, sitting on the benches with their logoed Polo shirts, studying as students would on any college campus. Each shirt, though varied in color, had the same "FBI" logo, and its bright seal stitched above.

The doors to the conference room were marked "No Admittance." Two other men, in black suits similar to Sergeant Carlson's, stood near the entranceway. Running diagonally across the bright blue passes clipped to their lapels was a bold red stripe with a small photograph in the upper right corner. Their passes—Will's, too—stood out from those of the few student agents in the yard, and earphones with wires running into the collars of their jackets emphasized the point. As he and Scott entered the room, four men and one woman stood up from their seats around a long, rectangular mahogany conference table.

It was the woman who instantly caught Will's eye.

"Colonel Parker, this is your training team." Scott stopped, turned, and waited for one of the security guards to close the conference room door. "I'll let each of you introduce yourselves," he said.

Will made an effort not to turn toward the side of the table where the woman was seated.

"I'm Steve Underwood," said the first man. "I'll be defense training and general physical fitness. Judging by your personal regimen, I understand I may have the easiest job."

"Sir," said the second, "I'm Lieutenant Jimmy Hamilton, Navy SEAL. I'll be working with you on underwater training, the ASDS, using rebreathers, insertion issues—things like that."

"I've had a little diving experience," said Will.

"I've seen your records, sir—USMC recon with training at our dive school in San Diego. BUDS school. Not much for me to do but update you. I imagine all I'll be doing is giving you an update on some of the comm equipment, and maybe exposure to ASDS."

"Great. I've never worked with the ASDS," Will said. The ASDS would be his taxicab ride from the Trident sub to North Korea.

"Also, I'll show you the Soviet version of the AN/PSC 10. There's not much to it, especially since you know Russian. You plug in a few cables, and it's ready to go."

Will turned to the next man, who was built like a fireplug—short and darkly tanned.

"I'm Mike Punaros, but you can call me Gunny."

"Marine Gunny?" asked Will.

"Yes, sir. USMC recon trained. Two tours

in combat, goddammit. Twenty-four years and out, sir."

Punaros was an old salt. Two recon combat tours meant membership in a small club. Few Marines had endured two insertions into the jungle well behind the Vietcong's lines.

"I know you've got a hell of a lot of experience, Gunny, but what's your specialty?"

"Weapons, sir, particularly the Soviet type," he said. "I'll teach you the Tokarev TT33 pistol, Type-64, and Makarov pistol from top to bottom. Also, I'm supposed to be the Agency's expert on Spetsnaz training and Spetsnaz forces. I'll teach you everything I know, sir."

"Thanks, Gunny," said Will, glancing to the next man to his right. Beside him sat the woman, her beautiful features a unique combination of Caucasian and Asian. Will guessed she was the child of some Army soldier on tour in the Philippines or South Korea, who had fallen in love with and married a local woman.

"I'm Frank Darlin," he said. "I'm your

expert on the intel you'll need in-country. I'll show you the topography, the escape routes, anything that'll help you get in and out of there." The voice was that of a New Englander, probably Harvard-trained, and just as probably the descendent of an old New England family.

Will had met the Darlins of the world before, and frankly, didn't always understand them. Harvard, or Yale, or Columbia, and then work for the CIA? It was an odd sequence. He supposed their intellect craved the challenge. But after the CIA, he wondered, wouldn't they find life on Wall Street—or anywhere else—boring?

"And I am Mi Yong," the woman said. "I'll teach you about North Korea and the North Korean people," she said. "I'll teach you Hanguk. Do you know what Hanguk is?"

"*Annyong hashimnika*, Mi-Shi." As a Marine Reservist, Will had done several language exercises in Korean.

She smiled. "And Russian. Do you know that as well, Colonel?"

"Actually, Ms. Yong, I know Russian, but have little experience in Hanguk."

"We got you the best." Scott leaned forward in his seat. "She's originally from the coast of Korea."

"I'll be spending every waking moment with you over the next several months," said Mi. "We don't have a lot of time, and the only way to make this work is to have you talk and think in Hanguk every day. Any questions?"

"No, Ms. Yong." He dampened the smile.

"Let's all have a seat," said Scott. "I have a proposed training schedule for you. It has a physical workout each day from seven until nine, intel classes from nine until noon, weapons from one until three, scuba and SEAL training until six, and language training until ten. We'll have other pop-up training as we go along."

"Mr. Scott, that's a good start-up, but—"

"But what?"

"I'll need two workouts and two runs daily. The first run will be ten miles starting at five. The first workout will be from seven to nine. Then another workout and run at four." Will knew that the one thing he would have going for him was the ability to do physically what the North Koreans never expected. If that meant covering a hundred miles of mountainous terrain in twenty-four hours on foot, he would be prepared.

"And Mr. Scott?" said a smiling Mi Yong.

"Yes?"

"Just a reminder that I need to accompany him to all his class work. As I said, he needs to be able to think in Hanguk, not just speak it. I need to use every class to talk to him in Hanguk."

"I don't know if that's possible, Ms. Yong."

"Make it possible, Mr. Scott," said Will.

"Colonel, you don't know the whole story," said Scott.

Mi cringed. She had heard similar comments before.

"I know this much," Will said. "For this to work, I don't need a tourist's knowledge of these people and their language. I need a whole lot more."

"Understood." Scott paused to return to his agenda. "The first week is to be spent in medical and dental. Starting tomorrow, any dental work will be redone, and I have Lasik set up for Friday."

Will had little need for glasses but was intrigued with the idea of vision correction.

"Let's show you around the place and get you settled in. Everyone knows the drill. Any questions?"

Choe Hak-son rarely used his office. On the top floor of the Nuclear and Chemical Defense Bureau, it was too ornate and oversized for his taste. He had learned to always appreciate less.

"Decadence feeds the monster within," The Supreme Leader had said to Choe on several occasions. And for this reason, Choe, a Kim disciple, preferred a closet-sized office in the government's main building several blocks away.

Choe thought of himself as the protector of Kim Il-sung's *Juche*—the art of self-reliance that enabled the people to overcome starvation, cold winters, and the death of their children. But the younger generation of leaders, especially Kim's son and grandson, were not as committed to the cause. Choe constantly had to push them toward self-denial and self-sacrifice even as the son, Kim Jong-il, savored the decadence of capitalistic living, smuggling in western movies and consuming more cognac than any other customer of Hennessy's. The grandson seemed to have some restraint, but many thought it only because the climb to power had not been completed.

Choe was committed, but with age, he learned that others expected the show of influence and power. A stark, antiseptic closet of an office did not convey to important visitors the fact that this man could affect decisions within the government.

"Vice Chairman?" said a young aide.

"Yes?"

The aide stood in the dark, mahogany double doorway across the room. Like a president, the elderly Choe sat behind an oversized table that served as his desk. Immediately in front of the desk were two small sofas, on a large Persian rug, that faced each other. And for every vase in the room, there was another across the room in a symmetrical location. It was this subtlety of balance that suggested control, power, and influence.

"Your guest is here."

"Let him wait a moment." After several decades of training, Choe knew the art of power. How to wield it. It was the military cadre, and especially the old generals, that had to be watched and controlled.

As Choe waited, he looked out over the city of Pyongyang. Wide-open boulevards led to large squares with little commerce. Gray was the common color—gray walls and gray buildings.

When will this succeed? he wondered. *Perhaps a century.* The western world thought in terms of years. The Asian world thought only in decades. *If it takes a hundred years for the plan to work, so be it.*

"You can bring him in now," Choe said over the phone.

A few moments later, the young aide again knocked on the door.

"Vice Chairman Choe, Mr. Astef," said the aide.

"Mr. Vice Chairman, it is an honor." The man wore a dark European-cut suit. The white shirt and dark tie were understated. Astef, too, was a true believer. He was here to bargain—to use his finances to wield power.

"Yes, Mr. Astef. You are welcome here, as always." They both spoke French—the old language of the world of finance. English would never be used here.

"You've been one of our finest customers," Astef said, "and have helped our common causes greatly."

"I understand the last shipment of guidance systems was received in Tehran, and is of great benefit to your people," said Choe.

"Yes, indeed. We now have missiles that can reach Tel Aviv. It will surely give pause to the infidel westerners." Astef was an arms merchant for small Muslim countries in the Gulf and Northern Africa.

"So why such an early return?" Choe knew to press the point. People in power had little time to dance—one had to get right to the heart of matters.

"I'm here on a most bold endeavor, Vice Chairman."

"I can only imagine."

"Yes, sir." Astef seemed hesitant. This was not like him.

"Let us have some tea," said Choe, standing up and clutching the telephone, ringing for his assistant. Astef sold several hundred millions of dollars a year in rocket weaponry to more than a dozen small Arab countries. Yemen, for example, had become a good customer with Astef's help, and Choe enjoyed the cat and mouse game that had entailed, but now, Astef seemed nervous.

"How are your children, Astef?"

"Oh, very good, sir. They are in school in Cairo and doing well." Mohammed Astef was an upper-class Egyptian by birth—trained as an engineer in the finest Egyptian universities.

"And how did you travel here?" Choe asked.

"Oh, through Moscow, Mr. Vice Chairman," said Astef.

The doors swung open as two young women brought in silver trays with thin, ivory china cups and saucers. They quickly poured the tea, offered cream and sugar, and left, with Choe's aide right behind them.

"Now," said Choe, "what is this bold endeavor, my old friend?"

"Mr. Vice Chairman, I represent a group of believers who wish to make a bold purchase."

"Yes, and . . ?"

"They wish to obtain one of your newest weapons," said Astef.

"We've always been most generous in offering our weapons to our comrades. We've shared our technology with a host of nations and peoples such as yours with the common bond of opposing Yankee oppression." The events of 9/11 had little affected the North's willingness to sell its weapons to willing buyers. "Which system do you have in mind?"

"Mr. Vice Chairman, we are interested in obtaining the Taeopodong 3."

Choe was taken aback. Everyone knew North Korea did not sell its front-line weaponry. And why did they think they had enough money to buy it? A TD-3 would be an expensive proposition.

"I imagine you're surprised about our interest in a program for such a long range weapon," said Astef, "and might be curious about the degree of our interest."

"The Unhar is something special," said Choe. The multistage missile, called the Unhar 3 or Taeopodong 3, was the pillar of their future nuclear program. The rocket was being developed to carry a load of as much as 1000 kg and its range included most of North America.

"I must apologize, but we've heard of the missile's projected capabilities. We know of the capabilities of Dr. Nampo from our past experiences. We know of the problems with the TD-2, but we also know that if anyone could make the TD-3 work, it would be Dr. Nampo."

Nampo had been directly involved in several of the previous No Dong missile programs.

"More importantly," said Astef, "Al Qaeda has enough funding to purchase two TD-3s—at three hundred million dollars per missile."

Choe tried not to react, but six hundred million dollars in hard currency did its own talking. Few North Korean leaders would or could refuse such an offer.

"Vice Chairman, we need a device that can be launched from within our border that can reach Europe and carry a hundred-kilo weapon."

So Astef did not need a nuclear weapon, but did require a mobile, intercontinental missile system. One sentence said a lot.

After a pause, Choe said, "Our project is only in development."

"Yes, sir, but perhaps with a generous down payment, we could fund additional work to improve it."

Choe leaned back in his chair and pondered the offer's many layers of significance, including what it could, or perhaps would, lead to. *An intercontinental missile fired from a remote location in Iran to the business sector of London would cause world havoc.* Another thought crossed his mind, and as it did, he smiled.

Astef, taking the smile as a good sign, said, "Vice Chairman, should we explore this further?"

"Of course, my friend."

"Good. I will report to my committee the prospect of a deal." The Arab was pleased and his body language showed it. Just the positive note of this meeting would carry with it special consideration for Astef.

"Sir, this project is our most advanced effort," said Choe. "Selling this weapon can affect us in ways I cannot presently anticipate. I must discuss this with the leadership." Choe could only imagine how China and Russia would react, but he had been surprised before by both countries' support of North Korean arms deals. The only conflicts that had arisen were those where China and Russia competed as sellers. Russia pulled off the sale of its MI-35 attack helicopter to Islamabad, but a short time later China sold them eight attack submarines for billions. Both were competing for the deals. Here, however, they would never be so bold as to have their names connected with an intercontinental missile deal.

"As a show of good faith, we're prepared to provide one hundred million to assist you in your development of the weapon system," said Astef.

"Well, yes, indeed, a sign of good faith."

"And we've been advised that much of this may benefit other systems you may be more anxious to sell, such as the portable ones."

"Yes," said Choe. "That would help us both."

Choe stood up as his aide entered the room. Walking with Astef to the door, he said, "I will advise you of the leadership's decision when I obtain it."

"Thank you, Vice Chairman."

Once Astef left, Choe went to his telephone. "This is Vice Chairman Choe," he said to the

operator. "Please ring General Sin for me."
Choe admired Sin—he was an old, ingenious,
hard nut who knew how to capitalize on an
event like this.

He heard Sin's voice at the other end.
"Sin," Choe said, "I have had an interesting
meeting that may have a positive effect on our
plan. We need our Western friends to get wind
of something."

General Sin asked to come immediately
to the NCDB.

"No, actually we'll meet at my regular
office." Choe preferred to return to the
comfort of his small, plain sanctuary.

"Ready?" Mi spoke in Hanguk as the elevator to the top floor of the FBI's dormitory opened. The two Agency guards looked up from their chairs at the sight of the woman in her gray, oversized sweatsuit. It was typical of one issued to new agents in training and disguised her shape well. On the campus, she appeared to be just another student out for a run before class.

Will wasn't dressed much better. "Yeah," he said, "let's go."

She noticed a limp. Will favored his right side.

"So the ten-mile run yesterday morning was too much for you?" said Mi.

"No." He pointed to the elevator as he

spoke, indicating he didn't want to talk, especially in front of the two sentries.

"Oh, you forgot your pass," said the younger of the two, who handed Will a blue card with a red stripe across it and a magnetic strip on the back. The guards kept the pass at night. If Mi had not held the elevator door open, Will would have had to swipe it through a magnetic reader, both to open and close the elevator door. The ninth floor was accessible only by pass.

The doors slid closed.

Will wore a white running t-shirt that hung loosely over his black running shorts. "Peachtree Road Race" appeared on the shirt's front and back. Will had made the Atlanta run every Fourth of July—until this year.

Mi was looking at the shirt's orange-pink peach logo when she first noticed the small red stain by the right side of Will's stomach.

"What happened?"

He pulled up the shirt to reveal a blood-stained bandage near his appendix, then held his finger over his lips.

Outside, as the early-bird FBI students walked by en route to the cafeteria, Will and Mi stretched like serious joggers. Scott would be satisfied to know they did not stand out. Two more FBI agents also seemed to be heading out for an early run.

The route for Will and Mi took them out of the FBI campus toward The Basic School and back to the campus by another road. The six miles usually did not take long, and they'd already gotten into the habit of running it twice. He hadn't pushed it very hard yet, but was already impressed with Mi. She was clearly dedicated to her own fitness—yet another thing Will liked about her.

"So what happened?" She repeated the question in Hanguk as they ran in the yellow pre-light of dawn.

A black Chevrolet Suburban followed them a hundred meters behind. Will didn't mind the nonstop surveillance as much as the nuisance of running with the vehicle's lights constantly shining on them.

"I was at the dentist for most of the

day." He stumbled on the Hanguk word for "dentist" and finally said it in English. "They said knocking me out was the least painful way to get the dental work done. After I woke up, I found this incision." He patted his right side as they ran.

"What is it?"

"Scott says it's a marker." The marker was a small locator chip that allowed satellites to trace Will everywhere he went. They could already follow him visually, by photo or by heat, but the marker allowed them to trace him, even inside buildings or caves.

At that very moment, only fifty miles to the north, the Agency was already following him. Buried well within the walls of the CIA, the last of the graveyard shift of technicians watched a large, rectangular panel screen, where a blinking light showed Will over an outline of Virginia. The light had a small number, "AGT4444," below and to the right. Quadruple four was Will's designation. Will only knew that he had a chip under the incision.

"Apparently it even has Soviet markings," he said as he ran.

"Yes, I would expect that."

"They said the microprocessor was from India," Will said. "The Soviets would likely use an Indian microchip for something like this."

He understood how they had made the chip insertion and why. That was not what angered him. It was that the admiral would do this to him without telling him. *That son of a bitch.*

But why was Will telling Mi? Her answers to his questions all seemed hesitant, as if she were holding something back, possibly against her will. As a foreign national, she would be at the U.S. government's mercy. Will had to assume that Krowl was pulling her strings and that she reported everything back to Krowl. But Will had to trust someone. Time was running out and he needed someone on the other side. He had to risk it. He felt a chemistry of sorts with Mi, and he trusted his judgment of people.

They picked up the pace as they neared the

Marine Basic School. Platoons of faces with boot camp haircuts ran by in tight formations, chanting cadence. Each was dressed in the same green running suit with a gray eagle, globe and anchor embroidered on the jersey. Only their running shoes were different.

Will smiled as he noticed the widely varied running shoes. When he had gone through The Basic School, everyone ran in black boots and utilities. Later, as the running craze took hold, the military hierarchy relented and permitted individual running shoes.

Individuality was not prized at The Basic School. For six months, Will had been taught infantry tactics for the individual rifleman and up through the squad and platoon levels, and he excelled. All the instructors had wanted to recruit Will to their specialty, including the most prestigious—infantry. Finishing at the top of his class, based on graded tests and leadership, Will had the option of selecting whatever military occupational specialty, or MOS, he wanted. Everyone expected that he would select infantry, the most direct route to the rank of general.

But Will surprised them on the last day, when he chose another MOS.

"O802."

"Artillery?"

"Yes, sir."

"But, why, Lieutenant Parker?" The company commander had been pitching for infantry. A couple of years in an infantry battalion, and Will could easily move up to Forces Reconnaissance.

"I think it ultimately gives me more options. It won't hurt to know more." He was referring to the ability to call artillery fire. Artillery was the high math of the military. Gravity, winds, weather, and a host of other influences can cause an artillery shell to leave the cannon's tube and land down range, far away from the intended target.

Will liked the mental challenge involved. An individualist, he also liked surprising management. Ironically, he had used the

Marine Corps as a means of expressing his individuality.

"One more lap?" Mi said in Hanguk

Will didn't understand the Hanguk word for "lap." "What?"

"Go around again?" she said in Hanguk.

"Oh, yes."

They ran the second lap at a faster pace. He would let her lead, but as they came to a hill, Will would surge past her. The lead danced back and forth between them.

As she ran, Mi started to slow. Will's pace had become too much. Will knew little of her background.

"Where were you raised?" He asked her in Hanguk as he slowed the pace some.

"Near the Taebaek Mountains along the coast."

"I know those mountains." Will had studied them with Op Plan 5015. It was the master plan for a strike back against North Korea after a North Korean attack. The Taebaeks jutted out from the shoreline, directly facing the brunt of the ocean.

"Do you like this country?" He was blunt.

"Yes, I do."

He thought of whom she might be reporting to. "And Krowl?"

She stopped running, and Will stopped with her.

"He told me once," she said, "that if I did anything he didn't like, it would be easy to tell someone where I was."

After passing through uncountable security measures and checkpoints, Scott arrived at Admiral Krowl's office in the Pentagon. Scott's security pass, after much use, had become entangled with the collar of his overcoat. The weather was beginning to change as fall settled into Washington. This day was rainy, damp, and cold. Scott's raincoat, tailored for him by a London shop, fit perfectly over his charcoal pinstriped suit and dark blue tie. He felt more like a finely-dressed funeral home attendant than a professional spook.

Pulling off his raincoat, Scott straightened his tie and announced himself to Krowl's gatekeeper.

The Navy lieutenant looked up from her desk, which seemed almost ceremonial—it lacked papers, notes, and all other evidence of work.

"Oh, yes," she said, "you're expected. Coffee or something to drink, sir?"

"No, thanks."

She nodded. "I'll tell them you're here."

Scott didn't expect the "them." Instead of taking a seat, he continued to stand, taking in his surroundings. A royal blue couch with gold tridents served as the centerpiece of this outer office. On each end of the couch were darkwood end tables and tall brass lamps.

Scott was more interested, though, in the photographs hung in groups on the walls. A series showed Krowl as a young officer in jungle fatigues. The man was far more impressive then—much thinner, with a smile more devious than happy. Another group of photos showed Krowl in the desert camouflage of the Gulf, a few years and many pounds later. Again, that same smile. All of the photographs showed him alone.

"Mr. Scott." The inner door swung open

and a bald Navy commander stuck out his hand.

"Yes."

"I'm Commander Sawyer, the admiral's assistant," he said. "Please come in."

Sawyer was Krowl's handyman. He often did the admiral's unpleasant work, Scott had learned, and gave Krowl protection. All flag officers, for better or worse, had a "Sawyer" to deliver their messages or to snoop out the status of certain sensitive matters. If a general were caught in an affair, the Sawyers of the military always found out first.

The inner office was a cavernous, wood-paneled chamber with two picture windows looking out on a boat harbor that led into the Potomac River. Any Pentagon office on the outer, or E, ring was valuable real estate in the world of military power. This remained true even after the attacks of September 11th and the destruction of certain E ring offices. It might entail greater risk, but most power-seekers would happily accept it.

Admiral Krowl had two small couches

facing each other and a square mahogany coffee table, bright brass hinges built in. Behind his desk was an enormous oil painting of two Revolution-era sailing ships engaged in battle.

"Mr. Scott, come on in," Krowl said as he looked up, taking one last draw on his cigarette before crushing it into the already full ashtray on his desk.

"You know Mi." He pointed to the back of the room, where she was sitting slightly out of sight in one of the leather chairs.

"Yes, of course." Scott was not entirely surprised to find her here.

"Commander Sawyer will join us. He has full authority and knowledge of these matters."

Again, Scott could not say he was surprised. People he distrusted by instinct rarely worked alone.

"Okay, let's review where we are," said Krowl. "What's the progress of training?"

Coming in, Scott had decided to limit his comments. "He's doing fine."

"You don't have much time left at Quantico. Is the team ready?"

"Yes, they'll meet him at Bridgeport."

"And how long will Bridgeport take?"

"About a month."

"Make it a week."

Scott nodded slightly.

"That would make them ready in just a few weeks," said Krowl. "They have to be ready as soon as possible. The boat will be available at Pearl by fifteen December."

"Yes, but——"

"No buts——fifteen December."

"The team may not be ready by then," Scott pointed out.

"Didn't Parker pick the team himself?"

"Yes."

"Well, then, they'll be ready."

Scott's blood boiled. His hand squeezed the arm of the sofa as he attempted to quell his growing irritation.

"Admiral, I don't mind preparing the bloody man for a job that holds the probability"——Scott pronounced the word slowly and quietly to emphasize the point—"I said the *probability* that he will not survive, or worse, be imprisoned for the rest of his life in a dank, brutal prison by an already starving country that considers torture an art form. But, to continually lie to him—"

Scott was still angry about the unannounced insertion of the tracking chip into Will's body.

"Mr. Scott." Krowl said it like a teacher about to send a misbehaving student to the principal's office.

"Yes?"

"He agreed to this mission," said Krowl. "And he's getting paid. No one in this building, nor the public for that matter, will be concerned about a paid mercenary being caught, imprisoned, or killed."

Before Scott could argue, Krowl turned to Mi Yong. "How about your end?"

"Sir?"

"Will he be ready?"

"Yes," said Mi. "He's already nearly fluent in Hanguk. He's knows Russian better than I do. He has been over the topography computer programs several times and knows every lake, stream, and valley within a fifty-mile area. He has a general sense of the vegetation, too, from the 3-D program."

Will had been taken to Langley several times. Always late at night, the van would pull into the CIA's basement parking garage, after which they would travel two floors up to the computer graphics room. With a 3-D headset and instructions from Frank Darlin, Will could walk, run, or even fly through the computer-reconstructed topography of the North Korean countryside. The programs were integrated with the latest information received directly from satellites, along with Darlin's personal expertise. Thanks to the latest advances in virtual-reality technology, Will could walk past vehicles parked that very moment on a roadway in North Korea.

"He's fully up on the camera and satellite relay computer." Scott had worked with Hamilton and Will for several days on the relay. Photographs were taken from several locations across Quantico and relayed directly, via satellite, to Langley.

"Good, okay. Anything else?" asked Krowl.

Sawyer had been sitting quietly in the back taking everything in, but this was his cue. He stood and opened the door to help move the visitors along.

"No?" said Krowl. "Then let's get him to Bridgeport now."

Scott grimaced. He picked up his raincoat and held it over his arm to make it more difficult for Krowl to shake his hand. This didn't faze the admiral, who remained behind his desk.

"Oh, Mi, stay a moment," said Krowl.

| | | |

"Anything else I need to know?" Krowl asked Mi Yong.

"No," she said hesitantly. "No, sir." She regretted not giving him something. A wild dog is easier to control when regularly fed.

"Good. So, from your viewpoint, he can get to that valley?"

The admiral, she noted, had a tendency to describe only half the mission. Krowl never spoke about Will getting back from the valley.

"I think Will . . ." She stopped. Another mistake, using his first name. It was not like her.

"Yes?"

"I believe he'll get to the valley, complete the mission, and get back."

"Okay." He said it flatly, without much enthusiasm.

"Anything else, sir?"

"No." He paused as he lit another cigarette. "But keep me informed. Your calls have been most helpful."

She was silent.

"Mi?"

"Oh, yes, sir?"

"Thank you."

Sawyer re-entered the room. A good aide always appeared and disappeared at the right moment.

"Miss Yong was just leaving," said Krowl.

| | |

Krowl called Sawyer back into his office. "Yes, sir?"

"I'm not sure about Scott. I want the CIA to order him to CINCPAC during the operation. Let him monitor it out of their SCIF. That'll keep him out of the way," he said. "We can say it's necessary so he can be closer to Korea if the need arises."

"Yes, sir. Good idea." The top-secret, classified operation center, or SCIF, at CINCPAC in Hawaii, would take Scott out of the action, but not outside of Krowl's influence. "What about her?" Sawyer tilted his head at the door.

"Yong?"

"Yes, sir."

"She'll be our little insider," said Krowl, "and when he moves on to the next phase, we'll be done with her."

"Doesn't she know a lot?"

"Yes." He leaned back in his chair, inhaling

his cigarette. Thin white smoke curled upwards to the ceiling. "That's a good point."

"Isn't she still high on their list?" said Sawyer.

"Oh, yes." Krowl continued to lean back and draw on his cigarette. "Let me think about this. Good job, Sawyer."

Sawyer smiled. "Anything else, sir?"

"No."

Exempted from all the usual restrictions, Rei had been allowed to keep his apartment for several years now. A single person living in such an expansive apartment in North Korea was unheard of, and initially caused his few neighbors suspicion. Rei, after all, was not a known party leader or a military commander.

His apartment was on the edge of what was called the Forbidden Zone or Forbidden City, where a high solid wall and armed guards kept everyone out but the elite. Plump, full-faced women in starched khaki uniforms and bright, red-starred hats, armed with machine guns, guarded the few entrances. It was here that the powerful members of the central committee, the generals, the admirals, and the many central marshals all lived—with ample food, Mercedes cars, and numerous Western amenities. It was here, out of sight of the ill-fed people of Pyongyang, that Kim Jong-il's select few lived in homes and apartments far above the city's crude, one-room, cinderblock huts, where packed-in families slept together on dirt floors. Those on the outside could never look in.

Several years earlier, the local block commander had demanded possession of Rei's apartment, which was on the top floor of a small building overlooking the Taedong River. The porch faced east, so its occupant could watch the sun as it rose across the river in the mornings. The apartment request had been summarily denied by higher authority, and the commander was never able to determine who the decision-maker was. As with all dictatorships, many had license to use nondescript superiors as authority to issue orders. Often, one would hear, "The Ministry of Defense does not allow it." In this case, the commander was simply told that Rei was to be left alone.

His curiosity ignited, the commander bribed Rei's housekeeper to gain access. One day, when Rei was gone, the commander slipped past the unlocked mahogany door into a small separate entrance room, which led to another set of dark, oversized, elaborately carved wooden doors. Rei could lock out the world with this double entrance. The commander removed his shoes as he swung open the inner door and looked inside. The expanse of the room was overwhelming and intimidating, with deep red Persian rugs, accented with crystal lamps and tufted leather chairs, representing opulence he had never before seen. On virtually every space on the walls were Western-style oil paintings. The commander quickly concluded that Rei was untouchable. He quietly closed the door, put on his shoes, and left.

Rei knew the block commander had been there. In fact, the loyalty of his housekeeper was absolute. The commander had been allowed to look inside only after Rei had given his approval, because he knew the old man's curiosity, unless satisfied, would only grow.

Rei's apartment in the Forbidden City stood at the end of a short alley with no street name or street signs. The lack of street signs was another example of North Korea's paranoia. It was intended to prevent an invading army from coordinating their maps to city streets. If a society didn't care whether Federal Express could find an address, the lack of street signs would be a powerful tool to slow down an invading army.

From one end of Rei's apartment, he could see the small islet in the center of the Taedong River, where the two circular towers of the high-rise, ultra-modern Yanggakdo Hotel blocked most of the enormous Yanggakdo soccer stadium at the other end. If he looked another way, Rei could see the behemoth *Juche* tower. One of the many memorials to Kim Il Sung, this was, by far, the largest and most dominant. The gray structure, with a gold flame at the top, was shaped like an enormous radio tower constructed out of stone, and was designed to be visible from all of Pyongyang. The city, in fact, was filled with monuments, massive tombstones, and behemoth buildings on open boulevards. It was an opulent graveyard honoring one man. Even from the grave, Kim Il Sung commanded constant visual reminders of his stranglehold on the people.

Rei thought of Pyongyang as special in its own, peculiar way. This place of nearly two million people was a quiet, open city that acted like a shy girl. She didn't bother you and often seemed to avoid you. One saw few cars, little air pollution, and few bicycles. And the city was immaculately clean. Teams of gray-haired women were constantly sweeping.

Here, Rei did not need to look over his shoulder. His one pass, a badge from the security police, gave him unlimited license. He could have anyone arrested without question, demand anything without payment, even commit murder without consequences.

Rei planned each of his missions in the apartment. Many years ago, it would take several months, but Rei had had his small study wired for broadband internet service. The internet was unavailable to most North Koreans. Less than a few dozen in the city of Pyongyang had access, and Rei was one of them. He found the internet an invaluable aid in plotting his foreign operations.

When he was ready to leave for a mission, a government driver would meet Rei at the end of the alley, always before dawn. Rei made a point of leaving well before the city awoke. Even in Pyongyang, Rei did not want to give anyone the opportunity to track his activities. He and the driver would rarely talk in the car.

The driver, much shorter than Rei, wore a gray-blue, plain zippered jacket, the common uniform of the Stalinistic state. Years of smoking had left him with stained teeth that he often showed with a broad smile. An employee of the state police, he had a reputation for trustworthiness. They would drive the twenty-four kilometers out of the city to the Sunam Airport, with no traffic during the entire ride. Pyongyang was largely without traffic on its busiest day, let alone before dawn.

Rei altered his air routes as much as possible. Pyongyang was mostly limited to three main portals. He would fly North Korea's Air Koryo to Beijing, Moscow, or Berlin. Occasionally, to break up his pattern, Rei would take the train to Wonsan, several hours to the east on the Sea of Japan, where he would board the cruiser *SamJiyan* and cross over to Japan. The *SamJiyan*, a small passenger vessel, traveled to Nagasaki, giving him the cover of a Japanese tourist returning home. Once in Tokyo, he could take flights to anywhere in the world. But this nautical route into Japan was available only once a month, and added substantial time to his journey.

The third route, by far his least preferred, was via the border. Every square inch had been mined, booby-trapped, or barb-wired. But the North maintained several tunnels—some much smaller than others—that permeated the line. Rei rarely used this portal and chose it only when necessary as an emergency escape route coming back from the South.

At Sunam Airport, Rei checked in, this time using the surname Nakada and a Chinese passport. The clerks at Air Koryo all worked for the state police and had a sense of who Rei was, but questions were never asked. When he passed through customs, his passport was never stamped with a North Korean marker. With their red and gold collars and shoulder boards, the airport's uniformed security guards were his last reminder of North Korea before boarding the airplane. The lobby was thinly filled with a few Russians who smoked incessantly and several Chinese dressed in military uniforms. Civilians were not seen. Once through security, Rei crossed over the terminal's spotless linoleum floor to vendors selling cold noodle dishes. Like birds waiting for crumbs, several old women stood in the corner, waiting just in sight with small brooms and dustpans to sweep anything that fell to the floor.

Rei enjoyed using the same vendor each

trip. He always bought a cup of red noodles with rice cakes, cucumbers, and salad. He sat in the corner, eating the dish while waiting for his flight. This was his final homeland treat before re-entering the outside world on another mission.

It didn't start this way, he thought.

During all his intelligence schooling in North Korea, China, and even Russia, Rei was taught that the spy game was more about subtle intelligence-gathering than assassination. To gain information, one was to recruit disenchanted secretaries or lonely wives, or hack e-mail or internet sites by stealing access passwords. Assassinating targets was the stuff of spy movies, not reality.

Yet Rei had grown proud of his work's violent nature. The generals respected him. They knew that if Rei were given a target's name, that person had received an irreversible death sentence.

Other nations and organizations used assassination to achieve their goals. Hamas in Palestine and Al Qaeda had ruthlessly murdered for years. Rei, however, participated in a bigger plan. He murdered to help his country gain a clear advantage. He killed for a specific purpose. Peter Nampo and his team would have few challenges when Rei was finished. *And it's so easy*, he thought. *A random killing by someone lacking repeated contact with the victim. Unprotected scientists who have no notion of their fate. They might have the rare ability to affect our future more than any politician, yet they remain as vulnerable as a street sweeper.*

Today, he would fly to Beijing on Flight 151, and then on to Hong Kong. There, he would change passports and catch a flight to London. His target taught at Oxford University, a brief drive from Gatwick Airport. He would rent a car and be at Oxford an hour or two later.

Rei had researched his target well. The old professor taught a class on Mondays and spent the remainder of the week at an engineering laboratory just outside London. He even knew where the professor usually parked his car and what route he would take to the lab. As in the past, his planned intersect point would be in a crowded area.

Once done, he would leave Heathrow Airport on a short flight to Paris. The passport he would use would be pre-stamped with a less recent entrance visa to England, and thus cause less suspicion.

Before the initial autopsy has even begun, I'll be gone.

From Paris, he would fly to Moscow, using yet another identity. In Moscow, his delay would again be very short. His Air Koryo flight left only an hour later, taking him home to Pyongyang.

And if he ever sensed the dogs on his trail, Rei would divert to Hong Kong and then to Seoul. Through Seoul, he had access to an underground network of people; if necessary, he could cross the border at a specific, hidden access tunnel that had not broken through the soil in South Korea. With a shovel and the right location, a quick dig would open the entrance and allow him to escape. Rei was among a handful who knew where the entrance lay.

And then back home to sleep, he thought as he swallowed the last of the noodles. Even cold-blooded murderers needed their rest.

As for the future, after this set of Peter Nampo missions, his superiors had promised him an instructor's position at the Academy. Just a few more names, and Rei, at last, would be home free.

The wind had changed direction since the morning, causing a drop in temperature, but Will would make the afternoon run no matter how cold. Over the past several months, the training had hardened his body more than ever. When the Virginia forest turned to bright oranges and reds and the weather cooled, Will extended his runs. He would often run with a backpack, carrying some weight and a camelback pouch that provided water without stop. His physical strength was constantly increasing.

Hamilton had pushed Will the hardest. It wasn't the weeks of swimming in the pool, or the laps underwater holding his breath. He had pushed Will through all of the SEAL training, with the constant threat that one failure, one letdown, would lead to his recommendation to kill the mission. BUDS training (his second time through) seemed much more difficult than when he'd been younger.

It was the final week that pushed Will to his limit.

"Come with me, sir," Hamilton said, almost gleeful. He led him out of the FBI building and crossed to a helicopter landing pad behind the main center.

"What's up?" Will asked, unsure what to expect.

Hamilton only looked at his watch. They stood there in silence for a short while until they heard the *whoomp-whoomp* of a low-flying helicopter. The Blackhawk cut over the tree line, just above the top branches, churning up the leaves in its wake. As it landed, Hamilton pointed to the rear.

"Get on board, boss."

As they strapped into the bird, it tilted up and then nosed down into forward movement.

"Here's a wetsuit, mask, and snorkel. You

better go ahead and change quickly," said Hamilton.

The helicopter flew across the base and then well out over the Chesapeake Bay. Far beyond the sight of land, it stopped, leveled low, and hovered.

"We're exactly twenty miles out. I'll see you when you get back." Hamilton pointed with his hand to the open door.

Damn, Will thought as he stepped out of the helicopter and plunged fifty feet into the cold water. The helicopter soon disappeared over the horizon.

All right, get a direction, feel the current, he thought as he began to move to the west. *Conserve energy*. He knew the wetsuit would give him the vital buoyancy he needed to survive the long swim. But quickly Will discovered that Hamilton had given him a rather thin wetsuit—less insulation from the cold water, and less buoyancy. Hypothermia would now be a risk. Hamilton had thrown everything he could at Will.

It took most of the day and well into the

night for Will to make it to shore. He stopped
at a farmhouse, and called a taxi, which took
him the final thirty miles.

"Mr. Hamilton," he said on his return to
Quantico, "you owe me fifty dollars for the
taxi."

Hamilton smiled as he reached into his
wallet.

In fact, the whole team had trained him
well. In a week, he knew, he would leave
Quantico and each of his trainers would
disappear, moved by Krowl to some distant
post. Punaros would be retired. Darlin would
be reassigned to Afghanistan or Pakistan.
Underwood, who'd overseen Will's twice-
daily workouts, would be sent to the ends of
the Earth. And Hamilton would be assigned
to a SEAL team on a submarine, kept out of
contact with the world for months at a time.
All would work far from one another so as to
leave as little trail as possible. Mi's fate was
the most precarious.

But of all the training, running remained
the most critical. If Will engaged the North

Koreans directly, he would fail. If he could flee, he might succeed. His physical training had given him the ability to run twenty to thirty miles at a pace pursuers would not expect. Adrenaline would push him faster and farther. And he had not yet reached his limit.

| | | |

"Mornin'," said Will, who seemed to startle the agent at the elevator. He was leaning his chair back against the wall.

"Oh, hey. Good morning."

After several months, even the best security would relax.

Will saw the agent radio the crew on the main floor. "He's coming down." As always, two agents would be waiting downstairs, the black Suburban running. Mi would also be on the ground floor, ready to go. She had not missed a step yet. Even on the longest runs, she had remained just one pace behind.

Downstairs, she waited in front of the elevator.

"Good morning," she said. "You have your

final class with Gunny Punaros today." She had gotten into the habit of calling Punaros by the affectionate Marine Corps title of "Gunny."

She and Will had worked together for some time, now. The full leap of trust had not yet been made, but Will had gained respect for her, despite knowing that she called Krowl periodically to report his every move. It's not as though she had a choice in the matter. Most of all, he appreciated her bright mind and curiosity. In some ways, they were kindred spirits. He liked to imagine that Mi was finding it tougher and tougher to call in those reports to Krowl.

"We have to go to a different TA," she added, referring to another training area.

The black Suburban took less than half an hour to get to an unfamiliar wooded area at the far end of the Marine base. The SUV turned off the main road onto a gravel path and passed through a gate with an armed guard.

Will looked up, taking note. In the past

several months, he had met the Gunny at either the pistol range or the rifle range several days a week. Will had become a far better shot, an instinct shooter who didn't simply take aim, but *felt* the shot.

Punaros had taught Will to fire the DPRK's best pistols and rifles. Most were Korean remakes of other weapons from around the world, like the Type-64, a 7.62-mm pistol and a Korean remake of the old Browning 1900; and the Korean TT-33, another 7.62 pistol. Punaros wanted Will to be comfortable with anything he found en route.

Then he'd have Will perform the same exercise at each session. Giving him a Makarov 9-mm pistol with a fully loaded clip of eight rounds, he would tell Will to lock and load the first round. Then he'd turn Will around, grab eight dimes, and yell, "Turn!"

He'd toss the dimes high into the air, and in the brief flash of time during which they fell, Will fired eight times. First, he hit four of eight, then six, then all eight. Now, he would hit eight with regularity.

"Okay, Colonel, come on," said Punaros when they arrived. He too couldn't seem to stop himself from calling Will by his rank.

He led Will into the woods, while Mi waited in the Suburban. She and the driver would not leave unless instructed by Punaros.

In a small clearing, a table had been set up with a DPRK Type-64 pistol. It had a long silencer attached—one of the few DPRK pistols machined to accommodate one. "The one problem with training," said Punaros, "is that it can't replace the experience of a bullet coming at you. We can spend all day long on a range, but what happens when those targets shoot back?"

Will knew Punaros was right. He might fire some of the best shots on the range, but miss the side of a barn when shot at.

"Here's how this one works." Punaros lifted up a clay target the size of a basketball. "Five of these are out there in red. There are twice as many orange targets. You'll be heading toward the red ones, but the orange ones will be in your way. Some are high, some are low. There are five live snipers on this course. You'll be traveling through the field of orange targets." He paused. "And they don't care if you get between them and the target. They ain't suppose to be aiming at you. Only the orange ones. But, if you're shot dead, the incident will be written up as a training accident."

Will imagined the newspaper headline as it would appear on page ten of the local paper: "Marine killed by errant weapon discharge in training accident." Few would read it.

"The course is one mile long," Punaros continued. "Once you hit a sniper's red target, he can no longer shoot at his orange ones."

Punaros, clearly concerned, looked Will directly in the eyes. He wanted Will to have the best chance, both on this test and in-country. As the training advanced, he had become less jocular. He was dead serious today.

"Now, this is a layout of the area," said Punaros. He pulled a board from the side of a small field table, featuring a large aerial photograph with a laminated cover. Taped on the lamination were yellow strips, forming a box. "Look at the terrain. You may not even have this much advantage when you're in-country."

The Virginia forest retained some of its summer vegetation, but the changing colors would give Will some protection during this dangerous exercise. He saw a rolling terrain that led down to a deep ravine at the end of the box. Two streams twisted through the base of two shallow ravines before reaching the last, deeper one.

"I get it. Essentially, hitting their red target is a kill."

"Exactly, sir."

"How much time?"

"Twenty minutes."

"Okay," said Will.

"And each orange is set up with the red in such a way that you can't hit the red without being in the path of the orange," said Punaros.

"I got it. The object is to put a round as close to my head without telling them to aim at me." said Will. He knew this came as close as possible to simulating combat. The bullets would be hot, low, and indiscriminate.

"Here's an extra clip. Each holds eight."

The 7.62-mm bullet was larger than most pistol rounds and made a deep, whomping noise when fired.

"The boundary of the course is marked by yellow tape. And, Will?"

Will looked up at the unusual mention of his name.

"You will have this in Korean if you want it." He handed Will a black, sleeveless ballistic vest.

Will was astonished by the vest's weight and size. It was as thin as a paper pad, and light—comparable to a sweater in size, weight, and weave.

"It's made from an experimental spider silk called Biosteel. Ten times lighter and tougher than old Kevlar. Virtually impregnable, but it protects only vital organs and doesn't do anything for that beautiful face of yours."

Only a Marine gunny could make Will feel so comfortable about getting his head

– 226 –

blown off. But the risk of that newspaper story was still there. Will slipped the vest over his Polartek top. He was surprised at how unrestricted he felt. Other vests made movement awkward and slowed you down.

"And, sir," said Punaros, "their weapons are a mix of North Korea's. They've got their Type-58s, -68s, and a Dragunor. The sound, the shells, everything will make you feel like we're doing this just north of the border."

The 58 was another North Korean knock-off of the AK-47, and the 68 was a reproduction of the Russian AKM assault rifle. But it was the Dragunor that caught Will's attention. The Dragunor was a SVD sniper rifle that could knock the nose off a squirrel at eight hundred meters. In all his months of training, during which he'd shot every weapon, the Dragunor had most impressed him.

"Let's go," said Will.

"The clock starts now."

Will took off like a flash, heading into the woods. His only advantage was a brief element of surprise—the snipers had been sitting in their positions for some time. Perhaps he could use his speed to get through the first few of them.

He ran straight for a large boulder, slamming to the ground just as the loud *whack* of a bullet flew past him. One orange target was only a few feet from his head.

Will paused, judged the angle of the shot, sprang up, and fired as the sniper sighted him again. As if piercing a heart, the bullet from Will's pistol split the red target.

He didn't stop or hesitate. Spotting the small stream below, he ran and jumped across it. Heading up the other hillside, he spied a flash of red at the base of a tree atop the next ridgeline. One shot popped the target before the sniper even sensed his movement.

"Come on," he whispered to himself as he moved across the slope.

Again, he heard the *whack* of a bullet above his head. It was an AK-47-type round. Will never stopped, knowing from combat that a fixed target meant instant death. He dropped to one knee, looked up, saw a flash of red, and squeezed the trigger. He had sixteen rounds in the two clips, but through three targets, he had fired only three rounds.

Now the forest crackled with arms fire. He could hear the 58, but not the Dragunor. The sniper had not been able to sense his pace, and was firing at any hint of movement. Often, it didn't belong to Will, but to a breeze or a squirrel. And this gave Will the upper hand. From the shots, he sensed where the shooter was—near another red target. The crack of the bullet had a certain sound that gave him a hint of the location of the shooter.

After half a mile, the terrain fell off to a

large, sandy stream a car's length or more in width. The area was open, giving the snipers more opportunity. But movement remained Will's best defense. Spotting a tree that had fallen across the stream, he immediately knew the target would be set, prompting him to ford the stream by the tree.

"The target is where I would be." Each location was a tactical decision aimed at putting an orange target where he would be most exposed.

He ran at full speed, jumping the stream at a forty-five degree angle, allowing his boots to hit two steps on the tree, as support, in the middle of the stream. As the bullet seared the Polartek, he felt the heat, but adrenaline was pumping now.

Will hit the other bank, rolled, and fired, hitting the fourth red target before the sniper's second shell was chambered in the weapon.

One left, he thought. *The Dragunor.*

He climbed over the next rise, moving slowly as he approached the top. It was always movement that caught one's eye in the woods.

A deer hunter would never see the deer but for its movement. With its natural camouflage, a deer was virtually undetectable until it moved.

Will moved very slowly as he pulled up behind an outcropping of rocks and trees. He peered over the ravine and saw an open field beyond the stream. The sniper would have an open space advantage to detect Will's movement.

"That son of a bitch." Only Punaros, he thought, would set up the last target in a way that made it impossible for him. Given plenty of time, Will could slowly cross the field like a good Marine sniper, an inch at a time. But the limited clock set stress at boiler-like levels.

Will saw movement in the tree line across the field. He stayed still, holding his breath.

The sniper moved again, very slightly, and when he did, Will saw a flash of red for less than a second. He smiled, sensing what was happening.

Punaros made this last one as tough as he could, Will thought, *and then that damn Marine decided to make it even tougher.*

The sniper, his body directly in front of the red target, supported the Dragunor rifle with the trunk of a fallen pine tree. For Will, the trunk blocked all view of the sniper except for the scope of his rifle and a small portion of his camouflaged head.

Will pulled back. He looked at his watch—five minutes remaining. As he looked up, he saw the yellow tape flutter in the breeze to his right.

| | | |

Although the sniper didn't know who the target in this exercise was, Punaros had given him the authority to do whatever he thought would make it tough on his opponent. He had walked the grounds before the contest and knew exactly where the target would cross the stream: it had only one point at which one could make a successful crossing.

The sniper also knew the only approach that would work would be a run—perhaps a zigzag—across the open field. Having set himself up in front of the red target, it would be a hopeless exercise for his opponent. The target would never get the chance to fix on him, while the sniper would have at least three clear shots. Only one would be needed.

At two minutes remaining, the brush near the crossover moved, and the sniper raised his rifle slightly, placing the butt of the stock into his shoulder. He had sanded the skin of his trigger finger down to raw flesh so he could feel the slightest squeeze on his finger. He braced for movement, expecting to sight, squeeze, and reload if necessary.

Whap. He heard the clay target break apart just behind his head. Out of reflex, he started to turn, but felt the cold steel barrel of a silencer against his neck.

"Oh, shit."

Will had cracked the target with the butt of the pistol, then turned the pistol on the sniper.

"Marine, you can assume you're dead."

"Yes, sir."

The old man always knew when there was something coming to the valley. At night, particularly during the rain, trucks would rumble down the road. Sometimes at dawn, he would hear a deep, thundering noise above the valley to the west.

He also knew of a much smaller, higher valley. It was actually more of a small plateau, about two hundred meters in length. A deep rumble caused a vibration in the ground. It always came from that same direction.

During the old man's lifetime, the valley had rarely been quiet. Not far from both Wonsan and the DMZ, it had been a battlefield many times over. The Japanese caused the death of his first child, a daughter, caught in the shelling when they tried to flee to the mountains in the east. Later, the armies of North Korea, the U.S., China, and again the U.S. ran through his small farm. Now, he sensed trouble coming again.

Off and on for several weeks, the rumbling had occurred nightly as the weather began to cool with the change of seasons. At night, the old farmer was often awakened by the rumble. At the same time, more and more vehicles passed down the road and through the trees at the other end of the valley. He heard the *thump-thump* of helicopters on a daily basis. He only wanted to be left alone, but this valley seemed to have other plans for him.

The helicopter flew lower than usual, barely clearing the tops of the pine trees near the hut, scattering the few chickens pecking in the yard. As the helicopter banked in a hard left turn, the smell of spent kerosene blew down on the old man and, as it tipped up into landing mode, a convoy of jeeps sped past on the road to the landing zone. Young Korean officers jumped out of the jeeps as a much older man walked from the helicopter to the lead jeep. The helicopter passengers met the others in brief conversation.

I   I   I

"General, welcome back."

"Yes, yes, again I am here." General Won had not expected to be back as early as he was. He had been on a vacation retreat with his wife at an official villa near Beijing when Army headquarters called to dispatch him to Pyongyang.

"Where is Dr. Nampo, Captain Sang?" The general remembered the young captain who met him during his last trip, now leading the entourage.

"With the launch imminent, he was detained, sir."

"Well, let's go."

The lead Soviet UAZ469 jeep had a red and gold VIP plate on its front. Won could have done without such attention. He always thought it odd that hardened combat veterans cared much less for pomp and circumstance than less experienced ones, and that the younger generals seemed always to have something to prove. And those who abused power the most were those given it most easily, and often, after only a short time.

The short convoy circled around the landing pad as the helicopter left, banking over the decrepit farm hut. Won glanced at the old man as his convoy sped past. He remembered him from the last trip.

"Is that your security guard for this valley?"

Sang chuckled. "Yes, sir," he joked.

"When is the launch?"

"Tonight at oh-one-hundred, sir."

"I didn't know you had a launch capability in this facility." He was not amused by the fact that the last tour had omitted that fact. "Will this be its first launch?"

"Yes, sir. Dr. Nampo and his staff will give you a further update."

"Yes." Beijing had already been given substantial amounts of information. As a result, two Chinese satellites had been moved to a more westerly position. One that arched over the U.S. Pacific fleet in Hawaii had been shifted to the west, behind the protective curvature of the Earth.

The jeep convoy pulled into the short tunnel below the grove of trees. More pine trees were now evident––not that it would matter after tonight. A missile launch from the silo would confirm the launch pad's existence, and by noon tomorrow, it would be on the newly revised target list of some American Trident submarine.

"You'll be in the same room this time, sir."

"Yes, thank you," said Won.

Entering the facility, the general noticed a much different energy. Last time, the young men and women glanced at him constantly, aware of a stranger in their midst. This time, they were too occupied to bother. The air in the space felt electric, not unlike that of a military force in its final exercise before an invasion.

"I'll come for you at midnight," said Sang.

"Yes." Before the captain left, Won asked, "But when will your Doctor give us the update?"

"He'll give the briefing at midnight."

"Yes, again, thank you," said Won.

The stainless steel door slid closed, and as he had done before, Comrade General Won used this opportunity to rest. He unbuttoned his tunic and draped it over the back of a chair. Midnight was not for several hours. As he lay in the bedroom, he again thought of another Korea.

"General?"

"Yes?" He sat up, realizing his brief doze had turned into a deep sleep. The captain was awkwardly standing just inside the door to the apartment.

"They are ready, sir."

"Let's go then." He quickly grabbed and buttoned his tunic, somewhat embarrassed that he had not been ready for the captain.

With Sang's help, he walked up two flights to a tunnel just wide enough for two lanes of electric cars, similar to American golf carts, going in opposite directions. The carts were separated only by a steel divider the width of a chair arm. Won slid into the back of one cart, facing the rear, and Sang sat in the front, next to the driver, a teenage girl. As they moved forward, Won could see the short length of the tunnel, which opened a few meters away to another large hangar-sized room, where the cars could exit the tunnel and turn around.

"I don't recall this from our last trip," said Won.

"It was not quite open at the time, sir."

"Yes, I imagine not." He was being courteous. He imagined it would have taken much more than several months to construct this tunnel, yet no mention of it had been made on his last visit.

As the cart continued at high speed, the general felt the whoosh of other carts pass in the opposite direction. He made a point of pulling his arms in, as if sitting in the seat of a small fighter, for fear that another cart would slam into him. Each cart made a horrible bleep just before passing another, as if to warn of its approach, but the warning always came too late. The bleeps echoed through the tunnel.

A moment later, his cart came to a quick

stop. The cart was perfectly aligned with another tunnel perpendicular to the main one. Appearing almost like a large bank vault, a massive round steel door opened to the next long tunnel, smaller than the main one, for pedestrians only.

"This way, General," said Sang.

"Yes." The general turned and bowed slightly to acknowledge his young driver. She smiled. With age, Won had learned how important his little gestures were to a young, impressionable soldier. It was one of the few benefits of being a general—to be able to make another's life feel special for a brief moment.

As they walked down the tunnel, the floor slanted downward slightly, then opened into another area and another vaulted door. In front of this one were two armed sentries. "This is our most honorable guest, General Won." The captain almost shouted the words. Both sentries came to quick attention.

Stepping in through the door, Won realized he was entering another long control room like the one he had visited several months ago, with one wall built from the natural gray stone of the nearby mountains, the other of thick, green-tinted glass looking out over a large bay cut into the rock. In the center of the open bay was a tall, gleaming white, multi-staged rocket with a bright red star a quarter of the way from the top. The letters "DPRK," boldly printed on the rocket's uppermost stage, appeared in white, blue, and red.

Surrounding the rocket, which sat on a stainless steel pedestal under a massive round opening in the rock above, were dozens of men and women, all dressed in white. All wore caps, and some wore masks, like surgeons preparing for a transplant operation.

"Welcome again, Comrade General." Dr. Nampo was also dressed in a long white surgeon's coat.

"Thank you, Comrade Doctor," said Won. "I never cease to be amazed at your resources and capabilities."

"Yes, well . . . ." Nampo seemed at a loss for words. He clearly had difficulty accepting a compliment. He bent his head down like a beaten puppy, then turned to his other associates.

"Let us begin."

"What are we doing here, Doctor?" said Won.

Nampo pointed to three large seats at a panel of television monitors above the main floor of scientists.

"We will launch our missile tonight to a target some six thousand nautical miles away, near the path of a west coast GPS satellite and in a GEO orbit."

"Yes, impressive."

"It will be absolutely clear, General," said Nampo, "that even with conventional explosives, we will be able to reach, intercept, and destroy any satellite in space, whether military or civilian."

General Won slumped into the chair.

He was not sure this was a power he wanted unleashed, even by a so-called ally. But, he thought, there was little that could be done to stop it.

22

"Congratulations, Colonel." Gunny Punaros sounded like a teacher who had given his star student all A's on his report card.

The last sniper, however, grimaced as he picked up his rifle and camouflage. He obviously knew as well as the Gunny that Will had not stayed within the field's boundaries. Then again, thought Will, he hadn't hesitated to cover the target with his body.

"What's next?" asked Will.

"That's it, sir. You're ready."

Mi came up to the small group, gathered near the sniper's final position. It was getting dark and cold as clouds moved in at a rapid pace. She pulled the collar of her black Polartek jacket up to block the chilly wind.

"How far out are we, Gunny?" Will said.

"I'd say about nine to ten miles back to the Academy, sir."

"Okay, we're gone."

With that, Will took off.

| | |

Mi smiled briefly at Punaros, then raced after Will down the graveled road.

Sometimes, during these runs, Will would talk, and after several weeks, Mi had begun to talk, too. At this point, they were both in such good physical shape that conversation, even while running, was effortless. But neither spoke now.

Will came to the paved road and turned right, heading back. As he did, snow began to fall—not a driving snowstorm, but a steady flow. Mi could feel the cold flakes as they struck her face and eyes. Then a dull flash of light lit a cloud, and they heard a rumble far in the distance. This was that rare storm—thunder, lightning, and falling snow as the temperature dropped.

They ran on in the lights of the following

Suburban, with Mi nearly in step with each of his long strides. His movement was a constant rhythm.

As darkness fell and they neared the final road that turned to the Academy, Will crossed a bridge over a small, bending creek—one they had passed over nearly every day.

Suddenly, he jumped right just beyond the bridge, down the embankment, onto a trail heading back into the deep, dark woods. Mi jumped, staying in his tracks, as the snow began to stick to the cold ground. She tried to follow within his steps, but his long, fluid stride caused her to be short every third or fourth step. When this would happen, she would feel her foot slip slightly, stamping through the newly fallen snow.

The black Suburban slammed on its brakes, then slid off the road to the other side and down the embankment. Mi could hear the slamming of doors and men cursing as she followed along the trail, deeper into the woods. Mi didn't remember this trail, but Will apparently did—he didn't hesitate. He ran in the dim light, with an occasional dull flicker of thunder illuminating the sky. The light reflected through the tree limbs and off the new, white snow, allowing Mi to see well into the woods. It would have been a lonely, scary view but for the fact that she could spot a cloud of hot air from Will's breath.

Will dashed down the trail until he came to a sharp bend in the creek running parallel to their path. He suddenly turned right, leaping up on the large outcropping of rocks the stream flowed over.

She kept pace, determined more than ever to stay in his footsteps.

Is he trying to lose me? she thought, beginning to feel both angry and exhilarated. Branches slapped her in the face and arms as he picked up the pace.

Another crashing boom of thunder and light struck nearby as the storm continued to build. The lightning was getting dangerously near, but Will continued up the hill.

Suddenly, as quickly as they came into the woods, they came out. They were near a line of rounded, tin-roofed Quonset buildings, all still, dark, and apparently abandoned. A sign on the side of one door, red with yellow lettering, said "CAMP UPSHER BARRACKS B." It was the second one down the line. The camp was empty of Marines—or any others, for that matter.

Will turned to the third one and slammed open the shed's door. Another boom of thunder sounded nearby, and the metal-roofed building shook with the force of the sound wave. She followed him into the building. Inside, two rows of bunk beds lined up straight. A few buildings away, a security light provided a dull yellow glow through small rectangular windows the height of a man's reach.

Again, a boom of thunder whammed through the building, and Mi saw another flash of light illuminate the barracks. As it did, Will grabbed her from behind. She jumped, startled. He brushed the snow off her back and arms and then turned her around, looking directly into her eyes, grabbing both her arms as he pulled her closer.

"Now it's time," he said, his blue eyes staring directly into hers. "It's time for you to decide."

She looked down.

"No," he said, raising her chin to meet her eyes. "What's it going to be?"

She was tired of deciding. All her life, fate had pulled her toward decisions of life and death. And she thought herself toughened by these decisions, both in North Korea and when working with the CIA. When she'd defected, it had cost several lives. Some died simply for being too close to her. But this time was different. He was different.

"Yes," she said.

"Yes, what?"

"This time, no government. This time—you."

Will kissed her and pulled her to the bunk bed. He reached behind her, pulled the mattress down to the floor, and leaned down onto the bed above her. They were both wet from the melting snow.

As the thunder shook the building again, they stayed locked in an embrace.

"This thunder . . . ." he said.

"Yes," she said, turning to face him.

"With snow like this?"

"Yes?"

"We have a name for it."

"What?"

"A northern thunder . . . a cold, northern thunder," Will said.

"What's next?" Mi asked.

"We're totally on our own," Will said. "Don't trust anyone."

Personal experience had prepared Mi well for this. She had been alone for years now. Not trusting others was the easy part.

"Yes, I know." This time, she grabbed him and pulled him closer, kissing him again.

Another boom of thunder struck nearby. He looked into her eyes again. "Now, this is what I need you to do . . . ."

The SIOC's operations center on the fifth floor of the FBI building was much larger than Tom Pope had remembered. Its 40,000 square feet of windowless, gray-carpeted workrooms were separated by a series of well-insulated walls. Massive fifteen-foot video screens covered much of the wall space in the separated work areas.

On his way to his office, Tom had often seen the one elevator with a guard in the back corridor, but had been called to the operations center only once before. This time, like the previous one, he had to get a bright red pass displaying today's date in bold letters, emphasizing his very temporary clearance.

"The director will be waiting." Dave Creighton was a man Tom Pope had known throughout most of his career; as deputy director, he was a heartbeat away from the top. Every agency within the government needed dependable professionals who could help the government make a transition from one administration to another. Creighton was in that small group of top executives who transcended politics and changing administrations. "Do you have a Powerpoint for him?"

"Yes, sir."

"And a hard copy?" For all executive-level briefings, the director was given a hard, printed copy as an aid and a record.

"Yes, sir," said Tom.

"It has to be classified," Creighton said.

"Yes, sir. It's already marked."

"If he doesn't want to keep it at the end, you must collect all copies and either keep custody of them or place them in a burn bag." Most secure offices at the Bureau had a red-striped, trashcan-like paper bag, similar to a small grocery bag, where sensitive documents were deposited every day and destroyed.

"Yes, sir."

"Are you ready?"

The procedural details made Tom nervous, but from his time in Washington, he knew Creighton to be a concerned boss trying only to help an underling do well.

"Yes, sir," said Tom.

The elevator door slid open to a wood-paneled entrance with two armed guards. Behind their desks hung a large, oversized seal of the Federal Bureau of Investigation. Below the seal was "SIOC" in large gold letters, and, below that, the label "Strategic Information and Operations Center." The "Sigh-Ock," as it was called, had started sometime in the late nineties, and was known by several other names. After the September, 2001, attack on the World Trade Center, SIOC became the FBI's main operational center when responding to a national crisis. Congress had authorized hundreds of millions of dollars to upgrade the center, its computers, and its communications.

Both guards stood at attention as Creighton flashed his badge. "He's with me," he said.

"Yes, sir."

Tom meekly lifted his temporary badge. He almost expected a laugh from the two, but they were accustomed to seeing guests on limited visits.

"Hey, thanks," Tom mumbled as he passed the men through another set of doors and into a hallway.

"Follow me," Creighton instructed.

"Yes, sir."

"Molly, this is Tom Pope."

"Yes, sir." A young freckle-faced woman with brown-blond hair, dressed in a blue pinstriped suit, greeted both men as they walked down the hall. Tom quickly noticed her nervous habit of pushing her wire-rimmed glasses up the bridge of her nose, and, as she did, he noticed her fingers—the nails had been gnawed to the quick, the likely result of nervous tension.

"She's our tech rep," said Creighton.

"Agent Pope, do you need any help on the briefing?" said Molly.

Tom pulled a CD from his pocket. "Powerpoint."

"Yes, let's do a quick walkthrough."

"Not much time," Creighton said with a frown. An overpowering man who had played all four years at Michigan as middle linebacker, Dave Creighton was not particularly tall. He had shaved what little hair remained on his head, giving him a Yul Brenner look.

Liked and respected, Creighton had a reputation for complete fairness. Never political, he was seen as someone who would help the Bureau survive bad times. During Creighton's rise to deputy director, the FBI had been confronted with several difficult incidents. Creighton had handled them all with great candor and aplomb, displaying a willingness to criticize and accept criticism when needed.

"It's okay. I'm ready," said Tom.

"Good deal," said Creighton. "He'll be more interested in getting specific questions answered than seeing a dog and pony show anyway."

The two swept their cards on a scanner at another wood door within the entranceway, this one marked with brass letters, "FBI Operations Center." Inside, several flat video monitors, massive in size and split-screened, immediately attracted Tom's eye. A large conference table stood directly in front of the screens. Far behind the table were several aisles of computer-laden desks, attended by an assortment of men and women. In a glance, Tom noted that the screens had a variety of maps, video surveillance displays, and several people talking from what appeared to be other centers, either across the country or across the world.

Tom came down to a rostrum next to the screens, to one side of the conference table. A large blue leather chair monogrammed with the Bureau's seal dominated the table. A glass panel, again with the FBI seal etched on, separated the conference table from the room with computer desks, and a set of sliding glass doors joined them.

"Okay, sir," Molly said to Tom. "This dimmer controls the light here on your podium. I'll control the lighting in the room. This clicker will control your Powerpoint. It'll be all set up. And if there are any problems, I'll be ready."

Tom looked forlorn.

"Have you ever briefed this guy?" Molly asked sympathetically.

"No, this is just my second time even being here."

She smiled. "He's okay. He won't embarrass you. Some of his assistants may take a swing at you, but he won't."

"Great." He breathed a sigh of relief, then a side door swung open and in walked several men and women.

Tom recognized the director from his many appearances on CNN, Fox, and other news networks, and from the evening news the night before, when the anchor had interviewed him. *Boy, will I have something to tell my family*, he thought. The director went right to the big chair, where a yellow pad, pencil, and coffee cup were set out for him.

"Okay, Agent Pope, what have you got?" the director said.

"Sir, we formed an integrated task force some time ago after a contact informed us of the deaths of certain respected scientists, and an apparent common thread connecting them."

"That's your Joan of Arc." The director was well-informed, which immediately impressed Tom.

"Yes, sir."

"Believed to be a DPRK employee."

"Yes, sir."

"Working at the United Nations?"

"Yes, sir."

"Why?" said the director.

"Why what, sir?" said Tom.

"Why is she helping us?"

"I don't know, sir, but she's been reliable."

"Okay, I don't see a downside yet. Keep going."

"Yes," said Tom. "She knew of the death of a Dr. Harbinger at Berkeley and a Dr. Walter at MIT. Since then, we've been tracking similar deaths with Interpol in Europe and with the Russians."

"The Russians?" The director slid forward in his chair.

"Yes, sir. We found out about the deaths of a Dr. Wiretrack at Oxford and a Dr. Boriskof at Russia's Ioffe Physico-Technico Institute in St. Petersburg."

"My God," the director said. All of his assistants rolled forward in their chairs and began taking notes.

Tom flashed another Powerpoint display showing pictures of the victims. "Each worked in advanced engineering."

"That's a little broad," said the director. "Anything more specific they had in common?"

"Each had worked, or was working, on advanced satellite engineering projects, including reduced payloads," said Tom.

"All were trying to apply developments in nanotechnology to reduce weight."

"Better."

At least this guy tosses out an occasional compliment. Tom felt a small uplift of pride.

"So, who's the culprit? The DPRK?"

The next slide flashed up on the central flat screen television. It showed not a picture, but a blank central box surrounded by lines of characteristics.

"Presumably, sir, but, other than Joan's tip, we have no evidence to this effect."

"Dave, have we had any discussions with CIA or DOD on this?"

Creighton leaned forward sheepishly. "No, sir. We're getting information from them, but to date we've only made very generic requests."

"Goddammit. I thought when I got here, I told everyone I wanted to break down these walls."

Tom knew the comment hit a nerve in the room. The FBI had inherited much from its father, J. Edgar Hoover, including the habit of keeping information internal. September 11th had proven the risk of that philosophy.

"Okay, let's get both CIA and Defense involved, and assuming it's DPRK, what's wrong with plugging in the KGB?"

"Sir, KGB leaks like a sieve." On this subject, Creighton was well informed by experience. Others agreed. "Given their past relationship with the DPRK," Creighton continued, "it's unlikely that any information won't immediately leak to North Korea. Virtually every DPRK agent is KGB-trained."

"But won't they be running their own investigation into the death of Boriskof?" the director asked.

"Not necessarily, sir." Tom inserted this comment and immediately regretted it. Such briefings were not the place to get brave. In this thin, high-altitude air, it was beyond daring to take too much of a leap.

"Why?" the director said.

"We didn't start tracking the relationship between the three scientists until Joan connected the dots for us. With only one of their scientists killed, it's unlikely the KGB will also have connected the dots."

"Okay."

"And, sir, this guy is using a very potent, advanced poison that acts very, very quickly and simulates a heart attack. That's how Boriskof's death was initially reported. The Russians still may not know it was an assassination."

"I see," said the director, "but if they don't know more, and thus suspect nothing, he'll be able to travel through Moscow and St. Petersburg without risk."

"Yes, sir, and that may be our best shot."

"Oh?"

"Yes, sir. We know where he'll feel comfortable. And, in that, we have an advantage."

Another Powerpoint slide popped up, this one showing a U.S. immigrations officer in a tie and starched white uniform.

"We did a scan on immigrations after Dr. Walter's death and ran across Immigrations Officer Benjamin Jones in Boston," said Tom.

"A member of my team, Agent Susan Wright, had come across the death of the Russian professor and cross-referenced it with the death of Dr. Walter at MIT. She then cross-referenced the time and dates with staffing at Logan's Immigrations and sent an e-mail to the officers asking for anything unusual. She found Jones."

"I'm listening."

"Officer Jones has been at Logan for twenty-two years. He remembered a traveler––a Mr. Chang––traveling from Paris to Boston shortly before Walter's death."

"Any luck with the random photographs at Immigration?"

"We got one photo, at a distance, of Chang passing through the Customs hall at Logan."

"And?" said the director.

"We did a cross-section of immigration records," said Tom. "Not only is there no Mr. Chang, but this man did not leave from Logan on his return."

"Okay, I've heard enough," said the

director. "Let's give Tom's group a higher priority and link them up with CIA and DOD."

"Yes, sir," said Creighton.

"And, Tom, I need to know the reason behind all these murders. Do we have an answer yet?"

"No, sir. But—"

"I believe I know the answer." The comment came from the side of the table at the far end—from a thin, bespectacled, older man in a vested brown suit.

"Yes, Doctor?"

Tom leaned over to Creighton. "Who's that?"

"He's the science advisor to the director," Creighton whispered, his hand over his mouth.

"It's a need-to-know issue." The science advisor said the words softly but clearly.

"Need to know" was the government's ultimate trump card. Even those with the highest security clearances might lack access to certain information because they lacked an official "need to know."

"Okay, Dr. Wilhelm, hold on a minute,"

said the director. "Dave, provide 'need to know' authorizations for you, me, and Agent Pope."

Tom's heart skipped a beat. He was being given access to the most secret information by none other than the director of the Federal Bureau of Investigation. It was like a land grant from the king.

"Okay, folks, everyone is excused for a minute. Molly, shut down this room and all portals," said Creighton.

"Yes, sir, Mr. Creighton."

The group stood up, and as the final man filed out of the room, the glass partition closed and a curtain slid down from the ceiling, sequestering the four men from the remainder of the center. Tom felt something strange—a surge of excitement, as if he were a teenage boy being allowed into the most exclusive club in existence. He came around from the podium and pulled up a seat just to the side of the director.

"Sir, this is a fairly long story." Wilhelm

learned forward and began speaking right to the director.

"Go ahead."

"In August of 1998, the DPRK launched a Taepo Dong-1 missile. It was their first attempt at building a multi-stage rocket and putting a satellite into orbit."

Both Tom and Creighton leaned forward to hear the low, quiet voice. As Tom began to make a note, Dave Creighton slid his large, athletic hand over Tom's, holding the pencil still. Tom took the hint and laid the pencil down.

"Some of us nicknamed the satellite the 'Trucker's AM Radio Station,' or 'TARS,' for two reasons: its purpose was to play music glorifying Kim Il Sung, and the frequency band was the same as truck CB radios."

The director smiled briefly. "Did it work?"

"They claimed yes, but the rocket's second stage didn't seem to have the required push. We had some tracking out of the North Hangyong Province missile base it was launched from, and the Kwangnyongsong-1, as they called it, was never confirmed in orbit."

"So, what's the point?"

"The K-1 satellite was about the size of a football," said Wilhelm. "We are limited in what we can track. If something's too small, we can't track it. For all we know, that satellite could still be up there."

"Is it a threat?" said the director.

"Oh, no, sir. As to the K-1, we scanned the band frequencies it was reported to be functioning on and never heard a thing. The point is, they were beginning to develop an intercontinental missile, and . . . they have been on the path of developing miniaturization technology. Later, they tested the TD-2. It was not much better. Broke apart over the Sea of Japan."

"I'm lost," Creighton piped up. "What's this all mean?"

"It means that they are decades away from developing a rocket that can carry a payload the size of one of our older, conventional nuclear weapons," said Wilhelm.

"Okay."

"But they are within reach of developing a smaller, intercontinental rocket, and possibly a 100-kilogram sixth-generation nuclear device. If they can reduce their payloads and still accomplish the same thing, they win twice. First, their rockets can carry the payload farther and higher, and——"

"And," the director interjected, "if it's small enough, we would detect the launch, but not the weapon, or whatever else they put up there."

"Exactly. We could monitor frequencies and command instructions, but they'd have numerous ways to get around that."

"And," Tom boldly added, "the dead scientists were involved in developing the same technology, and thus best informed on how to stop it."

"Again, exactly."

Creighton let out an audible sigh, underlining the point.

"Okay, so is that why someone's on a course to eliminate all these scientists?" The director raised both hands in a visual question mark.

"I haven't talked with the Agency lately on this subject," said Wilhelm, "but my guess is that North Korea must have someone trying to corner the market on some of this technology."

"And an elimination of competition would do what?"

"It would give them several years during which they, and they alone, could do a host of things."

"Yes, like exporting the technology, selling the technology, and——"

"Blackmailing countries without the technology." Tom again tossed in his comment without thinking.

"Yes, Agent Pope. Blackmail," said the director. "If any government in the history of the world has a reputation for resorting to blackmail, it's the DPRK."

"Does it matter to us and our investigation if they have a scientist of this caliber?" Creighton asked.

"The Agency will surely want to know

what's going on here, but all we really need is a clear sense of who this guy's potential targets will be," said the director. "We need to know who would be considered the scientist's competitors, and in that regard, some sense of who or what they're competing against." The director tossed his pencil down onto the pad, where it rolled off onto the shiny mahogany table.

"Sir, I suggest Dr. Wilhelm makes appropriate inquiry with his counterpart at the Agency, while we bring in our profiling team." Creighton sounded like the captain of a Michigan football team.

"And their purpose would be to develop a profile of the criminal?"

"No, sir," said Creighton. "In this case, they would develop a profile of the potential victim."

"Good idea, but we need to keep this very, very limited." He cringed slightly, seeming to realize that he was backtracking on his previous interest in breaking down interagency walls.

"Yes, sir."

"Agent Pope, for now, keep this limited to you. Let your team develop its thoughts and use this information to guide them." As he said it, he realized the potential cat and mouse game at hand.

"Yes, sir," said Tom.

"But don't expand it further than the absolute minimum."

"Yes, sir."

"Dave, I need an update on this one with extreme regularity."

"Oh, yes, sir," said Creighton. "We'll give Agent Pope the highest priority, and he'll let me know what's going on as it develops."

Tom knew an order from Creighton when he heard one.

"Oh, and Agent Pope," said the director, "I know this is sensitive to you, just as it would be to any agent, but we need to know how much information we can get from your source."

"Yes, ah, sir," Tom stuttered. Like a news reporter being asked about his source, a good field agent took to his grave the identity of a good informant. *Woodward and Bernstein probably felt the same when their editor asked about Deep Throat*, he thought. *But maybe I can give them what they need without getting into too much detail.*

The director sensed his hesitation. "I don't plan on pushing you too much, you can be assured of that. For now, let's just get this guy." He jumped up and crossed beyond the table, offering his hand to Tom. "Thank your people for me," he said.

"Yes, sir."

"Let them know they're greatly appreciated."

"Yes, sir." Tom's chest swelled with pride.

"It's quiet in both the Pacific and the Atlantic."

"How about China? Any planned launches today?"

"No, quiet there as well."

The Missile Warning Center was good duty. A small computer room buried deep within Cheyenne Mountain's Operation Center, the MWC was where sensors, satellites, radars, and surveillance equipment fed all their information from around the globe.

If something big happens, I'll be the first to know, thought Air Force Senior Master Sergeant Billy Algrade. *Which means I'm the one who gets to tell the president the shit has hit the fan.*

The Saturday morning shift at MWC had become rather routine for Billy, the senior non-commissioned officer of Bravo Crew CD. He enjoyed "being at this point of the spear," as his commanding officer often said, although it grated on him that the generals would all be out playing golf while he spent his Saturday morning at work.

"Why don't you run off that stale, old shit," Billy commanded his junior airman. Johnson and the crew always expected Billy to start each shift by giving them a certain amount of grief—and by ordering a new pot of coffee. This morning, Billy had managed to do both at the same time.

"Yo, Johnson," he said a few minutes later. "What the hell's taking you so long?"

At that same instant, the alarm began on the main computer—a shrill sequence of beeps—and in a split second repeated on the second, third, and fourth monitors. Dominoes seemed to fall as each computer sounded the same distress call.

"What is it?" Billy said.

Adrenaline coursed through the room.

"Launch detection," said Johnson.

"Okay, check list and location."

"Sergeant, it's the Pacific." At that moment, the Bravo Crew officer of the day charged into the room and pulled up a chair next to Billy's desk.

"Okay, Billy, what's it look like?"

"Satellite detection by USA394, sir."

"China launch facilities?" Satellite USA394 passed north to south along the eastern end of China, then across the East China Sea, the Korean peninsula, the Sea of Japan, and the Sea of Okhotsk.

"No, sir, and none are expected from China." Even with the strain of politics, the superpowers had gotten into the habit of giving each other a heads-up on future launches. For China, as with the others, there wasn't any advantage in keeping launches a secret. Besides, launch preparations were visible by spy satellites for months in advance.

"Where, then?" said the officer.

"DPRK."

"No way."

"It looks like that's it, sir," said Billy.

"We haven't had one from them in months."

"Yes, sir."

"Where in DPRK?"

"God, sir, this is pretty far south——almost at the DMZ."

A chill ran down Billy's back. Depending on the launch's direction, his first thought was that this was a North Korean strike across the DMZ. A missile flying south would have already traveled the thirty or so miles to Seoul and detonated. Even with the instantaneous reaction of surveillance satellites and their computers, the distances were too short in Korea. If this missile had been sent south, the death sentence to millions in Seoul, including thousands of American forces in close proximity to the border and the city, was already history.

"The DMZ?" said the officer.

"Yes, sir."

"What do the other systems show?"

"The launching station seems to be in the eastern coastal region," said Billy. "It launched in the direction of eighty-six degrees and will be crossing over one of Japan's northern islands."

The officer visibly relaxed, and so did Billy. It was trouble, but an eighty-six-degree launch that crossed over northern Japan was clearly a test missile, or at least not an offensive missile aimed at Seoul.

"Okay, CMOC will be monitoring this, but talk to them," said the officer. "Also, talk to SCC and OIW." He pretty much covered the bases. NORAD's massive bunker deep within a Colorado mountain had been reorganized several times since the Cold War thaw. It retained the Cold War responsibility of detecting what Air Force strategists called "air-breathing machines"—or jet aircraft— as they approached North America. But, as technology progressed, space had become a larger and larger part of the job.

The Cheyenne Mountain Operation Center (CMOC) took in, assessed, and coordinated information from a host of sources. The Missile Warning Center was one of several monitoring centers. Others were the

Space Control Center, known as SCC, and Operational Intelligence Watch, or OIW. It was to be moved to nearby Peterson Air Base in the near future. The old mountain had become expensive.

Space Control had the ever-increasing task of monitoring every detectable object in space. Already, there were nearly nine thousand operating "earth-space vehicles," as satellites were called, and countless other bits of space flotsam and jetsam. SCC folks were the space librarians responsible for precisely cataloging all such objects in space.

"Okay," said the officer, "by both computer and verbal confirmation, we need to relay to the big guys what we know."

He was referring to the never-ending layers of Operations Command Centers. The Missile Warning Center fed to CMOC at Cheyenne Mountain, and then to US STRATCOM at Offit Air Force Base, Nebraska, and then to the National Military Command Center at the Pentagon, and then to the Secretary's Executive Support Center. Finally, NMCC and ESC would be on a direct hookup to the White House Situation Room.

"Yes, sir," said Billy. The red phone on his desk was behind the framed photographs of his wife and son. He moved the pictures and picked up the phone.

"Offit, this is Cheyenne. We've detected an unexpected missile launch from the DPRK."

| | | |

Billy's words woke up several duty officers, who scrambled to contact their bosses.

Less than an hour later, General Kitcher at Strategic Air Command convened battle staff at his Operations Center deep below Offit, Nebraska. "Is the VTC online?" he said.

"Yes, sir," the young captain responsible for communications said from the back. A panel of screens showed a variety of men in various military uniforms. The attendees of the video teleconference, or "VTC," had one thing in common: Each was framed from behind by a group of others making up his staff, with the unit's seal on the wall behind them.

"Okay, this is Kitcher at Offit." He ran down the roll call as the varying television screens spoke. "Cheyenne Mountain Operations Center?"

"Yes, sir, Brigadier General Apps."

"Randy, do you have representatives from the Missile Warning Center?" said Kitcher.

"Yes, sir," said Apps. "We also have representatives from Space Control and Operational Intelligence."

"Great. And NMCC?"

"Yes, sir. Admiral Tony Vandergrift," said the next man down. "I'm duty officer at the National Military Command Center."

"And the Secretary?"

"Yes, this is Assistant Secretary Butler."

"Yes, sir," said Kitcher. "Then I'll begin this VTC. I'm told we're locked on for thirty minutes time. This brief is Top Secret—Need to Know. If we need more time, we can discuss that at the last minute or continue these discussions individually offline. MWC——or Randy——why don't you begin?"

"Yes, sir," said Apps, "I have a very basic Powerpoint to help." A map of North Korea appeared on a split screen as Air Force General Apps spoke.

"We had a launch at oh-one-hundred local Korean time from a previously suspected, but unconfirmed, underground facility approximately thirty miles south-southwest of the port city of Wonsan," said Apps. "That places it approximately thirty miles to the north of the DMZ. This is a new launch site. More importantly, the rocket appears to be a multi-staged intercontinental rocket, and may even be the TD-3X."

"I thought the Taepo Dong-3X was still in its developmental stages," said Kitcher.

"Sir, this is Colonel Thompson of Operational Intelligence," said a new voice. "They never really had a fully successful flight of the TD-2. This could be a refinement of it or the beginning of this TD-3X. It appears from initial data, however, that this has not only pushed beyond one thousand nautical miles, but has reached GEO orbit."

"Sir, we also had some other bad news," Randy Apps said in a deliberately low voice.

"What?"

"A West Coast GPS satellite in the same general path and orbit of this detected missile went offline at 0137 local time for about five minutes."

"What does that mean?" said Kitcher.

"We don't know yet, sir. It could be a coincidence, random failure, or something else. A GPS backup took over shortly after the bird went down. With an eighty-six-degree launch and a polar orbit, the Korean rocket could have passed very close to this particular GPS satellite."

"I have some comment on that, General and Mr. Assistant Secretary," said Thompson. "We know that a short while ago, the Chinese moved some of their more southern and eastern satellites out of their standard orbits."

"Yes, sir. We've been tracking that as well in SCC," said Kitcher.

"What are you suggesting?" said Butler.

"They may have been told to get their assets out of the way," Thompson said.

"Mr. Assistant Secretary, I suggest the Secretary be advised of this situation immediately," said Kitcher.

"Yes, General," said Butler, "I agree. I'll have him located by the ESC and get with him shortly."

One of the brass sitting around the National Military Command Center's conference room table, Admiral Julius Krowl, had a big smile on his face as he looked to his assistant. Krowl knew opportunity had just knocked at his door.

"Is there anything to add?" Assistant Secretary Butler asked.

"No, sir," said Kitcher.

"The TD-3X is bad enough," said Butler. "Let me know what the GPS folks think as soon as practical. And let's keep this off CNN as long as we can."

The several screens went blank.

The young sailor working the flight line heard the low *whomp-whomp* of the Marine helicopter before he saw it. When he turned, it took him a minute to realize two birds were flying closely together, low on the horizon.

"CH-53s?" he said.

"Oh, yeah," said another sailor, "from Bridgeport."

Fallon was a target range for Navy fixed-wing fighters needing space to play with their thousand-pound bombs. Marine helicopters rarely visited the naval air station except for maintenance or fuel. But the chief mate who ran the flight line at Fallon immediately knew why the double-blade helicopters were in Nevada.

The two machines touched down lightly,

their wheels collapsing and settling into place. Both the crew chiefs dropped their half doors, climbed down, and walked two-thirds of the way around their aircrafts, still tethered to the chopper by long intercom cables. As one chief watched, the crew signaled the pilot to shut down the aircraft, and the whine of the engines slowly purred to a stop.

A young Marine captain in flight gear put on his "cover," or "hat" as his civilian friends would call it, and walked jauntily from the helicopter. "The Flight Operations Office?" he said.

"Yes, sir," said the flight line sailor, "on the left side of the tower."

The captain swung open the door to Operations, not knowing it lacked a spring, and it slammed against the door stop with a bang.

The Operations personnel all glanced up.

"Sorry," he said. "I'm supposed to be picking up a transit passenger for transfer to Bridgeport."

"Sorry, sir. No one here," said the airfield operations chief.

"What about inbound?"

"No aircraft scheduled. A C-130 from San Francisco isn't due until tomorrow."

"Is that so?" said the captain. "Can I use your phone?"

"Yes, sir," said the chief.

At that moment, a voice crackled over the loudspeaker—one obviously tied into the flight tower. "Fallon, November One Six Seven for final stop."

The captain looked up to the old, brown speaker on the wall.

"November One Six Seven, please describe nature of your flight. This is a restricted military airfield." The airfield tower operator's voice crackled with static.

"Yes, sir. One Six Seven is a military-approved flight."

"Roger, you are cleared to land on Runway Sixteen. Winds out of the northwest at one zero knots. Altimeter two niner, niner two."

"Yes, sir, cleared to land on Runway Sixteen."

The sailors and captain turned toward

the windows facing the field. A long, thin jet banked across and above the runway as it turned for final landing.

"That may be my man," the captain said.

The airfield rarely saw the visit of a senior admiral, or even a Gulfstream V, and these arrivals were always announced and planned well in advance. But this mysterious, unannounced flight, on its final leg, was just now making its initial contact.

The shining, black, long-tubed jet landed, its oversized engines reversing to bring the aircraft to a quicker than expected stop. Then it taxied fast to the large open space across from the two Marine helos.

"Thanks, folks." The captain gently pulled the door closed behind him, then walked across the tarmac and signaled his crew chief with a thumbs-up. He spun his index finger around in circles. The helo engines began to whine in unison as their auxiliary power units ran up the jet engines.

Just as he turned toward the Gulfstream, the door opened, a stairway lowered, and a man in a Marine flight jacket hopped off. He didn't have a cover on, which was unusual for a Marine, but he walked like a colonel. He had no badges, no patches, no name tags.

"Sir, Mr. Parker?" ventured the captain.

"Yes," Will said.

"To Bridgeport, sir," the captain said. "CH-53 express."

"Let's go."

A youthful man in a white airline-style shirt with black epaulets and one gold stripe brought a canvas bag down from the Gulfstream and handed it to Will.

"Can I get it, sir?" said the captain.

"No, I'm fine." Will closely followed the captain as they approached the helicopter.

Will now relinquished the bag, tossing it to the crew chief as he approached the hatch.

The crew chief pointed to a row of web seats; Will grabbed the one closest to the door. The chief gave him a helmet—more for sound protection than for anything else.

Will felt the jiggle of the aircraft as the long steel blades swung above. Until they got to a certain speed, the helicopter wiggled around, struggling into a balanced spin. It began to smooth down and get into its rhythm, and Will felt the bird lift up, rise, then tilt forward. In quick succession, it rose above and over the Gulfstream, banked sharply to the left, and headed directly toward the mountain range in the near distance.

As the helicopter tilted again in a sharp bank, its sister aircraft pulled up in unison to the back left. Will had flown in CH-53s many, many times before, yet always felt the electricity of flight. He sank into his seat. As the second bird leveled off with his aircraft, Will saw the Gulfstream below taxi onto the main runway and then move down it, faster and faster until it lifted off. Like a missile, the G-IV shot up into the clouds leaving the helicopters below.

Will turned back around, catching the eye of the crew chief, and pointed to his watch. The *whomp-whomp* of the chopper blocked out all sounds, so they could only communicate via hand signs.

The crew chief held up his right hand, and flashed all five fingers once, twice, and then a third time, signaling a fifteen-minute flight from Fallon. The Bridgeport base was actually located several miles from the town, beyond Sonora Junction, and in a small valley called Pickle Meadow.

Will occasionally leaned forward, catching a glimpse out the crew chief's door as the helicopters banked and climbed into the Sierra Nevada Mountain range that bordered Nevada and California. It became colder in the body of the helicopter as they gained altitude amidst the snow-covered mountains. As Will zipped up his flight jacket and turned the fur collar up around his neck, he saw below a rocky ground, covered in deep snow. Occasional groups of pine trees dotted the sides of the mountains. Will Parker had learned to ski in mountains like this near Aspen. His father had sped down the steepest runs, with Will struggling to stay up.

Instead of trying to climb directly over the mountain peaks, the helicopter banked and turned back and forth as it made its way through the valley. Will turned over to his left side, looked out through the scratched, oval window and saw a small, two-lane highway just below the helicopter. An old truck seemed to strain as it climbed through the curves of the road below.

At the same time, he glanced to the rear of the helicopter to the opening above the ramp door and saw the second bird following. It was mesmerizing watching his helicopter bank, then the trace helicopter in tandem.

After a short while, his helicopter banked hard to the right as it passed from one valley into another at Sonora Junction, heading deep into the mountain range. It had been many years since he'd been on this small road—it broke off from the main highway and headed up the valley to the Marine Corps Mountain Warfare Training Center.

The helicopter now banked to the left in a continuous circular turn. Will sensed that the helicopter was in its final approach for landing at Pickle Meadow. Below, through the Plexiglas, he saw brown and gray rock and stone, and green-tinted buildings tucked against the side of the valley. At this altitude, the remnants of an old storm were evident in patches of brown-stained snow around each of the buildings. He saw the occasional Humvee jeep parked in front of the separate buildings and knew this was the place.

It had been decades since Will had last been at Bridgeport. As a young officer attached to the First Marine Division in southern California's Camp Pendleton, then-Lieutenant Parker had been assigned to a training unit here. He spent two winters in the Wolf Creek region above Pickle Meadow, teaching young Marines mountain warfare training and winter survival. In the second winter, he became officer in charge of what became known as the red hats—the instructors of one of the most difficult and challenging schools of the Marine Corps.

"Sir, we're coming in for landing," the chief shouted over the roar of the jet engines.

Will gave the crew chief a thumbs-up. The

helicopter completed its bank and then, as if proceeding down a slide, tilted its nose up and its back wheels down. The *whomp-whomp* of the blades increased as the pilot changed the pitch to hover mode. Will leaned back against the seat as the aircraft gently slowed down and collapsed on its wheels, the nose finally pitching down to a full landing position.

The crew chief unlatched the bottom half of the door and stepped outside as Will unbuckled himself from his seat and came up to the entrance-way. As he stood in the door, he saw a small greeting party of five. The blades slowed to a near stop as Will climbed down from the helicopter and crossed over to the group. "Well, Mr. Scott," he said. "It's good to see you again."

"Yes, Colonel," said Scott, "I thought I'd be here to make sure the second phase of your training gets off all right. You know these three Marines."

"Indeed," said Will.

"How you doing, boss?" The man who spoke first was a stocky, young staff sergeant

ANDERSON HARP

with a gold set of jump wings on his dotted green, black, and brown Marine utilities.

"Staff Hernandez, how're *you* doing?" He grabbed Hernandez's hand in a vice-like grip. "In fact, how are all of you doing?" Will turned to the other two Marines standing next to the staff sergeant. Each of the men was broad and muscular, with virtually no waistline. The Marine with black sergeant chevrons on his collar was by far the tallest and broadest of the three, the sleeves of his uniform tightly wrapped around the muscles of his upper arm like a taut rubber band. "Sergeant Stidham, I haven't seen you in a while."

"Yes, sir."

"Still playing some football?"

As a middle linebacker, Shane Stidham had been heavily recruited by sixteen different colleges in the South. The coach at Auburn University had called him the next Bo Jackson. Bad grades and an incident with the law brought him to the Marine Corps, and a tour in the Marines gave him the maturity to go back to school, get a degree in physical education, and become a teacher and assistant football coach at Jordan High School in Columbus, Georgia.

His service with the Reserves helped him stay in shape and involved. When he wore his dress blues, Shane Stidham also wore two bronze stars—recognition for deeds done with Will in the Gulf.

"No, sir," said Stidham. "I do more coaching than playing."

"And Gunny Moncrief." Parker turned to the last and shortest of the three Marines.

A muscular man, Moncrief made up for his shorter stature with a much taller attitude. "Yes, sir. Be just my luck to work for a colonel who would drag me out to a godforsaken, cold-ass place like this, sir."

"At least your attitude hasn't changed," said Will.

"Yes, sir. I imagine it won't, either," Moncrief said.

"Okay, Mr. Scott, what's the plan for us?"

"We thought we'd give you two or three

days to acclimatize," said Scott, "then move up into the mountains later this week."

"No, we're ready to go now," Will said.

"O-kay," Scott said, more a question than an acknowledgment.

"My thoughts about this phase are that we work on small unit tactics and get our coordination back up," Will said.

"Yes," said Scott. "And get familiar with some of our new cold-weather gear."

"Unless my team disagrees," said Will, "we're ready to go right now."

"Yes, sir, we're ready," said Stidham, his deep southern accent slow and thick.

"Me, too, sir," said Moncrief. "I've been here a week, sitting around staring at the four walls."

"Yes, sir. Me, too. I'm ready to go," Hernandez said.

"Okay," said Scott, "we'll go up to the gymnasium and outfit you with your cold-weather gear and then head on into the mountains."

Scott led the way to two Humvees parked at the edge of the helicopter pad. After sloughing through the melting snow at the lower base camp level, Will climbed into the front right seat of the first Humvee with Scott in the seat behind him, then covered his eyes as the snow-reflected sun temporarily blinded him.

"Here, you'll want these." Scott leaned over from the backseat and handed Will a pair of black wraparound sunglasses.

"Thanks."

Others would have immediately felt a shortness of breath as they adjusted to the seven thousand-foot altitude of the base camp, but not Will. While others would have suffered through frequent gasps for air, the fast pace of daily ten- to fifteen-mile runs had made Will more easily adaptable.

The jeeps pulled away from the helicopter pad and wound their way up the small mountain trail, past several stone and block buildings, to the upper road above the small base. More than a true military base, Bridgeport was a national park camp. In fact, for many years, it had been on loan to the Marine Corps from the Department of the Interior, with the hope that one day it would be returned to the Park Service. But the threat of North Korea and other cold weather war scenarios had the Marines constantly renewing the lease. With each renewal, the Marine Corps, like a cousin who came to visit but wouldn't leave, built more buildings. After September 11th, the Corps sought and signed a long-term lease for the space.

The two Humvees stopped short of the entrance to a gymnasium on the top ridge overlooking the small camp. Scott and Will exited the vehicle.

"Okay, Colonel, this is Captain Phillip Burke," said Scott.

A young Marine in white pants and white parka stood at the entrance to the gym. Aware of both the colonel's reputation and rank, he cracked a swift salute to Will. "Yes, sir," said the captain, "welcome to the Mountain Warfare Center. I'm in charge of the instructor team here."

"Yes, Skipper, I know all about your teams."

"If you Marines will come with me," Burke said as the rest of the team left the Humvees, "we'll get you set up."

They walked through a green metal door into a small gymnasium. In the center, on four tables, were parkas, other clothing, ropes, and MOLLE packs stuffed with gear. Strapped on top of the packs were titanium snowshoes only slightly larger than cold weather boots. All the equipment was white, including the boots.

"Sir," said Burke, "you'll find your equipment on the far left table. The gunny's table is next, followed by the two staff sergeants. We believe they correspond to your sizes."

"Good job, Captain," said Will.

All the clothing was made using the latest in Extended Cold Weather Clothing System technology. Will lifted up a Gortex parka with a mixed white-and-black camouflage pattern. The pattern had a broken patch of black, browns, and whites that looked odd in the building but would blend in well in the mountains. Each of the Marines stripped down on the spot and put on the ECWCS underwear and Gortex cold weather gear. From the table, Will removed a pair of white silk socks and two white boots. "Mickey Mouse boots," the military affectionately called them. Oversized and rubber-insulated, they did their job extremely well. Even when Will had worn them without any socks at all, his body heat soaked the tightly sealed boots. They were the same sort of insulated, cold weather boots he had used at Bridgeport when last here years ago.

The suited-up men walked out to the Humvees. In his MOLLE pack, Will found an arrangement of green suspenders and pouches with pockets and straps could be added or removed, another set of sunglasses, suntan lotion, and lip balm—all the essentials for sun exposure at high altitudes. This equipment was of the highest quality—little of it typical government-issue—and all altered to appear Soviet-made, complete with Soviet labels and stitching.

The two Humvees took off from the upper camp to Bridgeport and followed a gravel, snow-covered road up the valley toward Sonora Peak. The road led through the wide-open meadow, toward the pass that would connect summer hikers to the other side of the High Sierras. Deep snowdrifts had closed the road for several months. The Humvees made a rattling sound as their snow chains grabbed snow, gravel, and rock.

The men said little during the ride. Moncrief sat in the back of the lead Humvee, cleaning and checking his M4 rifles. Will sat in the front right seat, next to Burke, who was at the wheel.

"Sir, this is your Beretta." Moncrief handed the shiny new pistol, already in a shoulder holster, to Will, who removed it from the holster, dropped the clip from the weapon, and spotted fourteen shiny, brass rounds already loaded. When he pulled the slide back, another round popped out of the chamber, hitting the window of the Humvee and falling to the floor.

After a twenty-minute ride climbing farther up into the pass, with wheels frequently spinning in the snow, the two Humvees came to a small clearing just below a large cliff, where they stopped and turned around.

"Okay, Colonel, we're well within the pass." The captain leaned over the Humvee's center console, peering at a GPS map of the mountain range.

Will smiled grimly to himself, realizing by the captain's actions just how much a threat Nampo was to the U.S. military. Light was fading fast, the sun blocked out by dark clouds moving rapidly to the east.

"What was the original plan, Skipper?"

"We scheduled a week of acclimatizing," Burke replied, "some cold-weather survival classes, and then a five-day tactical exercise. Our hardest exercise is long-distance patrolling, with food available only at certain locations."

"Okay, let's go straight to that," said Will.

Moncrief let out a long moan.

"Sir, here's map coordinates for three locations of LRPs," said Burke, pulling out a map. "Each location will be heavily patrolled by our enemy teams. You want to eat, you have to get to the spots." The long-range patrol rations, or LRPs, were concentrated, high-calorie meals.

Will glanced at the coordinates as he pulled the captain's map toward the light of his window.

"Each of these coordinates is on a mountain top. Each has full exposure to both your teams and the worst weather."

"Yes." Will smiled, thinking this sounded like a Gunny Punaros mission. "Okay, what happens if we don't get to them?"

"No problem, sir," said Burke. "All you have to do is follow the lights down into the valley."

"You mean give up."

Moncrief let out a bellowing laugh. "Yeah, right, Skipper. You've never served with the colonel." He said this in as sarcastic a tone as possible.

"What's the weather doing?" said Will.

"Sir, here's the most recent fax," said Burke. The thin sheet of paper was covered in tight, circular lines from top to bottom, clearly showing bad weather moving from the northwest down to the southeast.

"Bad, bad snow." As Will said this, he looked up to see the first snowflakes coming down at a driving angle. "So, either quit or get through this storm for five days."

"Yes, sir. Nothing for fifty miles in any direction," said Burke. "And the exercise is through terrain so rough that some unfortunate wagon trains resorted to cannibalism 150 years ago."

"Thanks, Captain, we get the point," said Gunny Moncrief.

"Okay, when and where on the fifth day?" said Will.

"Twelve-hundred hours at that gym. You have enough food for half a day," said Burke.

As Will swung the Humvee door open, a gust of snow-driven wind pushed it back against him. He felt the cold, wet flakes strike both his face and eyelashes.

Once Will explained the plan to Scott, Stidham, and Hernandez in the other vehicle, the Humvee convoy, carrying Burke and Scott, headed back down the valley road. The four remaining soldiers looked like abandoned wayfarers grouped together with their packs and snowshoes.

For a moment after the vehicles left, the deep woods were completely silent. The cold, quiet air was a short respite for Will and his men, but it was rapidly getting darker and the winds were building.

"We know what to do. Visibility is going to go to zero shortly, so I'll lead and let's run a rope," said Will, pulling a rope from his backpack. "Each of you hook on with Moncrief."

"Yes, sir."

"You know what to do at the tail."

"Yes, sir, just like Greeley." Despite all his chatter, Kevin Moncrief was the team's second expert on cold weather survival. He had spent a winter as a Marine liaison instructor at the Army's cold weather survival school at Fort Greeley, Alaska. Moncrief grabbed the end of the rope, tied a loop, and locked on a carabineer. The other two team members grabbed the end of the rope, twisted loops, tied them off, and locked carabineers from their MOLLE packs onto them.

Will pulled the parka over his head and fixed his goggles. He strapped onto his wrist a compass with a large illuminated dial and pointed to a heading northwest.

Moncrief moved into Will's line-of-sight and gave him a questioning look.

The three peaks were more to the northeast of the valley. Will's course seemed to take them farther northwest and deeper into the Sierras.

"He's arriving!"

The petite young scientist belted the words out as she hung up the telephone at the console in Nampo's operation center. Like her, everyone in the operations center was ecstatic. The launch had succeeded, orbit had been achieved in less than fifty minutes, and the small explosion from the warhead had hit something—as it turned out, the target, an American West GPS satellite. And now, the nation's leader himself, Kim Jong Il, had come to visit the facility to award Dr. Nampo the People's Medal.

"Calm yourself, girl," said Pak Yim, Nampo's assistant director, his stoic face giving no hint of approval.

The underground command center rarely had more than the minimum number of people needed to man it: a Nampo directive issued at the project's beginning. But today, the large room was crammed with white-jacketed scientists and engineers, both men and women, many of them lined up against the rear wall.

"You know, the Americans just don't understand," Pak said to two of the engineers standing next to the main console. "If they had as their leader the son of George Washington, maybe they would." Since birth, the people of North Korea had been indoctrinated not only to respect the country's founder, Kim Il Sung, but to regard him with a spiritual reverence. And Kim Il Sung, in turn, had propagated myths about his son and grandson —both had been born under a double rainbow, their births marked by a bright star.

The young woman, barely out of her teens, hovered next to the command center door as if waiting for a rock star to arrive. As the visitors came down the tunnel to the doors, she felt the beating of her heart.

Enthusiasm energized the room, and the people moved closer to the door as a short, pudgy man with wild hair and oversized dark-rimmed glasses entered. He wore an olive drab Mao suit cut almost like a tunic, with matching drab-olive pants. The only things that made Kim Jong Il stand out were black, highly polished, European-style shoes, custom-made for him, by the dozens, in a Tokyo shop. The shoes contained lifts to compensate for his barely five-foot-three stature: another of the well-kept secrets of Kim Jong Il.

Trailing behind the leader was the undistinguished-looking Dr. Nampo and another young man with a round, pudgy face. Nampo wore a scientist's white lab jacket, a gold star medal on a blood-red ribbon hanging awkwardly on its lapel. Nampo had received the highest decoration Kim Jong Il could bestow on citizens. Kim Jong-un was dressed like his father, following the group.

"My comrades," Kim Jong Il said as he stopped into the center of the room, signaling to the people to back up and bow. "Today, after years and years of dedicated service by each of you to your country, we have tasted our first victory. Without Dr. Nampo and his team, this project would never have reached this great success. All citizens of our great democratic republic, including my father if he were still with us, are overwhelmingly proud of your accomplishments."

Kim Jong Il worked his way around the room like a Chicago politician, shaking hands with each of the scientists. This was rare for him. His security guards almost never allowed him to be so exposed, but this was as safe an audience as Kim Jong Il would ever see. Each scientist had been handpicked and trained by Nampo exclusively for this project and for this center.

"Attention," yelled a gold-braided North Korean general from the back of the room. The building's intercom system belted out North Korea's national anthem, and on the last note, Kim Jong Il turned, and with an escort of generals, left the operations center.

On the way out, he stopped and grabbed Nampo's arm again, looking the scientist directly in the eyes. "You have had great success here today," he said, "but we still have a long way to go to reach our goal. Can I trust you to ensure this is just the beginning?"

"Yes, Comrade General Secretary, it is just the beginning," Nampo said to the leader.

As soon as the dictator and his entourage departed, Nampo turned to his assistant and said, "We need everyone out of here except the essential steering committee." He paused, then yelled, "*Now!*"

As fast as they had scurried in, all but five gray-haired scientists filed out of the entrance and down the tunnel, away from the operations center.

Nampo walked to one sizable chair at the end of the conference table and sat, pulling out a cigarette, lighting it up, and nervously inhaling. Then he began bouncing his leg up and down, rattling the table with his nervous twitch.

The five scientists joined him at the table, two on each side. The last to arrive was Pak, who, after closing the doors to the command center, sat in the chair opposite Nampo.

"Let me see if I understand fully what we

know to have happened," Nampo said, again inhaling his cigarette. "First, launch was a success, and thirty-eight minutes into launch, we reached the GEO synchronization orbit."

"Yes, sir, thirty-eight and a half minutes into flight," said a gaunt, gray-haired scientist to the left of Nampo.

"And when it reached the GEO synchronization orbit, we thought it acquired the targeted west coast GPS satellite."

"Yes, sir," each of the scientists nervously chimed in, expecting the hammer to fall at any moment.

"But we also know that the rocket was at least ten nautical miles from the actual target when the conventional TNT explosive discharged."

"Yes, sir." Again, in synchrony.

"And because our payload weighs no more than ten kilos, the explosive sent out a shockwave that merely jolted the targeted satellite."

"Yes, sir," said the oldest scientist, sitting next to Nampo. "In fact, as best we can understand, the explosion probably flipped the satellite several times and changed its orbit slightly. Then, when it came back online, the satellite's computer reset the correct orbit."

"Gentlemen, what we have now," said Nampo, "is a three-hundred-million-dollar firecracker that's far from being a weapon of devastating impact."

There was no response from any of the scientists.

"In fact, either we have to improve our accuracy in acquiring the target, or we have to finish the miniaturization of a nuclear device and use a sufficient warhead, so we can overcome our lack of accuracy. Wouldn't each of you agree?"

Pak Yim leaned forward in his chair and intertwined his fingers on the desktop in an effort to show respect and deference to Nampo. "As always, doctor, you are both insightful and correct," he said in a whisper. "Your development of a nuclear weapon capable of being carried by our rockets is essential both to this great project and to the People's Republic."

"Thank you, comrades. I've heard enough. Each of you has your mission and you're fully aware of what's necessary. You may go."

With this command, each of the scientists stood at attention, slid their chairs underneath the table, and proceeded silently out of the room as if leaving a funeral.

"Assistant Director, one moment please," said Nampo.

"Yes?" said Pak.

"Please stay briefly. I wish to talk to you."

When the departing scientists heard that, they shuddered. They were not unfamiliar with Dr. Nampo's leadership style. Pak waited until each man left, and then pressed a pad on the door, sliding it shut.

Turning to Pak, Nampo said, "You know that the accuracy of the acquiring team is faulty?"

"Yes, sir," Pak said meekly.

"Comrade Nung-Say is in charge of the team. Can his assistant handle the requirements we expect of that team?"

Again, Pak was aware that only an

affirmative response would be acceptable. "Yes, sir, without a doubt," Pak said. "He has a young scientist, Ko My, who works as Nung-Say's direct assistant. Ko My is probably brighter than he is, and they have a complete team I believe can do the job."

"Then have Nung-Say removed tonight."

By this command, Nampo did not mean have him relieved, replaced, retired, or reassigned. Instead, the unfortunate scientist would be taken to the front entrance and placed on a UAZ Soviet jeep. He would ride the short distance to Kosan, where his wife and two young children would be picked up as well. The wife would see her husband's look and begin to cry. She would know why the armed guards were present. After a full day's travel to Wonsan and then by train across much of North Korea, the small family would be delivered to Haengyong near the Chinese border. Haengyong was also known as Camp 22. At Camp 22, the State Security Agency kept nearly 50,000 prisoners in brutal, frigid, famine-like conditions.

"Comrade, if we don't succeed, and I mean succeed quickly, each of us will make that journey to Camp 22."

"Yes, Comrade Director, your directions shall be followed explicitly."

"Good. Let us replace him quickly and move on with our tests," said Nampo. "I have come to the conclusion that we'll never be able to achieve the needed accuracy and efficiency with a conventional warhead. It's clear we must have a nuclear weapon that matches the Taepo Dong-3X's range and payload size. We don't have time to develop another rocket. We don't have time to develop a higher payload capacity. We'll have to develop a weapon that can operate within the payload capacity and still reach the GEO orbit."

"Yes, Comrade Director, you're absolutely right."

"And the clock is ticking."

| | | |

"Nampo is necessary to the survival of this

country." Kim Jong-il sat in the large lounge chair in the railroad car, smoking a cigarette.

"Yes, father." Jong-un listened intently.

"A nuclear equipped missile is the only thing that can keep the wolves away." Kim Jong-il looked white, pale and bloated as he finished the cigarette and lit another. "They had nearly a half a million participate in the last exercise."

The multi-force of South Korea, the United States and even Japan held their war game every year immediately south of the border.

"They want to kill us."

"Yes."

He leaned closer to his son. They were alone in the executive rail car.

"We rarely get the chance to travel together like this. I want to take this opportunity to warn you."

"Yes, father?"

"Watch out for Jang. Your uncle will make his move soon."

As the small team climbed through an aspen grove, Kevin Moncrief noticed, amidst an intensifying snowfall, that it was becoming more difficult to see Shane Stidham ahead of him on the rope. Stidham, stopping ahead of Moncrief, held his hand up high, then made a circling motion. He was relaying a signal. The colonel had stopped and was calling them to the front.

Moncrief moved rapidly up the line, grabbing the excess rope as he caught up to Stidham. From there, both moved forward together to Hernandez. The crew had spent years together and, as with riding a bike after a long hiatus, quickly reached the point where they could often anticipate each another's actions.

Moncrief felt the cold wet snowflakes each time he turned into the wind. He lifted his goggles, only to feel the sting as the increasingly dense snow struck his eyes. It wasn't the ice on his face that surprised him as much as how comfortable he actually felt. The few layers of Polartek and Gortex were infinitely superior to the equipment supplied during his last visit to Bridgeport. The Marines then had doled out Korean War-era pants and multi-layered parkas with fur-lined hoods. The old clothes covered them like heavy Mexican blankets, weighed as much, and were constantly damp, inside from the sweat and outside from the melting snow.

At the edge of the grove, the four men huddled low, their backs to the wind. "We'll be crossing a saddle about five clicks to the north, northwest," Will whispered to the three. The snowstorm may have deafened sound, but Will was taking no chances—a voice in the mountains could carry, and he assumed patrols were near.

Moncrief was again perplexed by the

direction in which the team was headed. Of the three peaks, one was to the southeast and the other two were south of that one. "The storm is worsening, and it'll be dark in about an hour," said Will. "I want to build two ice caves and ride out the worst of it here."

"Yes, sir." Moncrief knew well the coziness of a well-made ice cave. A break from the increasingly ferocious wind would probably add twenty degrees of warmth.

"Gunny, you and Staff Hernandez will take one, and Staff Stidham and I will take the other. Stidham and I will carve out both caves while you two cut some evergreens to line them."

"Yes, sir." Moncrief turned as he spoke to Enrico Hernandez. "Staff, this is getting worse. We probably need to stay tethered together so we don't get lost."

"I saw several pine trees on the edge of the grove about five hundred meters back," Hernandez said.

The two crews silently went to work building the two shelters. At the edge of the aspen grove where the face of the mountain rose sharply, Will and Stidham found a large boulder between two deep drifts of snow. In silence, Will pointed Stidham to the right, then began on the left. At the edge of his drift, Will bent down on his knees, removed his pack, took off one of his snow shoes, and dug like an oversized mole, using the snow shoe as a small shovel, first down a few feet and then into the drift. Meanwhile, Stidham dug on the right. Once down and in, both started carving out small caverns deep below the snow.

Will stopped after some time, climbing carefully out of the etched hole, and spotted a stick, the size and shape of a long broomstick, near an aspen tree. He crossed over, pulled the stick from the snow, and broke off a few branches, making a long straight pole. Carefully, he leaned over the cave's top and gently poked the stick down, through the roof and into the cavity, slowly moving it in a circle until he had created an opening the size of a golf ball. He then tossed the stick over to the entrance of Stidham's cave.

Will opened his pack, searching through it until he came across a small white candle. Any pack outfitted for basic survival in the cold, snowbound woods would contain one. Holding it, he crawled into the cave, lit the candle, and began making circular motions on the ceiling, causing drops of water to splash onto his face. The melting snow built a bond of ice molecules, and as the increasingly cold breeze flowed into the cave, the water turned to ice. The ceiling was streaked with light black marks created by the candle's smoke. When finished, he had melted and frozen a solid dome capable of supporting a man who might accidentally walk over its top.

As Will pulled himself out of the cave, Moncrief appeared at its entrance with a large pile of small cut evergreens. "Sir, you stay in there and I'll get these through to you."

Will slid back through the entrance and waited as the first of several piles of evergreens was passed through the entrance. Soon, the inside of the cave was covered with a deep, pine-smelling layer of small greens. After the last pile, Moncrief handed Will's pack to him. At practically the same time, Stidham came over and handed his pack through the opening to Will.

"Gunny," said Will.

"Yes, sir," said Moncrief.

"It's going to be totally dark in fifteen minutes."

"Can't see much now, sir."

"Yeah, I'm guessing it's zero visibility and that'll probably last through the night."

"What're you thinking, boss?" said Moncrief.

"We've got several candy bars in our packs," said Will. "Let's bed down for a few hours and then move out before dawn."

"Sir, the tail end of the storm will still be cooking then."

"Yeah, I know, but we need the cover. They've got people at the food stops, but they may be out patrolling as well."

"Good point, boss." Moncrief, now certain they were headed in the wrong direction, figured at this rate, they'd be off the military base in a few miles, and much deeper into the mountains. But he knew not to argue with the colonel.

"See you in a few hours." Will, with Stidham right behind him, crawled back into the cave. Like two wild creatures in a burrow, they wiggled tightly together, and in orchestrated fashion, Stidham pulled himself back out through the opening. Using a pine bough, he brushed the footprints near the opening, then gathered up a large pile of snow the size of a large playground ball and pulled it to the doorway, snugly plugging in the hole. In only a short time, the snowstorm would blanket over the remaining tracks and conceal any trace of this part of the team. A patrol, if it braved the storm, would walk across the domes of the caves and never realize the men were a few feet below.

The two lay in tight quarters, with the candle lit in the corner near the small breathing hole. The cave warmed up quickly, and both men soon unzipped their parkas and laid down on them.

"Well, it could be worse," Will said.

"How's that, sir?"

"We could be on that mountaintop, guarding the food."

"Yes, sir." Stidham laughed. He knew the misery.

As usual, Gunny Moncrief pulled the caboose, the last man on the tethered rope. For several hours without stopping, they had crossed down through a deeply wooded valley into another large aspen grove. Stidham again held up his arm to signal a stop. Moncrief, leaning away from the wind next to a large aspen the size of a street pole, felt a rough cut to the smooth aspen bark and noticed an etching carved into the tree.

"I'll be damned," he said quietly as he recognized not the initials "R.S." as much as the date—"May 5, 1908." Aspens had sat as silent observers on these mountains for quite some time.

A tug on the rope pulled his attention back to Stidham, giving a hand signal to move forward. It was only as he left the aspen grove that Gunny Moncrief first noticed the stream crossing to the left near the wall of the canyon. Only a few minutes later, he noticed the shape of a small, red-stained cabin next to the stream, followed by another and another. Will stopped at the third cabin while his team held tight to the tethered rope.

"I thought we were a little off-course, sir," said Moncrief.

"No, we were right on-course—just not their course."

Gunny smiled in appreciation. Under the rules of the exercise, they could hit the mountaintops for food, but only if they wanted to. As far as Will was concerned, 'wanting to' wasn't a necessary part of the mission.

"The cabins have plenty of bunks," said Will. "Each has a fireplace and stacked firewood."

"What about Pickle Meadow?"

"We're at least six clicks off their maps. By the time they even get curious, we'll be gone."

"Yes, sir," said Moncrief. "And food?"

"This place is still owned by a retired Marine gunner who lives in Reno in the winter," said Will. "He's got a pantry stocked in the main cabin, and it's not even locked. It's the code of these mountains that if you get this far back, you can use whatever you want. We'll leave a few bucks for him when we get back to Fallon."

"Yes, sir."

"Besides, he and I served together here in the early '90s. He'll get a kick out of the story."

In less than an hour, the crew had a fire raging in the largest of the cabins, cooking green beans, corn, and steaks that Hernandez had found in the back of a turned-off freezer still cold enough to keep the meat frozen.

"Okay, boss, what's this mission all about?" Moncrief asked after they'd stuffed themselves with the lavish meal.

"I can't tell you much right now."

Will's tone was more serious than Moncrief had remembered in a long time. He hadn't used the gunny's first name, especially in front of Stidham and Hernandez, in a decade. One night in Kuwait, when Will had just gotten word that their ANGLICO team would not be helo'd out, but would have to walk out past a regiment of the Iraqi National Guard, Will had used "Kevin" to explain the depth of the problem. They'd lost two men that night.

"Okay, boss."

"I can say this much—it'll be a limited insertion into North Korea."

Moncrief raised his eyebrows.

"I'll be the one going in. Alone," Will said.

"Goddamn it, sir," Moncrief's voice sounded more like a yell.

Will could feel the whole team openly rebel. "I'll need your help at the beach."

"Yeah, boss, but we can handle it."

"I know you can," said Will, "but a team will leave too many footprints."

"Yes, sir," said Moncrief.

"Boss, we can be pretty quiet." Enrico Hernandez, normally understated, prompted a laugh from the others when he offered the mild protest in his south Miami Spanish accent. Hernandez was an unusual addition to this crew. An inner city kid, he had been the leader of a Miami gang when the judge gave him and his mother the choice of five years in the youth prison system or enlistment in the Marine Corps. The judge had seen testing scores, which the Marine Corps later confirmed, showing him at a near-genius GCT of 138. Enlistment in the Marines endangered Hernandez's life but, at the same time, had probably saved it.

"That's not the mission," Will said. "And we're done talking about it for tonight"

"Yes, sir," said Hernandez, "I'm gonna crash in that bunk over there next to the fireplace. You need something, just let me know."

"We'll lay low here for another two days," said Will, "then work ourselves south, down the road, cut behind Lost Cannon Peak, and be back at base camp by twelve-hundred hours."

"Yes, sir, just in time to watch those teams come down off the mountaintops all frozen," said Moncrief.

"Let's make a point of not bragging about this, Gunny."

Moncrief nodded, relieved to have the colonel calling him "Gunny" again instead.

| | | |

Bridgeport was not very happy with the team when they came down off the mountain. On the fifth day, there was talk that search parties might be needed. A snow avalanche on the south side of Wells Peak had wiped out a valley of trees, and with no food picked up for days, speculation mounted that perhaps Will's team had gotten caught up in the avalanche while making a daring crossover to the second mountain. The worst of it, however, was that the team was not famished, nor even very hungry, when its members showed up shortly before noon. After brief showers and new uniforms, they were whisked off by choppers to Fallon.

Scott joined them for the journey to Hawaii and, upon reaching cruising altitude, swiveled his chair around to face them. "We'll get to

Honolulu in about four and a half hours. Once there, the U.S.S. *Florida*, a Trident sub newly outfitted for special ops, will be waiting at Ford Island."

"When's sailing time?" said Will.

"Midnight."

"Wow, a day in paradise." Moncrief scowled.

"We have quarters set up for you on Ford Island if you need them," said Scott, "but we'd like to keep liberty down to a minimum. Maybe a quick meal, a shower, but not much."

Will had things other than liberty in mind, but his team deserved one last run before hopping on the boat.

"We will have very little running around," he said, implying that his men could do *some* running around.

"A quick visit to Duke's on the beach at Waikiki, and I'll be ready for war," said Moncrief.

Will gave Moncrief a cautionary look, then turned away to the window. At 41,000 feet, the jet flew well above cloud cover. Will could see small dots of white on the Pacific below.

How strange, he thought. *Today, five miles above. Day after tomorrow, a mile below.*

This will be the final one, Rei thought as he glanced around the dark, wood-paneled room. Gold carvings of dragons and flowers surrounded the cornice, and dark, mahogany-colored leather chairs framed a table desk at the room's end. The desk's crystal lamp illuminated a deep swirling burl pattern of wood as if this was the finely appointed office of a Beverly Hills plastic surgeon. But then, utterly ruining the sophisticated ambience, the walls had taped to them a complex array of paper sheets, maps, photographs, and hundreds of small yellow post-it notes.

Rei surveyed the confluence of information, exactly as he had done time after time before, settling his gaze finally on the target. A poster-sized photograph was taped to the wall at the far end of the room. It was surrounded by numerous printouts and photographs from newspapers, all taken from the internet. The target was a gray-haired woman with a light smiling face and bright, curious Asian eyes. In the photographs, she often wore a white laboratory coat.

He reached over the desk, logged off the computer, then turned off the lights, only to see the blue screen of the monitor faintly illuminating the dark room and the target's face.

I won't have to do this again. Rei sighed in relief, yet felt unsure whether he could manage a new life without the adrenaline rushes of the past. He considered each kill a critical deed for his homeland, yet each had become easier than the one before.

I'll clean this all up later when everything can be shredded, destroyed, and removed, he thought as he swung the door closed.

The housekeeper would spotlessly clean Rei's apartment, but she rarely entered that room. Except for two other men, no one knew

who his next target would be. The evidence
in that room would tell all and thereby
endanger his life, but only the housekeeper,
whom he trusted implicitly, had access. She
and her husband, son, daughter-in-law, and
two grandchildren often had the only food in
their tenant building. They had eaten well and
suffered no hardships since starting work for
Rei more than a decade ago. His secrets were
absolutely secure with her.

Rei closed the inner door to the apartment,
locking it and activating an alarm only the
housekeeper could disarm. If sounded, it
directly signaled a small security cell in the
intelligence branch. A Western-style system,
it was the only one of its type in Pyongyong.
There was no great need for security in this
city. Few had anything to steal. Those who
had objects of worth were also those who
could easily have a thief executed.

In the predawn darkness, his driver waited
at the end of the block.

"Today, a short ride, friend," said Rei.

"Yes, sir."

"Potonggang Station."

The vehicle turned north, up a broad boulevard with wide-open sidewalks. Rei slumped down in the seat, thinking that only two weeks earlier, he had been summoned to the NCDB.

Sin Tae-sam had again been the messenger. "We have a most important mission, Comrade."

Rei placed both arms on the conference table in the National Chemical and Defense Bureau's uppermost floor. "Comrade, I am always ready to serve our leader and the state," he said flatly.

"We have other news as well."

"Oh?"

"Yes, you have won your reward."

"Comrade?"

"This will be your last mission," said Sin. "Upon your return, you will be appointed to an instructor's position at the National Defense University."

Rei had felt both elated and unsure. Like a

professional western athlete, would he end his brilliant career on his terms or theirs?

"Is there a problem?" Rei could not keep himself from asking.

"In fact, there is," Sin Tae-sam said, his face falling under the direct cast of a single light. His eyes seemed worn down by experience and time. "Our friends in Beijing have a source in Washington. It is apparently well-connected in their Federal Bureau of Investigation."

"Yes?"

"They have a sense of what is going on," said Sin. "They may know it's you or at least suspect you."

Another surge flashed through Rei's body.

"I have always assumed so," said Rei.

"We know they're still guessing, but it is enough."

"I understand, but if this is so, should we do another with me?"

"We have had that conversation," said Sin, "but this one is most important and most unique."

"Why?"

"Nampo believes this one scientist, who he has followed for quite a while, is on the verge of a breakthrough in nanotechnology," Sin said. "We have gained access to her work, and Nampo has nearly replicated it in his laboratory. It will allow him to reduce a ten-kiloton nuclear weapon to the size of a loaf of bread."

"That seems greatly significant."

"It is. It will solve our payload problem and allow us to place multiple weapons into the highest orbits. One rocket will be able to carry several different payloads, similar to the Americans' MIRV System. The multiple warhead system has been in existence for years, but it required a higher orbit than our North Korean rockets could achieve."

"Yes, sir." Rei wondered why the old man was being so open. Perhaps it was because, with the FBI possibly on his tail, he knew he was putting Rei at heightened risk.

"You have served well, Comrade," said Sin. "You deserve this appointment."

"Thank you, Comrade."

"And, also . . . ."

"Yes, sir?" said Rei.

"This one may be easier than any other."

"Why?"

"It is in Japan."

The taxi's short and sudden stop jolted Rei back to the present as he thrust his hand forward to brace himself.

"We are here, sir," said the driver.

The taxi had stopped directly in front of a large, block-shaped, cream-colored building. Outside, above the center of the front entrance, was an enormous framed painting of the Supreme Leader and his son. Below, in large letters, was the label, "Potonggang National Railroad Station."

The light of dawn began to illuminate the city, and for the first time, Rei noticed soldiers in their green uniforms, large saucer hats, and red shoulder boards standing around the station. Wordlessly, he nodded to the driver and left the taxi.

The station was waking up. It was clear

to Rei, however, that but for the military traffic, it would be virtually empty. A large blackboard, its writing in chalk, showed only three trains: two to China and one to Wonsan. The board's empty lines were reminders of future commerce that was no more than a hope.

How pathetic, he thought. *A city of millions with only three trains running?* Rei knew why the government was so determined to keep its borders closed. Comparing this main train station to any in Europe highlighted the pathetic condition of the North Korean economy.

Rei showed his security badge to a sentry, armed with an AK-47, standing near a stairway leading up to the train marked for Wonsan. "You will be on the priority car, Comrade," he said.

"Yes." He was aware of this important privilege. Even in North Korea, or especially in North Korea, there *were* privileges.

The train's final car had armed guards posted on each end, with curtains drawn shut.

Inside, a general, apparently from the army, sat in one of only a few chairs, intently reading *The London Times*. The general glanced up at Rei, then turned again to his paper. Because Rei was not in uniform, the general figured he was someone best ignored, and the two did not talk.

Rei's unwilling companion puffed on a long cigar. Rei recognized the sharp smell of a Cuban. *There's one pleasure a Communist country can enjoy—if one has the money to pay for it.*

It took until mid-afternoon for the train to reach Wonsan. The arrival was timed so that he and others could easily transfer from the Wonsan Station to the passenger ship *Mangyonghong-92* for the overnight voyage to the port of Niigata.

The early winter winds of the Sea of Japan were fierce that night, but Rei stood on the ship's front deck just the same, bracing himself against the wind and smoking a pack of his American cigarettes. *I need to get a couple of cartons*, he thought, realizing that this trip might be his last opportunity to do so for some time.

As the ship neared its destination, Rei worried that his entrance to Japan would telegraph his exit of North Korea. For precisely this reason, he had not been to the Japanese port of Niigata in several years, traveling through Beijing and Moscow providing him better cover. As he walked down the wooden gangplank into port customs, he immediately noticed a far greater scrutiny than he ever recalled seeing before. Japanese custom officials, accompanied by armed Japanese security forces, stood evenly spaced along the walls of a corridor leading to a large room. Each of four customs desks were situated behind thick Plexiglas shields. A loudspeaker announced a request for declaration of all goods, and amnesty for the tendering of any weapons, which Rei thought was unusual.

The 6:09 a.m. Toki Shinkansen Super Express train left Niigata Station exactly on time, just as it did every day. Rei usually enjoyed the first-class cabin with airline-style luxury seats, but today, he decided to adopt a lower profile, taking an ordinary car instead. In less than two and a half hours, the train pulled into Tokyo.

As soon as he descended the stairs into the main station, Rei felt as if he had been dropped into a giant ant farm: two million Tokyo residents passed through the station every morning. He was always amazed that no one ever touched, not even in the most casual of bumps. In Rome, Madrid, or Paris, he would have felt constantly jostled. But in their trams and subways, where people were packed together like sardines, the Japanese tried to respect each other's space and privacy by not touching or, if at all possible, even looking. It was a culture that stressed casual coolness.

The air was beginning to cool in Tokyo, so Rei pulled up the collar of his black leather jacket. He stepped out to the taxi stand in front of the backside of the station, an aluminum-and-glass structure that rose up to dominate the city block. A driver bowed briefly as he stood at the rear of his taxicab, opening up the trunk.

"Keio Plaza Intercontinental, two twenty-one *nishi-shinjuku*," Rei said in flawless Japanese.

"*Hya*," the Tokyo taxi driver said as he again bowed.

The more affluent hotels attracted less attention than some out-of-the-way places. Police around the world would scrutinize a dark alley hotel and keep a far more detailed account of who stayed in its rooms. Rei had even gotten his superiors at Pyongyang to authorize a gold American Express card in several of his cover names in order to carry on missions in this manner. The card's bill was mailed to a post office box in San Francisco, and always paid on time, through a San Francisco checking account in the name of an electronics company. The electronics company did not exist, and the corporate name changed on a regular basis, making it virtually impossible to trace.

Once checked into the hotel, Rei would

make a point of leaving every morning no later than eight o'clock and not returning until after four in the afternoon, to prevent any suspicions that he wasn't a businessman on a business trip to Tokyo. He often preferred to arrive in the target town about twenty-four hours before his attack, but this time he had arrived earlier.

Rei knew that Dr. Maka Aoano would be at the Tokyo Marriott Kinshicho Tobu, on the far eastern side of the city, for a symposium on silicon conductors for a brief 48 hours. The Marriott stood two blocks away from one of the city's smaller train stations, but it was also on the main rail artery to the Narita International Airport. In two weeks, RIKEN, Wako's Institute of Physical and Chemical Research, was scheduled to hold its annual conference at the Marriott. Based in Wako, Japan, the Surface and Interface Laboratory's director was the lead presenter. Her topic was using "Ersiz" silicon molecules to reduce the size of computers.

Rei's plan was simple. He would hit the

target at the Marriott, walk the two blocks to the Kinshicho train station, take the express train to the international airport, and be on a flight to Seoul on Korean Airlines in less than an hour.

Amazing, he thought. *Who would imagine that my last mission would be the simplest of all?* Because it was his final mission, he had planned to rent a car once he arrived at the Seoul International Airport, drive fifteen miles out of town, and take the hidden tunnel that he had thus far been able to avoid.

Tom Pope started the morning meeting in the SIOC Operation Center with this announcement: "Gentlemen, we have someone."

"Oh, really?" Dave Creighton dropped his pencil. The group was much smaller than it had been weeks before. Now, Creighton sat in the center chair, handling the senior supervisor's role, and while the group met every Monday, its composition had changed to include only Creighton, Pope, Dr. Wilhelm, Mark Wilby from the Agency, and one man in uniform from the Joint Chiefs—an admiral.

"Joan reported the coordinating of logistics for someone in New York going to Tokyo in early December—hotels, an American Express card, the usual," said Tom.

"So," said Creighton, "what are your thoughts?"

"Sir, we don't know if he's going on from Tokyo or if the target is someone in Japan."

"How many fit your profile of possible targets in Japan?"

"We have three for sure and possibly a fourth," said Tom.

"How about traces on the ports of entry?" The others remained silent as Creighton continued to bombard Tom with questions.

"We're monitoring the major airports and, although it's a stretch . . . ."

"Yes, Tom?"

"We're looking at direct vessel traffic into Niigata."

"They can't be that obvious," said Creighton.

The admiral made a small note on his pad, then continued to doodle in the margins— boxes within boxes. He smiled slyly as he took everything in.

"I may have some insight on the DPRK's use of that vessel, the *Mangyonghong-92*,"

Admiral Krowl said, rubbing his fingers over his mouth, making it hard to understand what he was saying. "I'll talk to one of my people and get back to you."

"Admiral, if it's significant, do it quickly. We don't know if this guy hasn't already gone elsewhere," said Creighton.

"I'll call as soon as we're done."

"What do the Japanese know about our interest?" said Creighton asked Tom.

"Only that we think we have a very big fish in the heroin trade coming through." Everywhere in intelligence there were the risks of leaks. With Japan's hatred of North Korea, there was too much of a risk for the Public Security Intelligence Agency to know too much. Japan's CIA might take action into its own hands.

"Good," said Creighton. "Let's meet daily on this, at least by VTC."

"Yes, sir," said Tom.

"Oh seven-hundred tomorrow, and if anything hot breaks, let me know immediately—twenty-four seven."

As the group disbanded, the Admiral stopped Tom at the door. "Hey, you have a secure phone I can use?" he said.

"Sure, Admiral." He pointed him to a red phone on a pullout drawer, next to the director's seat. "You can use this one."

"Thanks, it'll only take a minute." He dialed the Pentagon's direct number to the Executive Support Center.

"This is Krowl. I need to talk immediately, by secure line, to my deputy, Sawyer." He held his hand over the receiver, muffling his comments, although no one was close enough to overhear.

"Yes, sir, this is Commander Sawyer."

"Go secure."

"Yes, sir." A high-pitched tone sounded for a few seconds. As the phone began scrambling, Krowl pulled out a cigarette and stretched the phone cord, searching the room for an ashtray. A young secretary at one of the terminals brought over a large, brass ashtray imprinted with the Bureau's logo.

"Sir, I show secure," said Sawyer.

"Where is she?" said Krowl.

Sawyer paused, his hesitancy showing. "Sir, I got a call this morning. She missed reporting in."

"Shit!" said Krowl. Everyone in the center looked up from his terminal as Krowl, red-faced, yelled into the phone. "That goddamn communist flipping bitch! I'll let them have her. I'll be damned if I won't."

Sawyer maintained a calm voice. "Sir, does this mean the end to Nemesis?"

"No!" Krowl snapped again.

"With respect, sir, this mission was always dangerous," said Sawyer. "Now, it may simply be a trap."

"Not," said Krowl, "if I catch her ass first."

In its final approach into Hickam Air Field, the Gulf Stream came in low over the crystal-blue waters of Pearl Harbor.

The shadow of the behemoth battleship *Arizona* lay below the water. Patches of green and black outlined her long shape below the surface, and a bright white monument stood across her bridge.

"Look over there, to the other side," said Scott. "That's the *Florida*."

Will swiveled for a better view and saw another, larger shape tied up at a small wharf. The *Florida* was long, black, and tubular, with only its nose and tail submerged. The visible dimensions only hinted at the gigantic machine's proportions.

"That, gentlemen, is our taxicab," said Will.

"Not every day a billion-dollar Trident sub takes you for a joyride to North Korea," Moncrief quipped.

Three black Chevrolet Suburbans, waited in line as they disembarked, giving their arrival the appearance of a VIP welcome.

Scott bounded down the aircraft's steps, crossed over, and shook the hands of two men waiting beside the lead vehicle. Will felt the warm breeze, a stark change from the cold air they had left at Fallon several hours earlier.

"We can go straight to the boat," said Scott.

"Okay, Scott, let's go." Will and Moncrief got in the rear seats of the first Suburban as the two others climbed into the following vehicle.

"The Christmas lights are up," said Moncrief as they left the airport.

"Indeed they are." A series of lights, like strings holding up a tent pole, circled the bell tower at Hickam. The small government-issue homes, mostly for the senior enlisted, were decked out in all the reds and greens of Christmas.

As the lit bell tower receded, Will noted the gash marks on its side created by the spray of December 7th bullets. *Funny*, he thought, *we're always in danger. North Korea just wants to do it in a different way.*

As the caravan pulled up to the gatehouse that accessed Ford Island, the security for the *Florida* resembled that of a bank just after a robbery. Honolulu motorcycle police, in their wraparound Maui sunglasses, directed traffic past the long, two-lane bridge, the only link to Ford Island. Sailors and Marines in flak jackets, all armed with M-4s, stood near Humvees blocking the entrance.

"There's some nice real estate here, boss," Moncrief said, smiling.

"No doubt." Will and Moncrief, having rolled down the windows, felt warmer as they passed over the open harbor. A tropical breeze blew inland across the bay.

"The battlewagons used to tie up to Ford Island like horses at a stable," said Will.

"Yes, sir."

"Now, there's a few quarters for senior officers, a monument, and an abandoned airfield," said Will. The orange-and-white-checkered tower, with streaks of dark brown rust, stood out in the center of the field. Grass poked through the joints of a massive cement runway stretching several football fields long. The U.S.S. *Missouri*, the last of the great behemoths, rested at her mooring, a tourist attraction temporarily closed for repairs. At least, that's what its mainland tourist office told the public.

The Suburbans pulled up to a dock on the far side of the island. It had no buildings or structures, only a long, tall, chain link fence. Will noticed a sandbag bunker on the left, and another on the right—camouflaged—then the faint movement of men. As he got closer, he realized they were Navy boys. Dressed in gray shirts, blue trousers, bulletproof vests, and gray helmets, they were armed with pistols, shotguns, and M-4's. It was then he noticed the steel structure sitting behind the wharf, rising above everything else, as tall as the few trees, but pitch black. A pair of gray and black leopard-like camouflaged periscopes rose above the mainsail. The submarine's huge mast gave some suggestion of its size, but it was misleading. The vessel stood six stories deep.

Scott led the way out of the vehicles and quickly pulled Will and his men together. "From this point forward," he said, "use no names. All your names have been pulled from your packs and your uniforms." They had been given a new issue of utilities and packs when they left Fallon. "Tomorrow, when you leave, all remaining identification of any kind must be turned in."

"So, ah, Mr. X, what about our bills and all that other crap?" said Moncrief, who loved this spy business.

"It's all been taken care of. This is a special-operations boat, and they're used to handling all that."

"Sir?" A curly-headed and heavily freckled lieutenant commander interrupted Scott.

"Yes?"

"I'm Lieutenant Commander Mack Wade, executive officer of the boat."

"Where's your CO?" said Scott.

"He'll be joining us shortly. He's up at PAC." It was rare for a Trident to visit Pearl, and the Pacific commander was a submariner by training. He would likely keep the Trident's commanding officer for some time, the two submariners exchanging stories like long-lost fraternity brothers.

"The team is welcome to come aboard," said Wade.

Will grabbed his MOLLE pack and followed Wade, who came up the gangplank and stopped before an armed chief. "Permission to come aboard?" said Wade.

"Aye, sir."

Wade turned to the standard American flag on the vessel's tail and saluted.

"You, sir, are the team leader?" He addressed Will.

"Yes, sir."

"Sir, please come with me. The others will go to berthing in the aft section."

The team did not mind this minor distinction, not only because Will was their boss, but also because submarine duty was well-known for treating everyone well. All the bunks would be snug and fairly quiet, and the food would be good and unlimited.

Will followed Wade past the mast, looking up at it from the main deck and taking in its enormity. Immediately beyond the sail, the young officer climbed down into the vessel. Waiting at the bottom of the ladder, he signaled Will to pass his pack down through the hatch.

Inside, Will was amazed at the array of cables and pipes, small and large, that surrounded him. He could only sense the vessel's actual proportions when he crawled down to the first deck. Beyond the cables and pipes to the bow, the bulkhead curved out, giving the sense that its nose extended well beyond and below.

"Excuse me for playing tour guide," said Wade, "but the *Florida* is over 560 feet long and displaces almost 19,000 tons when submerged."

"Yeah, I'm happy you're on our side," said Will.

"Follow me, sir." He led Will down a short hall, past side rooms with men by computer screens and beyond the control and periscope room. As they passed, several young officers, along with a well-wrinkled boat chief, looked up from a chart board. Their eyes reflected their curiosity. The boat chief nodded. The crew had received no orders other than logistics and stocking requirements. The *Florida*'s officers would have only a general sense that this mission involved something in the Sea of Japan, or perhaps Russia.

"This way, sir." Wade hopped down a short steel stairway to the next lower deck deeper into the submarine's bow. Will glanced down the stairs, which continued down several more flights.

"This is you, sir." Wade stopped at a door marked "Executive Officers' Quarters."

"I'm bunking in with you?" Will asked.

"No, sir. You've got it to yourself. We got word to provide quarters to a colonel, no questions asked."

"Doesn't that violate your protocol?"

"Well, sir, not to be too glib about it," said Wade, "but I figure you're going to earn your paycheck on this one more than me."

Will smiled. Though he never expected special consideration because of his rank, he had to admit that it felt good. His room—no bigger than an oversized bedroom closet in a new upscale suburban home—somehow squeezed in a small desk, computer terminal, chair, and bunk bed, onto which he tossed his pack. Wade was providing him the only luxury on the boat—privacy. These quarters were no more spacious than those assigned the commanding officer, but in all boats, almost everyone shared rooms.

"Attention, CO arriving." The loudspeaker echoed throughout the boat. Will worked his way back upstairs to the command and control room, where the men stiffened up.

A six-foot man was climbing down the

front ladder where Will had entered. He removed his pisscutter hat, a naval term for the Boy Scout-styled cover, and turned, showing bright silver eagles on each collar.

"Attention," Wade yelled out.

"Carry on," said the CO, his unhesitating voice that of a leader. His brown hair was accented by slightly gray sideburns, his eyes were bright green, and his face was tanned, surprising for a submariner.

"So, you're our guest," he said to Will.

"Yes, sir." Will did not need to add the term of respect, but did so absentmindedly.

"Welcome aboard, sir."

"Thank you," said Will.

"Chief, my hat."

"Aye, aye, sir," said the well-wrinkled chief, his head well on the side of pudgy, retrieving a washed-out blue hat marked with a bright orange "AU" and the words "Auburn University."

"Excuse me—my old school," the CO said.

"It's a good one." Will smiled.

Captain J. D. Hollington, the commanding

officer, had graduated Navy R.O.T.C. with honors from Auburn University. It was not easy for a non-boat-school graduate to get command of a Trident. The Naval Academy, or boat school as it was commonly called, risked losing its supremacy when engineering students from ordinary universities were given such prestigious commands, but this was Hollington's second tour, and one for which he had been requested.

"This is the Gold Crew," said Hollington. "Gentlemen, the mission requires our not mentioning names, so this is the Colonel, and let's leave it at that."

"Welcome aboard, Colonel."

"Yes, sir, welcome."

"Okay, Colonel, let's go down to my room and discuss a few things," said Hollington.

Will followed the lanky captain down the stairs to another door, immediately adjacent to Will's room. Hollington's bunk bed had been pulled down to accommodate a couch. Hollington closed the door and turned to Will.

"Will Parker, you sonofabitch," he said. "You chose us on purpose, didn't you?"

"Absolutely, Skipper," said Will. "You're the only submariner I know who could pass Naval War College, and definitely the only one I wanted behind me in a fight."

"Just my luck," he said, smiling, "to have such friends." They had been roommates at the Naval War College in Newport, where they went on daily ten-mile runs around the points and mansions of the Rhode Island city. Some of the races became quite furious, and others at the college quickly realized not to accept their innocent invitation for an "easy" jog. "Now why's Krowl involved?" said Hollington. "That snake would trade in his sister for a promotion."

"Not my choice. He came up with this."

"Okay, but watch your back."

"Oh, yeah," said Will, well-prepared on that point. "When do we sail?"

"After dark, we have to float across the harbor to a SEAL base and pick up the ASDS." The SEAL mini-sub had been noticeably missing from the main deck when Will came aboard. "We'll leave right after that. It sort of telegraphs your mission to the world when you pick it up in Pearl. They're leaking the cover that SEAL Delivery Team One is doing some sea trials."

"That makes sense."

"It's supposed to rain tonight, which is a big plus," said Hollington.

"What's latest departure?"

"Zero-hundred."

"I need to get out of here for a few hours," Will said. "I've got a few errands, and I want my men to get one last beer at Duke's."

"This Scott guy's not too high on that. I'd recommend you be back by twenty-two-hundred max."

Will smiled. "I can handle that."

"And here's the keys to my car, with a CO's pass," said Hollington. "I've got some civilian clothes if you need 'em."

"No, I'm fine. Let me get mine and go."

The black Tahoe with a blue and white eagle sticker pulled out of Ford just before dark. The windows were tinted, but as it passed security at the Ford Island Bridge, the sentry saw four figures inside. He sharply saluted the driver. A half hour later, the Tahoe stopped in front of Duke's.

"I'll be back at twenty-one-hundred," Will told his men. "Sharp. And then this vehicle's moving. Got it?"

"Yes, sir."

"Okay, boss."

In another half hour, Will was back at the airbase, using the backdoor entrance to Hickam. The black Tahoe cut up to Vickers Avenue, and then a side road near the flight line. There, as Will's Tahoe approached, a man stepped out. The sun was setting, causing the shadow of the building to stretch across the side alley.

"Hey," said Will.

"This wasn't easy, sir."

"I can imagine."

The Marine lieutenant colonel in green-black checkered utilities climbed into the front seat. "Go around back of the CIL," he said.

Will drove the half-block around a modern one-story brown-brick building to a side entrance and loading dock. One of the doors was open. Above the door, the tan and blocked letter sign said, "U.S. Central Identification Laboratory."

"We had to do a lot of talking to our local contact, but they helped," said the lieutenant colonel.

"You know this is important," said Will. "It's also life or death that nothing's ever said."

"Yes, sir."

Will turned the Tahoe around, backing it up to the loading dock. Another man on the dock, with gloves on, lifted a black oil drum onto the rear of the Tahoe.

"Watch out. It's cold," said the lieutenant colonel.

"Got it."

"Other than that, you can't hurt it."

"Thanks," said Will. "Oh, let me borrow two sets of gloves."

"Borrow, sir?" He smiled. "I don't think I'll be getting them back."

"You may be right."

The Tahoe pulled out the main gate at Pearl, heading to the far end of the island. It took nearly an hour for Will to reach the last state park at Kaena Point. Highway H-1 was crowded with traffic exiting the football stadium at Aloha Stadium after a University of Hawaii game. It made Will realize how far he had come. The South would be in late fall, leaves changing, college tailgating parties winding down after a long season. He was a long way from what he had left.

Darkness was finally falling as he reached the dead end of Highway 930, which stopped at the small state park on the far end of the island. From there, he began walking the old Farrington Highway, which quickly deteriorated into more of a trail than a roadway. He hiked several miles along the cliffs and broken road. On the very edge of the deep blue surf, white spumes of water shot high into the air after colliding with the rocks. A bright half moon lit his path and a constant warm breeze blew in from the ocean like a large gusting fan. The road became progressively worse as large gaps caused the surf to spray up. Will worked his way around the rocks and gaps, smelling the ocean surge as he crossed up the trail.

Finally, after the road almost completely gave out, he came to a break in the ground, where it fell off several feet below. A large, barren mountain range paralleled his path, with nothing but sage and tumble-like weeds. This part of Hawaii was dry, brown, and unoccupied. Only a few tower lights marked the tops of the mountain, and a brilliant red and white light flashed farther down on the point.

At the gap, staked to the side of the rocks, was a chain that led down across a small rocky path to something dark. Will slid slowly down the trail, holding the chain, inching across the rocks to the end. The farther down he headed, the slipperier the rocks became from the spray of water and the moisture of the salt air. There, near the bottom, was a black hole with an opening the diameter of a man with both arms outstretched.

Will entered the cave, feeling the cool charge of air and smelling a musty odor of prior hikers or explorers. He went to a large outcropping of rock and reached behind it, struggling with his arm, feeling only the sandy floor until he touched the edge of something man-made.

"Yes," he whispered as he pulled out a green and black backpack from behind the rock.

I   I   I

The Tahoe pulled up to the U.S.S. *Florida* at precisely 10 p.m. local Hawaii time. Because most everyone was already aboard—the exceptions being a handful of security officers—few noticed Will and his men as they carried a drum and backpack onto the vessel. The chief of the boat was still topside.

"Chief, this drum needs to be stored in the food freezer."

"Aye, sir." Anyone else making such a request would have to go through several layers of command. The chief knew better.

"Sir," said the chief, "a Mr. Scott is waiting for you below, and when you get done with him, the skipper wants you on the sail."

"Copy that. I see you got the ASDS." A smaller black version of the Trident was locked onto the *Florida*'s deck just to the rear of the main sail. It may have been miniature, but its structure loomed well above their heads.

"Yes, sir. Newest version. High-speed. Silent-running."

"Great."

At that same moment, Scott climbed out of the aft hatch.

"Here you are," Scott said, looking more than a bit dismayed.

"Yes, Mr. Scott," said Will.

"Let's talk." They walked to the stern, standing on the black steel where rows of missile tubes used to be.

"Colonel, Krowl put me here at Pacific Command to monitor the mission," said

Scott. "So I'm essentially out of the game. The camera, along with a relay computer and satellite dish, are in your cabin. You've worked with them in Quantico. You know where Nampo should be. We're expecting a visit to the facility by a Chinese Army general on the 15th. That's probably your only chance—one photo, nothing fancy."

"Understood."

"Oh, and Colonel, as best you can, watch yourself."

Will wasn't sure what to make of Scott's last statement. Perhaps the training had developed a little loyalty after all.

"Excuse me, gentlemen, but we're moving." The chief pointed Scott to the gangplank as two sailors wrestled with it. Scott jumped onto the plank and, with two hops, was on the dock. He turned to Will and gave him a thumbs-up. As the rain began to pick up, Scott disappeared into the dark.

"Sir, on the sail," said the chief.

"Yes, Chief." Will heard the Auburn University fight song piped through the submarine. The skipper knew they wouldn't all be Auburn fans, but wanted to give the crew a reason to galvanize as a team. Each crew member donned a different version of an Auburn hat and roared in song, "Fight down the field, always to conquer, never to yield." It could have been Notre Dame or Southern Cal or Alabama. The power of that unity and pride made for a better crew.

Appropriate, Will thought as he felt the mass of steel gently moving under his feet. Then he smiled, knowing Staff Sergeant Stidham was at home with his old football team.

"Permission to come up?" said Will.

"Granted," said Hollington.

Will climbed up the series of ladders to the small opening on top of the sail. He felt the behemoth slowly move out from Ford into the main channel. Despite the increasing rain, the surrounding lights of Pearl, other ships in dock, and the warehouses surrounding the harbor painted a dull glow. Two small gunboats, one forward and one to the rear, followed the Trident out to sea.

In the close channel at Pearl's mouth, Will saw the lights of the Officer's Club. The music of a Hawaiian band carried as he watched, under the fluorescent lights of an open pavilion, people dancing in brightly-colored floral shirts. He wasn't nervous—just on edge.

"Okay, let's batten her up." Hollington climbed into the red-lit porthole, Will right behind. Will stopped, turned one last time, and inhaled the warm, gentle air, realizing it might be a long time before he did so again.

A short while later, after turning to the east for several miles, the U.S.S. *Florida* submerged. Once below the detection range of satellites, it turned back to the west and then to the north-northwest. In a few days, it would be past the islands of Japan.

33

"Give me a situation update." Krowl sat at the head of an elongated conference table in the Executive Support Center. At the briefing stand at the far end, an Army colonel dimmed the lights. Four large panel screens dominated the wall behind him. The far left screen had a familiar face. Scott sat in another briefing room on the other side of the world, alongside an admiral––the Pacific commander–– dressed in tropic whites. An Air Force colonel occupied another screen, followed by a map of the Western Pacific. The last screen showed a satellite view of a snow-covered road leading into a wooded area.

"Sir, we have Space Command online, and Pacific Command online," said Scott.

"Where's the *Florida*?" asked Krowl.

"The central map shows her tracking approximately 500 miles to the north-northwest of Hawaii."

"Scott."

"Yes, Admiral?"

"Any problems?"

"No," Scott answered succinctly.

I was right to put him at the Pacific Command, Krowl thought. It intimidated the PAC commander to take no action, and at the same time prevented Scott from interfering.

"How about going offline at the conclusion to discuss other issues?" Krowl said.

"Yes." said Scott without much enthusiasm.

"General, we are minus ten days," said Krowl. "Is the satellite up?"

General Kitcher, representing Space Command, appeared in the far left monitor. "USA82X will be as ready as we can make it."

"Colonel," said Krowl, "what's the intelligence situational awareness on this base?"

The Air Force colonel clicked on the aerial satellite monitor's button, zooming in on three trucks traveling in a short convoy down the road toward the wood line.

"The base has been given the identifier Nampo-1," said the colonel. "It is a confirmed multi-layered, heavily fortified research and launching facility."

No kidding, Krowl thought to himself.

"Admiral Krowl?" said the Pacific commander. His submariner's gold emblem glittered in the light. Scott scooted to his right and pulled his chair back behind the commander's.

"Yes, sir."

"Is the White House going to participate in this?"

"No, sir," said Krowl. "We have autonomy on this and will be the ultimate superior command. At minus two days, this cell will go on twenty-four seven and remain in that status until it's over," said Krowl.

"Any estimate of length?" The Pacific commander was the only one in the conference with the nerve to ask that of Krowl.

Before he spoke, Krowl took off his glasses

and rubbed his face to emphasize the point. "If he doesn't get it on plus two, it may be a year before we see Nampo again."

Intelligence had reported that a Chinese general named Won Su had made several trips to the Nampo-1 site on apparent military inspections prior to the early fall launch. The Agency's review had discovered that, on these trips, Won always went to the eastern DMZ south of Wonsan. It seemed an odd little fact until a multi-stage missile launched from this site knocked a west coast GPS satellite off orbit for a few minutes. Photo imagery of his trips placed him in the same valley at the time.

The CIA had also learned that another Won Su trip was scheduled for late December.

"What about weather?" said Krowl.

"A major front is expected in the Sea of Japan around the landing date," the Air Force colonel said.

"What's that mean?"

"North Korea is known for being cold, but not for a lot of snow. This front may produce the exception."

"Will it interfere with the satellite?" said Krowl.

"This is Space Command," said Kitcher. "Nothing will interfere with our bird."

"We need a representative in the Command Center who can have total control over that bird, General."

"Okay, that can be arranged." Space Command didn't usually relinquish control of a multi-billion dollar asset, but this situation called for different rules.

"Okay, we'll be up at twelve-hundred hours, Greenwich time, at D minus two," said Krowl. "Limited personnel with only top secret clearance need to know. And there'll be total restriction on entry at each of these operation centers."

"Yes, sir."

"In other words, no walk-in traffic."

Krowl anticipated curtailing the traffic even more. *They may raise a stink*, he thought, *but at the right moment, everyone except Space will be dropped.*

"Sir, the conference will time out in one

minute," said the Army colonel, reading a note given him by a young enlisted man.

"Okay, thanks. Scott, call me."

"Yes, Admiral," said Scott.

Just as each of the screens went blank, the red telephone at the end of the desk rang.

"Sir, Mr. Scott," said the tech sergeant.

"Secured?" said Krowl.

"Yes, sir."

"Everyone, I need you to leave."

The Army colonel and others quietly left the room, closing the soundproofed metal door behind.

I   I   I

Scott saw the next conversation coming.

"What's her status?" said Krowl.

"No idea, Admiral," said Scott.

Scott knew what "other issues" meant when Krowl had said it earlier. And, no, he did not have a clue where Mi was now. Intelligence gave no indication she had returned to the north. In fact, recent chatter indicated that North Korean agents had been told to be on the lookout for her and, if they found her, they had a blank check to take "appropriate action." Scott wanted to talk to her, though he was not as convinced as Krowl that she had turned; indeed, he was convinced a dime had been dropped to North Korea, and he knew who probably dropped it.

"How much damage can this cause?"

"Well, if she's turned, obviously, it would be a lot."

"You're damned right."

"But I don't think she defected back."

"Why?"

"Well," said Scott, "she was last seen coming out of her apartment in Alexandria two days after we finished in Quantico. She was told to take some leave. The Agency said you authorized it."

"Yes," Krowl huffed. When he approved the leave, he had simply been trying to get her out of the way.

"And then she was gone. But we know that DPRK intelligence has given its field agents a license to kill her on sight."

"Yes."

"If that was a ruse and they wanted to bring her in to talk, too many people have been given the green light to do otherwise. They couldn't call off the dogs even if they wanted to."

"So . . . ."

"My guess is she knew you'd never let her out of the game," said Scott. "She can't go back. . . ."

Krowl could hear the shrug in Scott's voice.

"Does Parker know?" said Krowl.

"Hell, Admiral, he's about a quarter mile down and heading to North Korea."

"Good."

"You know, I've got five years invested in recruiting her. Any idea who told them she was loose?"

"No."

| | | |

"Got a moment?"

Will sat in the officer's galley with his legs propped up. Ship life was testing his patience.

"Yes, Skipper," he said. He and Hollington had kept up the ruse of being distant. It benefited neither his team nor the *Florida* crew to know how deep their friendship ran.

"How about in my quarters?" said Hollington.

"Let's go."

The Skipper's quarters, not far from Command and Control, was close to the officer's galley.

Will followed Hollington in and closed the door.

"Okay, our orders are to get in close—about ten to twenty nautical miles south of Wonsan Harbor—and let you and the team off without endangering this multi-billion dollar weapons platform."

Will knew the last comment was customary for all commanders. One was to do the mission but not endanger the vessel—unless that was the only way to complete the mission.

"I'm in complete agreement."

"Meaning?"

"My team will take me in and then leave,"

said Will. "If I'm in the slightest trouble, I don't want you, or this boat, or especially my team, to come back for me."

Will's suspicious mind had served him well so far. If finding Nampo wasn't the only problem, he didn't want either his team or Hollington's boat to be at risk. It would be his problem to solve.

The knock on the hatch woke Will from a shallow sleep.

"Sir, it's midnight."

"Yes." He was more than ready. The time on the boat with no long jogs, not to mention anticipation of the mission, had made him feel increasingly like a penned-up animal waiting for the gate to open.

"Your team's waiting in the galley." The chief of the boat leaned into the room as he spoke from the well-lit corridor.

Will quickly put on his utilities and boots and crossed over to the galley, where J. D. Hollington waited with his crew.

"Steaks for everyone——it is our tradition." The galley chief brought in a platter stacked with t-bones.

"Finally an upside to this suicide mission," Moncrief said as he plunged his fork into the top steak.

"Skipper, can I talk to my folks?"

"Sure." Hollington closed the galley door, then the officers' mess door behind him.

Will pulled out a map and several satellite photos. In front of the men, he laid out the photos and a map showing their location.

"This is Wonsan, twenty clicks to the north. Your mission is to get me and my gear ashore at this location here." He pointed to a rocky area where a small stream flowed into the ocean from the mountain above. "I want to set up a well-camouflaged tent here. And that's it," Will said. "That's all I want you to do."

"Sir?" said Hernandez.

"No 'sir' about it. You'll do nothing more."

"What about in-country?" Despite what Will had said initially, Stidham had clearly expected to go inland with his boss.

"There's no need. If I need you, all I want is your availability after the landing in the

ASDS," said Will. "And . . . no matter what happens, if you've not heard from me by 2200 the day after tomorrow, you're to return to the *Florida*."

"Sir, we can't leave you."

"Moncrief, that's a direct order. No word by me by 2200 on D plus two and you, Gunnery Sergeant, are directed to return to this boat."

"But—"

"No buts. That's a direct order."

"Sir—"

"Again, a direct order."

"Yes, sir," said Moncrief.

"Okay, let's go down to the ready room."

They wolfed down the steaks, knowing it would be their last real meal for some time, then convened in a small room two doors down that had nothing but four empty duffle bags, one on each of four metal chairs.

"Now, take everything off." Will began to strip, removing each item of clothing and putting them into one of the duffle bags. "Rings, watches, necklaces—everything."

The four naked men then went through

another hatch into a room with four small tables lined up in a row—each with an issue of uniforms, boots, and underclothing.

"We're Spetsnaz now," Will said. "Put on your wetsuits, seal up the Spetsnaz uniforms in these waterproof pouches, and grab your weapon."

The men suited up in the plain black wetsuits and slung their packs and weapons over their backs. Now they moved to the third cabin, directly below the open hatch to the ASDS.

"Let's go." Turning to Hollington, who had entered the room, Will told his men, "Whatever you do, don't endanger this boat."

Hollington smiled at the comment. "That won't be a problem. Good luck and Godspeed."

Will felt a small flutter of emotion. All was in place, and all was beginning. He climbed up into the mini-submarine, where the men sat in two rows facing each other, alongside their packs and the black, lightly frosted 50-gallon barrel.

"Sir, we have direct contact with PAC."

The Navy lieutenant who skippered the mini-sub sat in a seat directly behind its operator. Gauges and scopes, similar to panels on the Gulfstream, were all in blues and greens. He handed a headset, tethered to a long cord, to Will.

"PAC, this is the team. Go," said Will.

"Team, this is PAC and ESC." Even over the headset, Will recognized Scott's British accent. He thought of Scott sitting in a vault-like room in the basement of the newly finished glass and brick building at Camp Smith. Pacific Command's new headquarters stood on a hilltop looking out over the mountains of Hawaii and the expanse of Pearl Harbor.

Once more, Will thought of Krowl, silently listening in from the Executive Support Center deep in the heart of the Pentagon.

What hour is it? Will thought absently, looking down at his Soviet watch with its small red star and deep green dial. *It's another day in Washington*, he thought as he did the mental calculation of time zones

"You have perfect weather," said Scott.

"That is confirmed," said Will. The weather officer of the *Florida* had given him an update as they left the galley. A gale-like snowstorm was following them as they headed ashore—"perfect weather" indeed for going undetected. Will could expect at least ten hours of blizzard conditions, followed by sporadic snow flurries and then another storm. The temperatures would be in the thirties.

As the small submarine rocked to the side, Will grabbed the panel of electronic boxes. He felt the rise of the vessel like an elevator ascending.

"Are you go?" said Scott.

"We are go." Little else needed to be said.

"We have the satellite ready for reception of your transmission."

"Affirm last." Will again imagined, somewhere in space, a satellite's small boosters going off in a syncopated motion as the satellite itself moved to a location in the geo-orbit directly above the Korean peninsula. The satellite might even be able to capture the shadow of the ASDS parked offshore from the North Korean coast. "Lieutenant, what's your plan?"

"Sir, the *Florida*'s about twenty-two nautical miles offshore." He pointed to the scanning screen of one of the sonars. It showed a green outline of the shore and a fixed larger object well out to sea. "We'll park this on the bottom about 500 meters offshore."

"How long will you wait there?"

"We can sit on the bottom, parked and anchored, for as long as needed," said the lieutenant. "We have some lithium batteries that keep us charged up, and a snorkel, if needed, for air."

The $250 million price tag for the Advanced SEAL Delivery System bought a dry, warm transfer vehicle that allowed the big boat to stay as far as a hundred miles offshore. The young lieutenant was clearly proud of his new command.

The lights in the small submarine switched to red. The lieutenant stepped past Will and pulled down a small periscope as he pushed and held down a red bar. A small motor ran for a few seconds. The lieutenant circled with the periscope.

"Here's the coast of North Korea, sir." He pointed to the scope and stepped aside so Will could look through.

Will saw darkness and the shape of a stark, rocky mountain. As his eyes focused and he turned the periscope, he spotted the faint, yellow light of what appeared to be a guard structure. He looked above the periscope to see an LED compass heading of one-hundred sixty degrees toward the south. He swung it around to three-hundred fifty-two degrees and the north. A large jetty of rocks extended out from shore, framing a small bay. Beyond the rocks to the north were the diffuse, yellow lights of a city reflecting off the low cloud cover. With the clouds and lights, Will could tell that snow was driving toward the shore.

"Perfect," he said.

"Sir, let's go 'ready.'" The young lieutenant reached beyond Will to a hatch in the center front of the mini-submarine. He pulled the hatch up and over, revealing a black water hole. The pressure in the submarine kept the water down in the hole.

"Moncrief, you lead," said Will. "I'll be last. Once out with our gear, I'll take the lead." Will took his Type-64 pistol and spun the silencer onto the barrel. He then pulled back the slide to chamber a round and carefully put it back into a waterproof pouch, which looked much like a bag for shirts returned from the dry cleaner. Moncrief and Hernandez chambered rounds in two 68 Russian AKM assault rifles while Stidham wrapped up the Dragunor SVD sniper rifle in a similar waterproof bag.

Moncrief slid over the edge and worked his way down into the black, cold water. He slid the re-breather mouthpiece over his mouth, tilted the black Russian facemask to let a little water into it, and headed down the ladder.

As two hands reached up to pull it down into the water, Stidham slid a backpack wrapped in a black plastic bag into the hole. Then both Stidham and Hernandez slid the black rum-shaped barrel down over the edge. It had little buoyancy and clanked on the sides as it slid down into the water. Black straps encircled the drum, providing a good grab-hold.

"I'll go next," said Hernandez. He slipped down into the opening, followed by Stidham.

"Thanks, Skipper." Will smiled at the lieutenant and slid his feet into the hole. He saluted as he descended into the black water. The water's coldness penetrated the suit, feeling like a cool dip in an unheated swimming pool in early summer. Will was impressed with the suit's ability to keep him comfortable even as the shock of cold water hit the exposed parts of his face.

As he slid down the ladder, Will felt his feet touch a sandy bottom. He saw the red circle of light above him, and as his eyes adjusted, the red illuminated the ocean's floor in a large circle. Round, smooth boulders dotted the ocean floor. He turned toward the nose of the submarine to orient himself toward shore. Will detected the shapes of the others, then saw them donning long black fins. His eyes quickly adjusted to the low light, and touching each man on the shoulder, he pointed toward the west.

In silence, they headed in a snakelike motion toward the shore. Will felt the sea surge as he swam across the increasingly rocky floor. In the dark, his only senses were the taste of rubber in his mouth and the sound of air sucked in from his re-breather. The Soviet device, similar to that made for U.S. Navy SEALs, released no air bubbles. After some time, he stopped, gathered the team together, gave them a hand signal to wait, and slid up to the surface.

The cold air struck his face as Will broke through a wave. Icy snowflakes hit his cheeks as he turned toward the shoreline. He was just out of the breakers, feeling the ocean as it ran past him. The shore was barely visible beyond the white foamed waves crashing into jagged black boulders. Will quickly circled several times, unable to detect the slightest movement.

Searching the shoreline for a break in the rocks and surf, Will quietly kicked up-shore for several meters, toward the north, until he saw a small beach no longer than two men laid end to end. Strapped to his wrist was a digital compass, from which he took a bearing. He backtracked to where he had surfaced, then submerged. Finding his team, he signaled them to the north.

After several minutes, they moved up-shore. Each man swam in below the surf until they could stand with only their heads above the water. Will led them through the tumbling waves and driving snowstorm to the break in the rocks. There, they quickly pulled their packs and barrel ashore, and each took a point.

Will signaled Moncrief that he was going forward, then silently slipped around one truck-sized boulder and quickly disappeared. The roar of the surf pounded on the rocks surrounding them. Each slipped their weapons out of protective covers and held them locked outbound from the center. Moncrief scanned the rocks above.

"Gunny."

Moncrief was surprised by Will's sudden

appearance behind him. "Damn, sir," he whispered.

"A small river runs into the bay about fifty meters to our right. It goes up into the mountains just over there." Will pointed up, toward what appeared to be a divide in the rocks. "There's a bridge on the coastal highway." Will had remembered this spot from the countless hours spent in the training room with the three-dimensional VR maps.

"What's the plan?" asked Moncrief.

"Simple. We erect the tent in those rocks at the base of the bridge and you get out of here before first light."

"Okay." Moncrief clearly still didn't like the idea of the team breaking up, and his tone said as much.

Will led the team, one by one, in a slow, quiet move around the rocks and boulders and up off the small beach. Only a few meters up, Moncrief saw the outline of an old, gray cement bridge. In the driving snowstorm, a flat roadway that paralleled the coastline was barely visible. He could tell it was a road only because of an occasional post marking its outline. He pointed to Stidham to keep a lookout to the north while he scanned the roadway to the south, expecting a coastal surveillance vehicle at any moment.

Near the base of the bridge, sheltering a small patch of sand, were two giant boulders, both capped with freshly fallen snow. Will pointed to the spot and used hand signals to direct the next move.

Hernandez and Stidham pulled up one of the oversized packs and took from it a small mountain tent. In a flash, the tent was up, snow quickly accumulating on its camouflaged sides.

"Sir, I'm not sure this is the best spot," said Moncrief.

"It's fine," said Will.

"But anyone looking from that bridge can see it."

"The snowfall should camouflage it well. Put the barrel there," he told Moncrief. To all of them, he said, "Give me the two other packs, and then run a quick scouting mission north and south."

"Yes, sir," they replied, piling up the extra packs and barrel next to the tent. Then they moved north, then south, for several hundred meters. Each man made every effort to move on the rocks at their base so as to leave little imprint, although the snow was now coming down in sheets. They doubled back to Will.

Will suited up in the Spetsnaz winter uniform, a hooded, one-piece KLMK coverall, its patterning a patchwork of white, black, and brown. When he pulled down the hood and facemask, he became part of the blizzard pelting him. Over his left shoulder, he hoisted one pack, also camouflaged in white, black, and brown streaks; another pack went over his right shoulder. A black shoulder holster held the Type-64 pistol. Its long silencer extended well below the holster. The black 50-gallon drum lay on its side near the tent.

"Okay, return to the mini-sub and wait for my signal," said Will. "Remember: If no signal by 2200 tomorrow, return to the *Florida*."

"Yes, sir." Moncrief picked up the pack as the other men grabbed the remaining gear and worked their way down to the water's edge. They slid into the surf, backing out and dragging the big empty drum and the remaining packs behind them.

"Gunny," said Hernandez, grabbing Moncrief just as a wave hit both of them in their backs.

"Yeah."

"The barrel's floating. We'll need to take off the lid to sink it."

"Do it."

Hernandez pried the lid off the black oil drum. As the water rushed in, it gave off a white cloud of steam. The next wave caught its open face and sent it to the bottom.

"I hope he didn't want that," said Hernandez.

"Nah, he already emptied it. Let's go."

Good luck, boss, Moncrief thought as he took one last glance at the North Korean coastline, pulled his mask down, and slid quietly into the surf.

"Do you need two keys to your room, sir?"

"No."

The hotel clerk bowed to the guest as she gave him the key. "Do you have an interest in our symphony?" she asked.

"Possibly, yes."

"Our concierge may have tickets remaining for tonight. She's at the desk on the other side of the lobby."

The clerk was referring to the Tokyo Orchestra. The Kimshicho Marriott, part of an interconnected row of modern silver and glass buildings, included the symphony hall. It was the tallest part of a commercial complex in the center of one of suburban Tokyo's many commercial districts. This particular district was to the east of Tokyo, along a growth of buildings and suburbs that connected the city to Narita Airport.

Rei was not a music fan, but attending this concert might serve a good purpose. The day before, Rei had taken the Tokyo subway to the Kimshicho station and walked the two blocks to the hotel complex. There, he'd noticed something he did not like: a well-dressed young man reading a Japanese newspaper in the Marriott lobby. It was not the newspaper that disturbed Rei. It was the small and barely noticeable earpiece he'd been wearing.

Rei had passed him quickly, making a point not to glance back at him. As he rode the taxi back to Key Plaza, where he had begun his Tokyo stay, Rei realized the only way to penetrate security was to be on the inside.

"And I have you down for a five-day stay," said the hotel clerk.

"Yes, that's correct."

"And this is for business?"

"Of course, yes," said Rei.

"We're required to examine your passport."

"Yes." He handed her an American

passport with another false name. This time, he was pretending to be a Japanese-American returning to Tokyo on an annual visit to the corporate headquarters of a Japanese electronics maker.

Rei took his passport back and approached the concierge. "Madam?"

"Oh yes, sir?"

"I'm interested in two tickets to tonight's symphony," Rei said, playing the odds. Buying two tickets would be less suspicious, even if the seat next to him remained empty. More important, a concert in the building adjoining the hotel would be a likely social activity for the science-conference attendees, thus potentially affording him his best opportunity.

"They're rather expensive," she said. "The concert's nearly sold out."

"Yes, how much?" He did not want to appear too easy or too quick.

"Two in the orchestra for thirty-two thousand yen apiece."

"Anything less?"

"Two in the second balcony for twenty-eight thousand yen apiece," she said.

He paused for a moment. "Let me call you." This suggested he had to consult with someone else, though not his wife—he wore no wedding ring.

Rei took the elevator to the sixth floor and checked into room 606. His window looked out over the vast expanse of Tokyo. Directly below, a bright red express train running between Tokyo station and Narita Airport flew through the Kimshico station. He knew this for certain. Such express trains were always bright red. In the distance, a Ferris wheel that rose as high as any skyscraper dominated the city's skyline. At the harbor near Odaiba, a suburb of Tokyo, the lights were a circus of red, yellow, and blue.

Sometime later, Rei called down to the concierge and ordered two tickets. He bought the less expensive balcony seats to further lessen any attention. The tickets would be delivered to his room before the concert began. Rei took a hot shower that steamed up the windows to his room, then lay down to rest before his big night.

│   │   │

Several time zones away, the net was closing. The Saturday morning meeting in the FBI's SIOC operation center had been scheduled, albeit at the last minute, for 6 a.m.

"Tom, what's going on?" Dave Creighton knew the agent well enough to know that an impromptu meeting suggested a major development.

"Sir, I was contacted last night by Joan."

"It's been some time, hasn't it?"

"Yes," said Tom, looking as sharp at six on a Saturday morning as he would at a Wednesday afternoon meeting. "I understand our man has remained in Japan."

"Oh?" said Creighton.

The two other men in the room leaned forward in their chairs. The meeting had taken a new direction, and possibly a new urgency.

"Who are the likely targets in Japan again?" asked Creighton.

ANDERSON HARP

"There are four," said Samuel Wilhelm. "Two in Kyoto, one in Wako, and one in Tokyo. But the one based in Tokyo is presently attending a conference at Cal Tech."

"We need to tell PSIA."

"Yes, sir."

"They can help protect their scientists."

Keeping Japan out of the loop was acceptable until it became clear that their own could be hurt.

"What about DOD, Commander? Any comment from them?" Creighton looked to the black-sweatered naval officer.

"Nothing yet," said Commander Sawyer. "And I should apologize for Admiral Krowl's absence. He's presently involved in a top-secret mission and is on twenty-four-hour watch at the operations center."

"Understood. So, the scope narrows. Any suggestions?"

"Sir," said Pope, "we can send a team to Japan to coordinate with Japanese Defense and the police."

"I don't have a problem with that," said

Creighton, "but, Tom, I need you to stay here. If anything starts to move fast, I don't want you 8,000 miles away."

"Yes, sir."

| | |

At that same moment, Rei slipped his coat on, straightened his tie in the mirror, and slid a bright gold dragon ring, backwards, onto his finger.

As the elevator door opened to the Marriott's marble and glass lobby, a throng of symphony-goers—men in black ties and suits, women in long, sparkling dresses—milled around. In the fringes of the crowd, Rei noticed several young men, separate and alone, their small ear devices barely visible. Rei made a point of staying in the center of the throng as they moved up the escalators and toward the walkways connecting to the symphony hall.

As the crowd merged through the symphony hall's entry doors, Rei saw an older woman, surrounded by three young men dressed like the other security men. He immediately recognized her face.

Well-protected, aren't you?

All was to his advantage. Despite the ring of protection, the target was out of her element. The large crowd would give him cover and opportunity. He slumped down in his seat, well to the rear of the balcony's railing, but with a good view of the entire hall. His target had been seated—sans her security detail—in the fifth row of the orchestra section. As the orchestra played Beethoven, Rei leaned back, his hands together, feeling the bulk of the ornate ring against his palm, patiently devising his plan.

Just before the concert ended, Rei worked his way down to the hall's main floor, spotting an empty seat near the rear wall and well in the dark. Shortly after he sat, the lights came on and a rush of people converged on the main exit. He remained seated, casually talking in fluent Japanese to the couple sitting next to him, suggesting that an ill family member had caused him to miss much of the concert.

He purposely stayed, waiting and watching as the professor made her way up the center aisle by herself, her security waiting in the lobby.

Now, he thought. He stood, bowed to the couple, worked his way into the exiting crowd and waited, not turning toward the main aisle until the last possible second. Then he moved toward the professor and turned the ring around.

She was close—so close now he could smell her sweet floral perfume. He reached forward to touch her, but just as he did, a short, balding Japanese man stepped in front, forcing him back.

Damn, he thought, as she smiled at him. He took the lead in front of her and moved past Rei, watching the crowd for trouble.

Perfect, he thought, now steps behind the professor. He nudged past other concert-goers until he was shoulder to shoulder with his target. The pin of the ring just brushed her arm, above the elbow, inflicting what felt like a mere scratch. She barely noticed it, no more than when one brushes against the lip of a counter and feels, ever so briefly, a rough, pointed edge. She walked a few more steps before suddenly arching her back, then crumpling to the floor.

The crowd parted, trying not to step on her, while others pushed forward, unaware, like drivers piling into one another while gawking at a stalled car on the shoulder. Rei knew what would happen now. He had no desire to stay and watch, and easily moved through the crowd and out onto the street.

Rei walked at a normal pace, as if in no hurry, passing by the entrance to the Marriott Hotel. He had planned to abandon what few clothes he had in his room. It would be too great a risk for him to be seen leaving the hotel with a bag shortly after the concert. A day later, the housekeeping crew would report that his bed had not been slept in the previous night. By that point, Rei knew it would not matter.

En route to Kinshicho Station, Rei, still on foot, merged with the crowd, passing the lights of several department stores and the brighter, circus-like atmosphere of the Pachinko Ginza Parlors. Noisy, flashing lights from these gambling halls lined the street toward the train station.

Rei pulled up his coat collar, blocking the cold wind, and moved with the crowd into the station. He smiled as he passed his transit card, already paid for, through the gate.

It's over, he thought, satisfied that his final mission had been accomplished.

He didn't take the next train to Narita. Instead, he took the blue line, back toward Tokyo station. There, he moved quickly up the stairs, through the crush of people and several hallways, to a down escalator marked "Narita Express." Rei had already reserved seats on several of the express trains, across a spread of times, knowing that one would coincide with the timing of his escape.

As his train left Tokyo station, it built up such speed that Rei could hear the wind whistle in the connectors between the cars. He leaned back and closed his eyes until he felt the car brake. Above the train, he saw the high rise of the Kimshicho Tobu Marriott and, looking forward, the lights of Kinshicho Station, which he had left only shortly before. The station's several platforms were now covered with police talking to every traveler. Many of the male travelers were dressed in tuxedos, and the women in long gowns.

The Narita Express slowed but did not stop, its destination far, far away.

| | |

"Tom?"

"Yeah?" Pope's voice sounded drugged with sleep. He had left the SIOC's center only a few hours before, another grueling sixteen-hour day behind him.

"This is Mac Howard."

"Yeah, Mac."

Howard, who worked the SIOC's graveyard shift, was in the loop on Pope's operation. "No need to send the team," he said.

"Oh?" said Tom. He had wondered whether they might be too slow responding to the lead in Japan.

"Dr. Aoano died of what appeared to be a heart attack at a concert in Tokyo earlier today."

"Damn! I thought she was the one in Wako," said Tom.

"She was apparently at the conference in Tokyo. He somehow eluded her security."

"Do they have anything?"

"Not much. A couple spoke of a man in his thirties, Asian, fluent Japanese, at the concert by himself."

"Yeah?"

"Seems he took a seat out in the lobby a few minutes before the concert ended. That's why they remembered him."

"Are the Japanese gonna get a sketch of him?" said Tom.

"Yes, sir. Unfortunately, that's the only lead. He's gone."

The prevailing winds drove the snow toward shore with such force that Will could barely make out Kevin Moncrief's facemask as he submerged beneath the water. He held his hand out just above his eyes, blocking the power of the wind and the cold, icy spray. Finally, after Moncrief's dark outline disappeared, Will turned away from the wind and toward the mountains. As he turned, he glanced at his watch. It showed 0336.

Only an hour and a half to first daylight, he thought. As he twisted around, a large boulder separated him from the beach and the ocean. His small tent was now almost completely white from the sticking snow. Will pulled the flap down and zipped it up almost to the top, leaving only a few inches open.

In the dull light, the water tumbling over the rocks at the streambed bottom appeared nearly black. Will moved slowly at first, allowing his eyes to adjust. He climbed onto the side of the streambed and underneath the gray, chipped concrete arch of the bridge. He moved silently, each step carefully placed. With time, he gradually built up his speed, moving from rock to rock. Soon, Will was climbing through a green pine forest as he followed the streambed up into the mountains above the beach.

They're well-named, Will thought as he scanned the span of jagged-tooth peaks extending both north and south. The Diamond Mountains of the Tieback range looked as sharp-edged as their brilliant namesake.

After an hour, he stopped at an outcrop of rocks, noting that the stream came from farther up into the mountains. Looking back, he saw the white caps of the waves as they broke on the rocks of the moon-shaped beach. It was from this vantage point that he could see the road as it followed the bay, off to the

north and left. He could also make out the few
lights of Wonsan in the distance.

As he looked to the south, the road turned,
and there he saw the faint flicker of a dull
yellow light. He stayed on the rocks for a
while and gazed at it, until he realized that
it seemed to blink on and off because of
movement between him and the light. Only
after staring for a few moments could Will
make out the shape of the bunker and see the
several North Korean guards surrounding it.

On a clear day, Will thought, *Shane
Stidham could have thrown a football from
where we'd landed and struck the center of the
guards.* As he adjusted the pack on his back
and the shoulder holster holding the Type-
64, Will looked at his watch to reconfirm
his westward bearing. The watch told both
time and direction. Feeling on his back the
increased wind of the snowstorm, he flipped
up the straps of the green and black backpack,
tossing it over his right shoulder. He could
feel all the pent-up energy of the past several

weeks released. This was the beginning of a marathon for which he was ready.

It was shortly before the yellow gray hue of dawn's light that Will crossed over the top of the mountain and found the small lake that fed the stream. *Better not move much during daylight*, he thought to himself. Will worked his way around the edge of the streambed and the lake to a large stand of pine trees clumped together. Sharp, jagged granite cliffs and peaks seemed to buffer all sound.

Below the cliffs, a forest of pine trees encircled the lake. He stopped, smelling the pine needles and whiffing the pine boughs as the snow continued to accumulate on the trees and boulders. He looked around at one particular boulder lodged next to the base of an ancient pine tree. Its trunk was the size of a pillar and could probably support a bridge. Between the rock and the tree was a small opening out of the snowstorm. There, Will shoved in his second backpack, the one from Hawaii, and pulled himself in behind it. The Type-64 silencer stuck into his hip and he had to twist the weapon. *If I ever have to use this, I'm in deep shit*, he thought. He wiggled around so only his hooded head stuck out near the entrance to his sanctuary.

Will wasn't tired, but forced himself to doze. Years of combat had trained him to fall into a short sleep and wake at a given hour, with his subconscious always alert to sounds. He would look at his watch, think two hours, imagine the time to get up, and wake near it.

| | | |

Several thousand miles away, the second shift at the Executive Support Center had just begun when the door swung open and Krowl entered.

"Give me a status," Krowl huffed as he pulled up a chair at the end of the table.

An Air Force sergeant worked one computer terminal while another worked another one nearby.

A young Air Force captain with a deep dimple in the center of his chin stood at attention. "Sir, I'm Captain Beardon and I have the second watch, sir."

"Yes, so what's the status?"

"Sir, Satellite USA37X has a fixed location on him presently in the Taebaek Mountains south of Wonsan." The young captain pointed to a large screen on the right that showed a detailed map of the mountains. High in the mountain range was a small lake, and just to the side of the lake, two blinking, bright-blue x's crossed virtually on top of each other. A thin diagonal blue line extended from each of the x's, which were marked X-1 and X-2. "Yes, sir, he's been stationary at that position now for six hours. It'll be getting dark in North Korea in about an hour. My guess is he's waiting for darkness to fall before he moves out again."

"That would make sense," Krowl said.

"Our other Air Force tech sergeant here is responsible for USA82X, the second bird, which is positioned in the GEO orbit." The captain turned to another large panel that showed a map of the Korean peninsula and a dotted tracing of two satellites, which appeared to converge as they ran from north to south.

"What about the convergence of those paths, Captain?" Krowl asked.

"Sir, they're on two drastically different orbits. The GEO orbit of 82 will stay fixed in its current position. We may lose the picture of this other bird, but we have another satellite that'll pick up on the window at 0800 Zulu."

"All right, the only thing is, I want to make sure we can use 82 directly from here."

"Yes, sir," said the captain. "We have complete capability from here to use 82 and do whatever you deem necessary."

As Will woke from the short nap, the snow continued to pile up in small drifts. Even in the submarine, he never heard the depth of quiet that he sensed in these mountains. "God," he said, rubbing both hands on his face.

Pulling out of the hole and quietly dusting off the snow that had accumulated on his shoulders and hood, he took the larger pack and slid it back into the hole, covering the entrance with a handful of pine needles. Looking around slowly in a circle, he adjusted the smaller of his two packs and his shoulder holster.

Amazing, he thought, recalling the times during his three-dimensional training he had walked the circumference of this small lake.

He knew this stream branched out from the lake at the center of its mass. If he circled around it to the right, he knew he would find another stream that fed into it from above. Slowly, as he gained his sense of footing and his body warmed, Will worked his way past the rocks of the streambed and around the edge of the lake.

This snow is not a bad thing, Will decided. It would provide him an extra blanket of camouflage and cover any trace of his presence.

After some time, Will came upon another stream flowing down through several rows of pine trees. He bent down below the sagging branches of one tree, which leaned under the weight of the accumulating snow. The stream's water was cold and crystal clear. Will traced it uphill, climbing the rocks like a continuous boulder stairway. Ahead some distance, he came across a surging waterfall, its sound echoing in the stillness of the forest and snowstorm. *Utterly amazing*, he thought, *the unblemished beauty of these mountains.*

Will slithered with his chest against the boulders as he climbed over the rocks above the waterfall. Snow continued to fall, his uniform turning into blotches of white, black, and green. It surprised him that, a few hundred meters beyond the waterfall, he could see the shape of a small valley off to the right. He knew he was on the mark, but his distance estimates hadn't put this valley so close. Will split away from the stream and worked his way through ancient pine trees, moving more slowly as he came out just above the valley. He saw a large outcrop of rocks several feet below him and slid down the hillside to below the rocky overhang. There, a small ledge extended out and away.

Perfect, he thought, scanning the valley and sensing the snowstorm slowing. Just then, Will heard the shifting rumble of a vehicle from the valley below and to his right. As he slowly turned his head in that direction, he saw two trucks with small convoy lights barely illuminating the road. *I'll be damned*, he thought, observing the speed of the vehicles. This had to be a highly improved road, because the trucks were moving fast, despite little illumination from their convoy lights. The drivers were obviously very familiar with both their vehicles and the road. Until the sound of the trucks slid well past him, Will stayed still.

In the darkness, he pulled below the ledge, removed a pack, and retrieved from it a black computer no bigger than a library book. He pulled out two tripods, both no larger than small lamps, and, using their pointed cleats, fixed them into the ground. On one tripod, he placed a small black metallic dish that looked like a kitchen colander. Finally, he pulled out a camera about the same size as a standard point-and-shoot digital.

He slid back out from underneath the overhang to the edge, placed the satellite dish back behind him to the left, and aimed it up at the sky. After attaching a cable from the satellite dish directly to the small computer terminal, and then from the computer terminal directly to the camera, he set the camera on the other tripod and slid it near the edge, aiming it down, roughly into the center of the valley. He bent the lid of the computer down low, took off his shoulder holster and camouflage jacket, and slid underneath the jacket so he could see the computer screen without illuminating any of the area.

He reached out with his arm and slowly tilted the satellite dish, playing with the computer keys until a long red band on the screen showed a high intensity. *Got it*, he thought as the satellite dish and computer homed in on the U.S. satellite. The computer showed a test screen and verified that the camera was fully online and ready to transmit. Will then took some dry brush and carefully slid the camouflage around the dish to cover all but the face pointing up toward the sky. He also pulled some brush around the camera so only the lens protruded. He turned again to the computer, and received a message back confirming the link-up. The message was entirely in Russian Cyrillic. "Good," he whispered.

Will slowly slid his parka back on and curled up in a ball underneath the overhang in the rock. *So, this is it*, he thought as he looked down at his watch, then up at the first light of Day 2. He lay there quietly for several hours until he smelled smoke coming from the valley below. Again, with the silence of a deer working its way through the forest, Will pulled up from the ledge, moving slowly and deliberately until he could see down in the valley. There, in the nascent daylight, his eyes focused on a curling, twisting column of smoke.

Will followed the smoke downward, then crawled nearer to the edge. He traced it to an opening on the roof of a small, crude hut on a patch of dirt surrounded by a snow-covered garden and two browned, rectangular, diked rice paddies. A dirt path connected the hut to the road, which Will could tell stood well above the rice paddies.

Will heard the swing of a door and the bang as it closed. An old, bent-back man crossed from the hut to a pile of wood nearer to Will. He watched as the old man struggled to swing an oddly-shaped axe, then heard the *thump* as it struck the wood. Splinters of wood flew up with each stroke. *He survives simply*, Will thought. *No livestock—just the rice he raises.*

Scanning the valley again, Will saw the road shift to his left and south, curving around an outcrop of rocks, their shape broken by an occasional grouping of small, young pine trees. The road turned also in another direction—to the north, more toward the coast and probably Wonsan. He hadn't noticed it at first, but beyond the old man's rice paddies and his path to the roadway, there was another well-improved road cut in a straight diagonal line. He followed it upward, across rice paddies on the other side, to a flat rectangular mound nestled against the valley wall. He studied this mound for some time and slowly moved the camera lens. Through the camera, he spotted a sizable cement pad. *That's it*, Will thought. *The helicopter landing zone.* He moved the camera to focus on the center, carefully pushing the tripod down to stabilize it.

His watch showed nearly ten in the morning. *Now, we wait*, he thought, slowly sliding back under the overhang, then pulling some of the brush up to cover much of his shape. If, by chance, the farmer wandered up the steep hillside, he would have to be virtually on top of Will before any of his shape or equipment would be evident.

All day, Will watched the twisting smoke float up from the hut below. Through early morning, it would climb a short distance above the hut, then blow west toward the other side of the valley. Now it climbed straight up into the sky. For hours, Will watched the old man scratch away at his dirt patch of a garden like an ant.

It was sometime after noon when Will first heard the low thumping sound of the Mi-8 HIP helicopter. From underneath the overhanging rock, he slowly crawled out to the edge.

He had still not seen the helicopter when he saw three Soviet UAZ jeeps coming from the south. They sped along in a convoy, as if late for some function. Will felt his heart, pressed against the cold dirt, beat more quickly. Slowly, he slipped forward, closer to the edge. As each jeep hit the same bumps in the road, it hopped up like a caterpillar. The old man stopped and watched as the jeeps zoomed by.

Will leaned back slowly, expecting the helicopter to appear above. He pulled up the lid of the computer and typed the Cyrillic code identification.

| | | |

"He's up," said Scott, sitting in the small, vault-like computer room in the security center, well below the Pacific Command's headquarters. Covering the wall were two flat panel screens; exactly as in Krowl's set-up in the ESC, one showed a satellite view of the valley and the other the track of satellites over the Korean peninsula. Unlike Krowl, however, Scott did not have a third screen's transmission of the second satellite.

"Okay, Mr. Scott, your boy's on station," said Jess Markeet, the only other person in the room. Tall and thin, his prematurely gray hair cut high and tight, Markeet, the resident CIA agent assigned as liaison to PAC-COM, would have looked odd anywhere but in Hawaii.

"What's he saying?" Scott asked.

"He's giving the code to stand by."

"Will we get the photo relayed here?"

"No sweat." Markeet hit the keyboard and a small split-screen appeared on the larger satellite overview. "When he hits his photo, it'll instantly relay up to the satellite and show up here, at Langley, and at the Pentagon."

"Is Krowl up?" said Scott.

"Oh, yeah."

"Can we VTC him?"

"Yeah." Markeet hit a few more strokes on the keyboard and another split screen appeared in the corner of their main screen.

"Can Krowl hear us?"

"One minute," said Markeet, typing some more. "Okay, go ahead."

Scott leaned forward into a table microphone, which looked like a small black ashtray. "ESC, this is PAC. Do you copy?"

With this comment, he saw Krowl turn around with the others and look at their screen.

"Scott, we have a relay that he's ready." Krowl looked drawn and haggard. It would be near dawn in Washington.

"Yes, Admiral. We're close."

"Good. It's about time."

Scott shook his head while the smirking Markeet, offscreen from the VTC camera, muted their audio feed to Washington. "Yes, Admiral, it's bloody well time."

| | | |

As he lowered the lid on the computer, a rush of air and noise blew over Will.

"Goddamn." Will froze as the Mi-8 helicopter, banking from his side of the valley, blew barely above the top of the short pine trees around him. He looked up, seeing the rivet lines in the underbelly of the helicopter. It flew so close he could see a forearm of the helicopter's crewman sticking out the side door. If the helicopter's path had taken it a few meters to either the left or right, Will would have been looking directly into the eyes of the crew chief.

Will remained frozen in place, trusting he'd remain invisible as long as he stayed immobile.

As the helicopter began to flare in landing directly across the valley, he slowly moved, lifting his head, watching it pass. The jeeps had turned up the small path of a road, heading toward the helicopter landing zone.

Will slid to the camera, watching the old man below as he leaned on his hoe, staring toward the commotion on the other side of the valley.

The helicopter continued to flare, pitching sharply upwards, on line for the center of the landing pad. Will saw the three jeeps stop, and several men—some in uniform with Kalashnikovs, others in olive green Mao-styled jackets—hopped out of the jeeps.

His pulse rate redoubled as he put the camera online.

One shot and I'm out of here, he thought, breathing deliberate breaths to slow his heartbeat. The camera had a simple crosshair, much like a deer-rifle scope. Similar magnification as well. He had worked with it countless times at Quantico. *Just pick the right Nampo and snap*, he thought as he focused the viewfinder. The camera's electronic lens whirred as he spotted the faces of the men, now standing in a small group. *Well, it's been some time*, Will thought, the camera focusing sharply on all the faces one by one.

Peter Nampo. He stopped on the face of a man he hadn't seen for many years. It was a thin, flint-hardened face with jet-black hair. Peter hadn't aged well.

Just as he began to squeeze the shutter trigger, another similar face appeared—then another, then another. Will held off, taking in the four virtually identical men. *Damn*, he thought, acknowledging the impressive accomplishment of finding—or creating— three Nampo doppelgangers. The quartet of Nampos stood together next to their jeep, awaiting their guest of honor.

Will stared at each man, moving the camera

from face to face. *They're perfect matches*, he thought, frustrated. The seconds ticked away.

A general with gold and red epaulette boards on his shoulders stepped down from the helicopter as the blades continued to swirl, but at a slower rate. Will watched the men, waiting for a reaction. There was none. No single man moved forward to greet the guest. Each of the four stayed with the others, making no individual movement. He thought of Krowl waiting impatiently, thousands of miles away, cursing Will for being unsure.

"Come on, goddammit," he whispered. *Peter Nampo's standing there—a man so dangerous they brought me halfway around the world to get one stupid photo of him.*

The slowing blades of the helicopter started to cast shadows over the men. The seconds stretching into eternity. Will knew the entourage would greet their guest, take him back to wherever they had come from, and Peter Nampo would disappear, not to be seen for months. The opportunity was slipping away.

Then Will saw it. The second Nampo moved and did something Will hadn't seen for years: he subtly leaned to the side, briefly adjusting his weight from one leg to the other. Nampo, he remembered, had always worn an elevated shoe to compensate for his shorter leg. It was a characteristic that the others would surely not share.

"Got him." Will aimed the crosshair at the center of Peter Nampo's forehead. The camera could focus down to the smallest detail. Will zoomed in on the other figures once more, studying their bodies, their movements. One moved his left hand toward his face, but no other Nampo readjusted his weight.

Shifting the camera back to Peter Nampo, Will felt the beginnings of another snow flurry. The valley suddenly became dark and much colder. He could see the breath of the men as they spoke.

Will waited again, just to be certain. And again, Nampo shifted his weight off the shorter leg. Will could see the rotation of the slowing blades above Nampo's head.

No doubt, Will thought as he squeezed the camera's trigger. But the camera neither clicked nor snapped and, for a brief moment, it seemed to do nothing at all. He held the trigger down again, holding the crosshairs on Nampo's forehead. *Goddamn it, it must be——*

The flash of brilliant light stopped him in mid-thought. Then he heard the boom. The flash, followed by the boom momentarily blinded and deafened him. *A bolt of lightning in the midst of a snowstorm? A bout of northern thunder?*

He looked back through the camera and saw Peter Nampo no more. A small cloud of smoke appeared where Nampo once stood. A few of the men who'd been closest to Nampo lay on the ground. The other men, clearly in shock, wandered around aimlessly. A thin blue streak of vapor, like a pencil, extended into the clouds momentarily before dissipating in the air.

"What the hell…?" He decreased camera magnification to pan the tableau. The old general sat on the ground, looking dazed. The blades of the helicopter were still rotating, but off their center, each blade now a few feet shorter than before.

"I'll be damned," said Will.

Some sort of laser, he guessed, in vaporizing Peter Nampo, had also sliced through the metal blades as they rotated over his head. Presumably, the beam's heat had exploded a body made up mostly of water molecules. At the same time, superheating the water molecules in the clouds above, it had caused an explosive clap of sound: thunder in a blizzard.

Will slid back under the overhang, slightly dazed himself. *Krowl never wanted a photograph. He wanted to assassinate Nampo. I was marking Nampo with the camera. Painting a digital target on his head. And that son-of-a-bitch Krowl never told me a thing about it.*

Will's next realization was more chilling: *Now, I'm truly alone.*

Krowl couldn't risk the assassination pointing back to the United States.

"Jesus, what happened?" Scott saw the camera focus in on a man who appeared to be Peter Nampo, then watched as the screen went blank.

"ESC cut off all feeds," said Markeet.

"How about the VTC to Krowl?"

"We're still hooked up."

"Turn up the volume."

Scott could hear Krowl's voice.

"Everyone leave except the airman on USA82," said Krowl, sounding even more intense than usual.

Scott heard the slam of a door.

"Okay, now turn to Target One," said Krowl.

"Yes, sir." It was the squeaky voice of a very young man, maybe one just out of puberty—obviously a young technician caught in the storm.

"How long before the laser's online again?" said Krowl.

"Two minutes, sir."

"How much time left?"

"Sixty-two seconds."

Scott imagined what was going on in the ESC. He saw Krowl standing over the technician and his computer, breathing down on him as the computer's targeting lined up for the second shot.

"Turn off the VTC," said Scott

"What's up, Scotty?" Markeet looked up at Scott.

"Just turn it off. We don't need to hear this." Scott understood now, and he didn't like it. He didn't want to witness it. He also knew there was nothing he could do about it.

I   I   I

There wasn't much Will could do, either. He pushed back below the overhang as machine guns fired sporadically, shooting at shadows. Bullets whizzed toward the other side of the valley.

Will peeked out and saw that two soldiers were firing at the already twisted and dead body of the old farmer, lying in his garden. Others fired at the old man's hut, riddling the walls with bullets. Their only convenient target.

Will slunk back farther, underneath the rock.

The snowstorm worsened as the sky grew darker. The firing of the Kalashnikovs echoed off the walls of the valley.

Another blinding flash of light. The second boom lifted Will up and threw him against the rock to the side of the overhang. He looked up and saw nothing but sky. The second laser shot had struck and destroyed the rock overhang.

A white, pencil-like vapor streak went directly up into the sky. The laser had heated the humid air as it passed through, leaving a direct marker at Will's location. If the laser didn't kill him, its trail would. The "pop" of bullets suddenly surrounded him like a swarm of bees.

As bullets continued to crack all around him, Will pulled out of the rubble, ran up the side of the hill, and jumped behind a downed log.

The laser recharged.

Parker took off.

Another flash. The third flash struck behind the log where he'd had just been. This one was closer. The force knocked Will to the ground. He began to count. Two minutes had elapsed between blasts.

Will made it to the stream, moving fast, working through the rocks. The cold water fazed him little. The snowstorm's intensity increased. On his face, he felt a pelt of ice, immediately melted by his sweat. He heard the rumble of the waterfall ahead. The cold penetrated his legs and arms, which he could hardly feel. He knew time was slipping away.

Past the waterfall, Will slid down, slipping under its icy flow, briefly out of sight.

First things first, he thought. *I can hide*

from the North Koreans. I can't hide from that laser.

It suddenly occurred to him. Will felt for the small scar on his abdomen, recalling the visit to the dentist's office arranged by Krowl. Just below the skin, he felt a metal disc, the size of a quarter. It was like a bullet in his side. He knew what it did. *I need something sharp,* he thought.

Will reached down into the bottom of the stream bed. Feeling through the round, smooth stones, he found a single sharp one resembling a piece of flint. He tugged with his icy cold, blue fingers. Then he grabbed the flap of skin, feeling the small disc in his grasp. He pulled the skin tight between his fingers, and held it in the flow of icy water from the waterfall.

Fifty-five seconds left before the next satellite shot. He gave himself a five-second leeway on his count. Between the cold water and his tight grip, the skin turned blue, numbing slightly.

"One, two, three." He cut into the flesh,

blood dripping down his side. Will exhaled with the pain.

A bright silver disc popped out, plunking down into the water below the pool of the waterfall. Without pause, he resumed running, moving quickly over the snow accumulating again on the rocks. Blood poured down his side from the open wound. Far worse, the numbing effects of the cold crept through his body, the first harbingers of hypothermia.

Blood droplets stained the white snow as he worked his way down the stream. Will could hear the commotion of the men following his trail. An occasional rifle shot rang out. They were still shooting at shadows.

Another brilliant flash of light. The boom of the fourth strike knocked him down again, this time into the cold stream. He looked back, several meters upstream, where a cloud of steam rose from where the waterfall once stood. It was now a crumble of rocks.

I haven't much time, he thought.

No, he had two far more deadly enemies

now than the laser: the cold and the North Koreans.

Will worked through the stream, hopping from rock to rock, ignoring the cold, moving at a marathoner's speed. The men behind him were moving but not closing. The snow and stream rocks slowed them. He was able to maintain a constant, rhythmic pace—until the lake.

I can go around it, but I'll only leave a longer trail, Will thought. No choice—he jumped headlong into the icy water. He couldn't feel the wound at all now, the ice cold water erasing any conscious thought of pain. Knowing time was running out, Will stroked steadily across the center of the lake. He maintained one conscious thought: *I will survive.*

| | | |

Captain Sang led the lead patrol, hot on the trail down the stream bed.

"Captain, he's hurt," said one of his soldiers.

The droplets of blood led down the stream.

"Do not kill him," said Sang.

"Yes, sir."

"Pass that word."

"Yes, sir."

"Captain, they're bringing up the 112th battalion," said the radio operator, following Sang closely.

"We're heading toward the shoreline," said Sang. "It's getting dark. Tell them to bring up the naval patrol to cut off any escape."

"Yes, sir. A patrol from Wonsan Harbor is heading south at this time."

Sang looked up at the cliffs above the stream bed, but his target remained hidden.

| | | |

Will shivered uncontrollably as he dragged himself out of the frigid water. The trail would stop on the other side, causing the North Korean patrol to split up and to go around both sides of the lake. Darkness would slow them further. Still, he had to get some protection to survive.

The cold water had flushed and numbed the wound, but it soon began to bleed again. He had to act fast.

Will worked his way up the stream bed on the other side, crossing behind the large, round boulders to the group of pine trees—the pine trees where he'd left his second backpack.

He was shaking, his teeth chattering beyond control. Barely able to maintain consciousness, Will was now a blue tint from head to toe. He pulled aside the pine boughs, grabbing the backpack from the hole.

From inside, Will pulled out two silver, plastic packs, ripping them open. Two large patches, similar to brown oversized Band-Aids, were marked—one as nutrition, the other as glucose/maltodextrin. He pulled the tape off each, sticking them to the sides of his neck. Both subcutaneous feeds pushed high-energy fuel into his bloodstream, directly through his skin.

Will also removed a small clear tube, no bigger than a tube of superglue. It was marked "permabond." He broke off its white cap and clinched the two edges of the wound with his fingers. He winced as he squirted the clear, glue-like substance onto the edges of his wound. Will held the skin together for slightly over a minute as the wound sealed. He used a handful of snow to wash off the remaining streak of dried blood.

A noise of men clattered through the woods to the north side of the lake. They were close and getting closer. It didn't matter––his most immediate problem remained still the cold.

Will ripped open another unmarked package. He knew it was from SEACU. The Army Research Lab was devoted to supplying the best military equipment in the world, and this was it. Will's hands shook as he pulled off his clothing and put on an olive brown, rubber-like jumpsuit––black soled shoes, gloves, and a hood, all built into a single garment. Will slipped the suit on, covering everything but his eyes, but the olive brown color stood out, even near the stand of pine trees.

On the left forearm, the suit had a velcroed flap of material. When Will pulled it back, a small LED panel was revealed. He aimed it at the snow-covered woods, pressing on the LED of the personal integrated area network. The suit, employing its microprocessor, scanned the snow-white and brown terrain. Like a chameleon, the suit instantly turned to a matching snow-white and brown color. He lifted up the backpack, pulling a small cable from a side, velcro-closed pocket. As he plugged the cable into the suit, the backpack changed to an identical color—white and brown.

Will turned nearly invisible, and just in time.

Sang's patrol had rounded the lake and neared the stand of trees. "Captain, we have lost the trail," Will heard one of them say.

Sang looked around the lake, seeing the other half of the patrol approaching from the south side of the lake.

"Where should we go, Captain?" said the soldier.

"Follow this stream to the beach. He must be heading toward the water."

Will, understanding the Korean perfectly, moved out of the tree stand and toward the stream, heading due east. As darkness fell, he stepped into the streambed. Again, he reached into his backpack, pulling out a pair of wraparound glasses, also from the SSC Natick Laboratory. The lightweight night-vision glasses gave him a daylight view of the stream. The clamor of the troops closed from behind as the snowstorm continued to build.

At the point where Will had stopped two days before, he felt the full brunt of the snowstorm, the winds blowing in from the Sea of Japan. Below him, he saw the lights of an increased number of soldiers at the point to the south. He also saw the lights of men closing from the roadway to the north. In the dark water, lights bobbed up and down near where the ASDS was anchored. North Korean patrol boats were criss-crossing the bay.

Will had scores of DPRK troops on all

sides of him, with Sang's patrol now less than fifty meters behind. The patrol had spread out, and was now on both sides of the streambed, behind and up the rocky slopes. They would search and search until they found him.

Will turned toward Sang's net of men, back up the streambed, to the west. A few meters up the stream were three snow-covered boulders, still within sight of the rocky beach. The soldiers were close—close enough that, in the green glow of his night-vision glasses, he could see the stars on their hats and collars. He saw their Kalashnikovs. He could see their eyes.

Wedging in between two of the boulders, Will used the suit's LED microprocessor to match the color of the rocks. He pulled off his backpack, removing from it a small black remote control device shaped like a deck of cards.

Will punched in a series of numbers, put the device back in the pack, placed the pack underneath his chest, and leaned over, using the suit to camouflage his presence. He bent down, trying to breathe slowly and relax, forcing his mind elsewhere.

At that moment, Sang stepped onto the rock above Will.

"Captain, he must be between us and the beach," said the soldier.

"Slow the men down," said Sang.

"Yes, sir."

"No, stop the men. Tell them to be totally quiet."

"Yes, sir."

Will slowed down his breathing, forcing himself to hear only the water bubbling past.

"Let's wait," said Sang.

"Yes, Captain."

Sang pulled out his pistol and chambered a round. From atop the rock, he could see the stream, the beach, the road bridge below, and the patrol boats in the dark water beyond.

"He's between here and the water."

"Yes, sir," the young radio operator whispered as Will heard the crackle of radio traffic. A swarm of patrol units chattered back and forth.

"Turn the radio off," said Sang.

Then silence covered the woods. The only thing heard was the stream of water running over the rocks. Sang waited, and Will remained as still as possible, less than an arm's reach from the captain's boot.

I   I   I

"Sir, look." The radio operator pointed down the stream, to the other side of the bridge. There, between the rocks, was a flash of light. "That's him."

"Let's go," said Sang. "Radio the units to close on the bridge now!"

The radio operator's radio buzzed with traffic as others converged on the bridge. The patrolmen moved out, clamoring with excitement now that the prey was in the trap.

Sang stopped the last of his patrol as his men moved downward to the bridge. He turned back upstream.

"Captain," said a soldier, "they found a tent, and they think he's still in it."

A shot rang out as an impatient Kalashnikov fired at the small, snow-covered tent.

"Damn it! Stop all firing!" cried Sang.

A bright flash halted the radio operator's chance to reply. The explosion lit up the pitch-black sky, momentarily blinding the army. As the darkness returned, Sang's radio chattered loudly as they closed in on the remains of the tent. A billow of smoke floated up between the boulders. Sang and his men ran down the rocks to the road and bridge just above the debris and smoke.

"Captain, we have him," said a soldier.

"Alive?"

"No, sir." The North Korean held, by the wrist, a severed, bloody arm.

"Form the men up," said Sang. "I want every man accounted for."

"Captain?"

"I want to be assured that's the arm of our prey, not one of ours."

The units formed up on the road. No one was missing. Sang now canvassed the guards to the south and to the north. No one was missing there, either, or unaccounted for. They continued to canvass the nearby units until well after first light.

"Sir," said a soldier, "we have debris of a Soviet frogman's suit, another Spetsnaz uniform, and a Soviet Type-64—all destroyed by the explosion."

"Then maybe we got him," said Sang.

"Not maybe, sir."

41

"Oh, my God." Kevin Moncrief saw the flames streak across the sky. From the ASDS, it was odd seeing the explosion—the water above them muffled the sound.

"What's up, Gunny?"

"We lost him, Hernandez."

"Bullshit," said Hernandez.

"No, it came from the tent."

"Gunny, we need to go in there." Stidham, now standing, rocked the mini-submarine with his large frame.

"Men, we got orders to beat it back to the *Florida*," said the lieutenant.

"Lieutenant, I don't know," said Moncrief.

"Gunny, we got a swarm of patrol boats overhead, some with sonar. They can't get to us right now, but they *are* looking for us. We've got to get out of here now."

Moncrief knew the lieutenant was right. He could hear the churn of propellers above him from several different directions. The beach, from north to south, was swarming with lights.

"Okay."

"Gunny." Both Hernandez and Stidham stared at Kevin Moncrief.

"Gunny, staff sergeants—the skipper said to get back to the boat. He's got to protect the boat," said the lieutenant.

Moncrief knew it was the thing to do. "We're outta here," he said.

Neither Hernandez nor Stidham could believe what was being said—not by Kevin Moncrief.

"Guys," Moncrief said, "follow me on this. The colonel's orders."

The two men sat back down as the navy lieutenant pulled the hatch over, sealing the opening. The boat floated up from the sea floor, turned, and headed west into deeper waters.

"She's moved," the lieutenant said.

"How deep?" said Moncrief.

"Two hundred feet, thirty miles out."

"Are we being tracked?"

"I don't believe so." The lieutenant had taken the ASDS back to the submarine the day before, recharged its batteries, then returned to pick up Parker's men. Running on batteries, the craft remained perfectly silent and undetectable by sound.

"I don't want to lead them to the *Florida*," said Moncrief.

"We should be fine. Fifty meters down," said the lieutenant. "We're heading north for about thirty minutes."

The mini-submarine tilted over and banked as it headed north. The lieutenant sensed that the patrol boats' attention was still toward the shoreline. In deeper water, North Korea had limited assets. At best, they had one diesel submarine, 1950's vintage, on the east coast.

Most of their submarine assets grouped in the west.

After some time, the ASDS tilted again to the west, banking as it turned.

"The *Florida's* on the move," said the lieutenant. "It'll catch up to us ten nautical miles to the north."

Minutes later, the mini-submarine slid up alongside the Trident, slightly above and behind. It pulled up over the moorings and floated down, clanking as metal connected with metal.

Moncrief felt the floating sensation cease as the ASDS came to rest on top of the much bigger boat. He heard the rush of compressed air and felt his ears pop as the mini-submarine sealed itself onto the *Florida.*

The hatches banged as they swung open. Moncrief led the way into the brightly lit mother submarine.

"Stow your gear. Not much time," said the skipper. "We need to move to deeper water."

The *Florida* headed east, making time and

depth and putting distance between it and North Korea.

"Ah, Skipper. . .?" Moncrief caught up with the skipper at the control room.

"Yeah?"

"I need to talk to you."

"No need," said Hollington.

"Skipper?"

"As soon as things quiet down on shore, we'll turn back to the west and check things out. We're following orders now."

"What exactly are those orders?"

"Abandon mission," said Hollington. "Leave area immediately. Straight from the Pentagon."

"When did you get them?" asked Moncrief.

"Just before the explosion."

"*Before?*"

I   I   I

The wind continued to blow inland, driving snow toward Will harder and harder. He waited behind the two boulders until well after the explosion. He stayed still long after the North Koreans had left the area. Just before dawn, he moved inland, back up the stream, toward the little lake.

At the lake, he moved south at a constant pace, building up a rhythm through the snow. As he did so, Will kept the Diamond Mountain peaks to his left, traveling through deep stands of pine trees and drifting snow. Will stayed up high, well into the mountains and far from any roads. He kept moving past daylight as the snowstorm continued to rage, almost instantly covering his tracks behind him.

At midmorning, Will came to a road that cut into the mountains. He stopped at a culvert under a gravel road that headed east. Here, the stench of open sewage forced him to breathe shallowly through his mouth as he crawled through the culvert. North Korean farmers fertilized the rice fields with whatever nutrient they could find.

Will felt the rumble of vehicles as they approached from the west. He looked down into the water pooling around the culvert and saw ripples form from the vibration. After the last vehicle, Will pulled out toward the western edge of the culvert—the convoy was heading up the valley. As he watched the Soviet-built supply trucks move south, Will noticed the movement of a North Korean soldier, just west, to one side of the road. He appeared, and then as Will watched, disappeared behind a snow-covered mound. He did it again and again.

Will then saw another man in a similar olive-colored uniform appear from another mound. As he made out the shape of the first, Will spied a series of mounds stretched across the valley.

I know what these are, he thought, cupping his hands around his eyes. In countless briefings, Will had been told that he'd know he'd gone too far south if he began to run into North Korea's hardened artillery sites—vast bunkers for their long-range artillery, called HARTS. Embedded deep within each bunker's concrete- and steel-reinforced walls were M-1978 Koksan 170-mm self-propelled guns and 240-mm MRLs. The multiple rocket launchers could spew out hundreds of chemical shells over the border, saturating square miles with deadly poison gases for lengthy periods of time. And the self-propelled guns could lay down a formidable barrage of hot steel.

Will was nearing the rear of North Korea's DMZ defenses—hundreds of sentry posts, troops, and detection devices. If he somehow passed through this maze, he would come upon miles of minefields, layered in crisscross patterns, each device capable of blowing a man to shreds.

I'll wait until dark and head to the coast, thought Will, leaning back against the cement culvert and ignoring the stench.

His mind drifted, wondering where she might be now—and if he could beat the odds stacked against him.

The conference room of the Nuclear and Chemical Defense Bureau was filled with military men of the highest rank, as well as the top leaders of the civilian government. Choe Hak-son, science chairman, sat on the far end, beside the vice prime minister. Also near Choe were Admiral Myong and General Hokoma, the army's chief of staff, whose scowl bespoke his contempt for the others in the room.

On the other end, near an empty chair, Comrade General Jo-Si, chief of the air force, smoked his French Gitanes, one after another. Several other comrade generals of artillery and logistics had chairs near his. The bright, shiny gold insignias of their respective branches of service stood out on their red shoulder epaulets. Several others sat in chairs away from the main table. One, dressed in a dark-olive, Mao-styled jacket, was Sin Tae-sam. He, along with the others, sat in silence, as if this were a wake.

The military and government leaders were joined by a balding, aged man in a brown, western-style suit. His pug nose dominated an ashen white face, alongside a blackened mole on the right of his forehead. Ambassador Vershinof was no stranger to anyone in the room.

"Attention." The young orderly sharply kicked his heels, then swung the door open for the Supreme Leader.

The short, frazzle-haired man with huge, black-framed glasses always appeared more comic than deadly. It was only by his pedigree that Kim Jong Il ruled the most dangerous country in the world.

Kim's chair was oversized and raised, allowing him to look down at the others. His fingers, held together tip-to-tip, touched his chin, like a Buddhist monk contemplating a prayer. The gloss of polished and manicured fingers reflected light from the chandelier.

"It's been assumed that the assassin of Peter Nampo was a Soviet Spetsnaz, perhaps from a submarine out of Vladivostok. A source in Moscow suggested that Russian arms manufacturers had been growing frustrated with Nampo's success in developing new weapons," said Kim Jong Il. His face was more placid and pale than in the past. As many in the room knew, or had heard rumors of, the leader's heart was slowly failing. Today's events wouldn't add to his longevity.

"That's what you were meant to think," said Vershinof. "But it was not a Soviet Spetsnaz." Vershinof spoke loudly to ensure there was no confusion on this point.

"And I'm told you have more," said Kim Jong Il.

"I do, Comrade General Secretary." Vershinof pulled a large manila folder from a beaten leather satchel. "I've brought copies. These are prints from one of our satellites taken over the Americans' Pearl Harbor only a few weeks ago. Moored to the backside of what they call Ford Island you'll see a Trident submarine modified for special operations."

The clarity of the photo showed several men on the deck of the submarine. Three in the conning tower wore baseball caps. Several on the deck carried rifles.

"You'll notice the fittings behind the submarine's sail or tower," said Vershinof.

The North Koreans circulated the photos around both sides of the room like schoolboys receiving assignments from their teacher.

"I have another photograph taken with sensitive, low-light film by one of our people nearby." He referred to a KGB agent, a Hawaiian importer who conveniently lived in a house on Halawa Heights Road with a hilltop view of all Pearl Harbor.

The submarine appeared to be crossing back from the other side of the harbor. A cigar-shaped object was affixed to its back.

"This is a new ASDS mini-submarine used for SEAL team deliveries. Their navy let it be rumored that the submarine was at

Pearl for testing, but it left late at night with the ASDS attached."

"Go on," said Kim.

"It has not returned, either to Pearl or their West Coast harbors, and. . . ."

"Yes, Ambassador?"

"As we compute things, like speed and sail time, it could easily have been along your coastline three days ago."

"So it was the Americans," said Kim. "But how did they do it?"

"Our scientists would appreciate any opportunity to help investigate. In fact, we——" Vershinof's comments were cut short when the young, uniformed orderly at the door approached the general secretary, bowed deeply, and handed him a note. Kim Jong Il appeared astonished at what he read. He quickly folded the note and laid it down. "Thank you, Ambassador. I'm sure we'll have further discussions on the matter." Kim finished his cigarette and stamped it out in the ashtray.

From many years spent in the Foreign

Service, Vershinof knew when not to press a point. To persuade any in doubt, he left the photographs behind for further examination. Then he gathered up his old, tattered satchel and left the room.

"The body parts of the corpse our patrols found contained frozen tissue," said Kim Jong Il once Vershinof was gone. "The man may still be out there. We need him dead."

43

A deep cold swept through the valley as the sun's last light started to fade. The SSC Natick Laboratory suit had kept Will well-camouflaged and relatively warm so far, but it was not designed for extreme cold weather, and the temperatures were dropping.

He began to shiver in the pitch-black culvert, seeing only faint gray light at each end. The suit, adjusting to the environment, was now a coal black that matched the interior of the culvert. Only a small patch of white around his eyes gave any hint the shape might be something human. And if he turned away and looked down, he would have been undetectable even to someone with a flashlight.

Well after dark, Will slowly moved out,

beyond the culvert, to a low, snow-covered ravine, where he again adjusted the suit color. The miniature computer on the forearm scanned the white and gray surfaces in the low light, and in a few seconds, the suit changed to a matching, mixed pattern of gray and white.

The stars lit up the sky, clearly illuminating the valley. Will did not like this level of light. It might allow his pursuers to detect his movement.

But they won't be looking north, he thought, referring to the hundreds of DPRK soldiers sitting in their bunkers only a few hundred meters away. It was their preoccupation with the south that gave him an advantage.

The mountains to the east stood black and jagged against the sky, like a broken pane of glass. They went from his left to his far right. But their rapid ascent and sharp topography gave him both protection and camouflage.

Will moved in the bottom of the ravine, again at a runner's pace, quickly building up heat as he kept low. Gradually, the terrain changed until he was climbing up a staircase of rocks and boulders. He set his course for the far right of one peak where, well in the distance, a faint yellow light indicated an observation or listening post. Will stayed low, stopping only briefly throughout the night, as he climbed up over a small jagged line into the next gully and again up over more jagged rocks.

It was well after midnight when Will realized how thirsty he had become. His power fuel packs had given him a continuous surge of adrenaline, but his mouth was now dry and parched. He followed the line of rocks, spotting a turn and drop to the south, indicative of a possible stream bed.

Beyond an outcrop of rocks, Will heard the movement of water. It was a small stream coming down from the last peaks to the east. The water did not have the smell of the lowlands.

Will stuck the fingers of his gloved hand into the icy pool, using the other hand to again open the velcro covering on his forearm. The LED screen of the uniform's computer displayed a code of letters in a light blue light. The computer confirmed that the water was untainted and drinkable.

So Will drank. His thirst seemed minor until he first tasted the clean, melted snow water. Then he sat on his knees and gulped through his cupped hands.

After a lengthy replenishing, Will began again, heading east over the final range of the Kumgang peaks. It would soon be the beginning of his fourth day in-country, and he knew he was short on time. He had perhaps one opportunity for escape, but even then, his timing would have to be perfect.

It was shortly before dawn when Will crossed the last line of peaks, spotting both the shoreline and surf crashing into the rocky shoals of the Kumgang. The craggy rocks shot the icy blue water of the Sea of Japan high into the air. As he crossed the last line of rocks, the cold current of wind from the water struck his face. It smelled of the sea.

The ocean seemed in turmoil, but it wasn't the surface of the water that caught Will's eye. The roadway to the north seemed like a disturbed ant bed, covered with small black dots moving back and forth on the ground. And they appeared to be expanding to the south. A beehive had been awoken. It was clear that they now knew the invader was still alive and somewhere within their borders.

I don't have much time at all, he thought, realizing that the North Koreans hadn't abandoned their search. He couldn't head north—the searchers wouldn't be satisfied until someone was found. Heading south would likewise be futile. The layers of men, equipment, weapons, and minefields would be impenetrable. Now, with so many on the lookout for him, Will's odds were drastically reduced. The water's currents would not allow him to swim past the patrol boats in the ocean to the south. And heading east would only postpone his problems. There was no refuge in this country. Every man, woman, and child was trained from birth to report the unusual.

But Will had considered all this before arriving. Both the date and time had been carefully coordinated for an exit strategy, but he could escape only if he kept moving.

Just to the south, he saw a washout leading, below a bridge, to the water. Will moved quickly, retreating south a few hundred meters across the rock-covered peaks to a position that protected him from sight. There, he crossed back over, again checking his suit to ensure that it matched well with the rocks, broken snow, and gully. Closer to shore now, the added humidity from ocean and snow made traction much more difficult. Occasionally, Will stopped, looking south. The first troops were less than half a kilometer away and moving rapidly up the coast toward him.

As he crossed under the unmanned bridge, fortune smiled on Will. The closer one got to the DMZ, the more sentries and observation posts one encountered. Yet, the bridge was unmanned. He kept moving, knowing speed gave him the best chance of not being caught.

It felt strangely good to him to feel the sand under his feet as he moved behind one rock, and then another, until he was within meters of the shoreline.

The backpack contained one last set of items for his survival. It took only a short time for him to don the black dry suit, the rebreather mask, and short fins. Over the dry suit, which had been designed for frigid waters, he slipped into a harness. Velcroed to his chest was a black, round metal disc tethered to the harness. His source at the Natick lab had provided Will with the best of advanced equipment.

It was well past midday when Will slid into the frigid ocean. The cold front had brought a cloudless blue sky, though that was of little benefit to him. Several hundred meters offshore, he surfaced, twisting around in a 360-degree arc, spotting the North Koreans as they swarmed along the shoreline. Far up the rocks, near where he crossed over the peaks, Will saw a commotion—they'd discovered a print. Will continued to turn around, soon spotting the faint outline of a small torpedo-like boat to the south. With the surge of water, he was lifted higher, where he saw the faint outline of another boat near the first. The North Korean military drew near. Will looked at his watch and the GPS locator on his wrist.

Another 1.5 kilometers to go. Will began swimming on the surface, feeling the sway of the seawater as he headed farther and farther out. It took most of the early afternoon, but he was surprised at how warm the suit kept him. Only an exposed part of Will's face below the mask felt the cold. Occasionally, he adjusted his hood to cover the spot.

But he would not stay warm forever. The suit gave him twelve hours of protection. After that, the frigid waters would have the upper hand.

As the late-afternoon sun began to settle down toward the horizon, the GPS indicator showed Will was on his mark. There, he inflated a small buoyancy flotation device on the harness and leaned back into the water. He would try to rest as much as possible, saving his energy for one last push. And there he stayed, floating in the water, waiting, constantly looking at his watch and the setting sun.

Come on. The watch showed 1600 hours local time.

Again, he did a 360-degree scan of the horizon. And again, he saw the military boats to the south. He still saw nothing to the north. Occasionally, Mi-8 helicopters crisscrossed the water at levels so low their props churned up the water. When one came close, Will slid below the surface, releasing the air in his device.

The rest of the time, he waited, floating in the cold water as the sun moved toward the coastal mountains in the west. The frigid water numbed his face, which he occasionally rubbed to keep the circulation moving.

At least I'm still alive. Braving the ocean was a better option than risking being captured in the North. At least, so long as he evaded capture in the water.

Finally, on another search of the horizon, he saw a faint dot to the north. Immediately, Will judged the distance and resumed swimming out to sea. Like an Ironman racer, he matched the pace, looking to the north as the object became clearer and larger.

Will would have only one opportunity, and he had to aim for dead center. As it got closer, he noted the distance, and finally submerged with the re-breather. He still did not want to be seen.

First, Will heard the churning, rhythmic noise of the propellers. He tried to determine their location. The noise, which grew increasingly loud, let him know this ship was far bigger than any military patrol boat.

Will surfaced one last time to get his final bearing. The boat was close, churning up the water from its bow, but to the far right.

He submerged and began kicking rapidly. From his chest, Will pulled the round black disc and held it forward with both hands, kicking quicker and harder. A miss would throw him into the propellers of the ship.

The noise became louder as he surged forward. He could now feel displaced water pushing him backwards, but Will fought it with all the power he'd gained from months of training. He kicked feverishly until a metallic clank indicated contact.

The passenger ship was returning to the eastern South Korean port of Tonghae from Changjon, a North Korean port just south of Wonsan. Following protracted negotiations, the head of the Hyundai Corporation had agreed to pay millions of dollars to the Pyongyang government to own the only vessel allowed to travel back and forth across the border. Its ostensible purpose was to allow passengers to visit the Taebaek Mountains. Thanks to the passenger ship's run, millions of tourist dollars poured into the North. Still, North Korea periodically threatened to restrict the tourist voyage, or cancel it altogether.

Today was all that mattered to Will Parker. Thanking his lucky stars for vessels than ran to schedule, he let the hull-locked magnet yank him forward like a large hooked fish. He adjusted the harness and moved just below the waterline. The re-breather allowed him to breathe as he deflated the buoyancy device and slid out of sight. If he tried to board the ship, one of the many North Korean spies on board would either alert others or disable the ship. He was far safer riding the hull, bouncing against its side.

Sleep, he knew, would not be possible. Nor would hydration. He settled in for the long ride and tried to relax.

The *Solbong* was actually running slightly

late, thanks to a bow-to-stern search the North Koreans had carried out in the port of Wonsan. The South Korean captain had never seen such an intense search, every space, every bag, and every passenger being checked and rechecked several times by the DPRK military.

Apparently, even that had not been enough. "Sir, three patrol boats from the DMZ are approaching." The voice of the first mate usually sounded far calmer. The repeated inspections had shocked the entire crew.

"Yes," said the captain.

The three patrol boats, lights flashing, approached, two on the port side and one on the starboard.

"They intend to board," the first mate said.

"That's not agreed upon."

The North Koreans had the right to conduct whatever searches they wished upon entry into Wonsan and prior to departure. However, when the ship left, the North Koreans had agreed it was to be left alone so long as it kept to a specific route, exactly 6.5 kilometers offshore.

A spray of machine gunfire cut through the water just in front of the bow.

"All stop," said the captain.

"Aye, sir."

The vessel slowed, pitching in the heavy seas. A North Korean captain climbed onto the deck, followed by several soldiers carrying machine guns.

"This is not allowed."

The North Korean struck the vessel's captain across the face with his Type-64 pistol. The older man sank to one knee. "We'll determine what is allowed," said the North Korean.

A new spate of machine gun fire erupted at the fantail and two bloodstained bodies were thrown over the port side.

"Under what authority is this outrage?" said the captain, rising from his knee.

The North Korean struck him again. "You'll muster everyone to the bow." He signaled to the first mate, frozen in shock, with a wave of the pistol. "Now!"

In short order, the few crewmembers

and all passengers were huddled together on the cold bow. Most of the passengers were elderly South Koreans visiting the Diamond Mountains they remembered from their youth.

"We have someone on board who has done our republic a great wrong, and we'll shoot each of you until we find him."

"We have no idea who you are seeking," the captain said.

"Thirty minutes."

As the ship came to a stop, Will sank lower and released the electronic magnet. Using a re-breather, he could stay there, without any signs of bubbles, for hours.

| | | |

When the thirty minutes expired, the North Korean pointed to a young woman dressed in the uniform of a crewmember.

"Take her there." He pointed to the port side of the bow, and two soldiers leaned the sobbing woman over the edge. "I warned you." He chambered a round and aimed the pistol to the rear of her head. The others remained still, stunned.

An instant before he squeezed the trigger, the *Solbong* shifted to its starboard side, a move so sudden and so violent that everyone on deck fell over, like bowling pins, and slid against the other bulwark. The North Korean fell backwards, and as he did, a pistol shot rang out in the air.

The vessel rocked back again violently to the port side.

The captain looked over to that side, spying the black fins of a massive structure passing by. It was as if a giant Orca had come out of the deep. One of the smaller North Korean patrol boats pitched up in the air at the sound of a machine gun firing aimlessly, then flipped over like a child's bathtub toy.

The Trident submarine broke through the surface just to the stern of the last patrol boat, and the North Korean soldiers on the *Solbong* scrambled into the last vessel, which fled to the north to escape being capsized by the American sub.

"All ahead, full, now!" The captain's order sent all *Solbong* crewmembers scrambling back to their stations.

As darkness fell, the *Solbong* entered the waters of South Korea protected by a fleet of South Korean destroyers.

CNN's lead story that day was of another international incident caused by North Korea. The following week, North Korea cancelled the ship's permission to visit the ancient Diamond Mountains.

When the cruise ship docked in Tonghae, South Korean investigators swarmed the ship, focused on the aftermath of the afternoon's bloodshed on the main deck. No one noticed a ripple of water near the ship's hull.

On the other side of the port, near a breakfront, a dark figure pulled up on one of the rocks and removed what looked like fins and a mask. Only one person was watching as he left the harbor and walked up the dirt road.

"Thank you," said Will, soaking the overcoat of Mi Yong as he pulled her close.

45

"I just don't know."

Will smiled as he leaned back into his seat at the hotel restaurant in downtown Seoul. The Western breakfast of eggs, toast, and coffee saturated his senses after three days of super fuel patches and adrenaline. He still felt a bit groggy—doubtless, the result of severe sleep deprivation. Mi and he had traveled by rental car through much of the night to cross the peninsula of Korea. She had rented the car, thus eliminating all evidence that he'd arrived in Korea or was traveling in it.

The local radio news station was reporting that Pyongyang had accused the United States of violating its territorial waters with a Trident submarine, thus raising fears of a possible nuclear attack. The U.S. Navy acknowledged that a navigational error had caused one of its vessels to be just north of the DMZ, but went on to explain that it surfaced only to lend potential rescue and aid to a South Korean vessel under attack.

In the restaurant, Will swallowed another long gulp of coffee as he took in Mi Yong's presence. It had been a long time since Quantico.

"You obviously got the backpack in Hawaii," Mi said.

"Yes, thank you again."

"Your friend from the Natick lab said he wanted feedback on all the equipment on your list."

Will smiled. "It couldn't have worked better. How about our ride out?"

"We have two tickets on a KAL flight to Los Angeles at 1500 hours."

"Immigration?"

"You have a Marine Corps uniform and endorsed orders."

"Charlies?" He referred to the relaxed

Marine Corps dress of khaki sweater, shirt, and gabardine pants.

"Yes," said Mi, "you'll be traveling as a gunny."

Will smiled. He liked impersonating a Marine gunnery sergeant, though he knew one gunnery sergeant on a submarine right now who'd be chagrined to find out.

"It seemed less obvious that way," she explained.

"Yeah, a colonel going through customs on both ends might stand out."

"Because you're on endorsed orders, you need no passport, and none would be entered into the system on either end. It wasn't too hard getting an identification card." She handed him a wallet, a white military identification card, several hundred-dollar bills, and the papers representing his orders.

The United States military was allowed to travel through customs in South Korea solely on proof of orders.

"A conference on SsangYong?"

She smiled.

"Ironic," he murmured. She had him attending a conference on the annual joint military exercise that trained forces to stop a North Korean invasion. It involved thousands of South Korean and American soldiers, who "gamed" the movement of troops in response to a North Korean attack. Numerous such conferences occurred between December and August every year. Now, with the international incidents he'd been involved with, the exercise was at risk of turning into the real thing.

"We need to get to the airport," said Mi.

Will had grown to care greatly for this woman, and not just because of her bravery. He wanted Krowl to pay as much for what he'd tried to do to her as for what he'd done to Will.

"I'll go change," he said.

It wasn't at all unusual for a Marine Corps gunnery sergeant in Seoul to check out of the high-rise Seoul Lotte hotel, especially in the company of an Asian-American woman presumed to be his wife. American forces had stayed in Korea now for more than five decades. When the two checked in at Inchon International Airport, many similar couples were already there.

Mi was traveling as Will's wife, and her passport under that name had been accurately stamped upon her arrival a week earlier. In addition, her passports and visas were correctly listed in the Immigration computer system, so there was no suspicion at all when Gunnery Sergeant Donald Ruskell's orders were reviewed.

"Here on the exercise?" said the Customs official.

"Yes, sir," said Will, alias Donald.

"I guess we'll see you back in a few months."

"Probably several times."

A television in the background had a flashing red newscrawl at the bottom of the screen as a CNN reporter was speaking in a muted voice.

"What's going on?" The South Korean Customs official turned to the screen as everyone else did in the room. The words then flashed on the ticker tape.

"North Korean Dictator Reported Dead of a Heart Attack."

Will looked at Mi, trying to show little reaction.

They kept moving. Both passed through to the third floor departure concourse. "We're flying business class," she told him.

"I knew there was something I liked about you." He wanted to say more, trying to connect the dots from the news bulletin. Was it coincidence? Or could the missile program setback have caused the dictator's death. He could read her eyes.

"The business class lounge is on the fourth floor." Mi led him across the Inchon air terminal to a steel-doored elevator, identified by a black-lettered sign marked "Lounges."

"We've got about an hour until boarding," Mi said.

He smiled at her again. "Before we go, I've got to call an old friend in Georgia."

"Who?"

"A guy named Gary Matthews. He's not involved in this."

The elevator, though empty, felt cramped. As they entered, Mi turned to the sliding doors, glancing through them into the open terminal floor, at the mass of people.

"Oh."

"What's wrong?" Will looked at her face, which had suddenly turned white. She slumped back against the wall of the elevator.

"Nothing." Mi tried to appear as normal as possible.

"You look like you just saw a ghost."

"I thought I saw someone I knew a long time ago." She leaned her back up against the wall for support, trying to remain calm.

"What do you need me to do?" Will said.

"Nothing."

They showed their boarding passes and entered Korean Airline's opulent teak and gold business class lounge. *This is quite a distance from the conditions of the past few days*, Will thought as he headed toward one of the telephones. He dialed the international operator, placing a collect call to Georgia.

"I'll be right back," Mi said. He barely heard her as she headed back out the entrance. The telephone rang on the other side of the world.

"This is Harold Wilson, calling collect," Will said. Wilson had been one of their professors in law school; it was his agreed-on alias.

I   I   I

Mi, in the elevator, took one look at Will, sitting back in the oversized leather chair by the phone, intently concentrating on the conversation. She knew that this whole thing had been so unsafe. She knew it would end soon.

The elevator opened onto the main floor of the massive terminal and Mi crossed it, openly, certain her every move was being watched. Fear had occupied much of her life. Today was no different.

"Can you tell me where the ladies' room is?" she said. She purposely didn't use the one in the lounge.

The KAL clerk smiled and bowed slightly as she pointed to a side hall. Mi walked directly toward it, finding it nearly abandoned. She knew she was the target. It was important that it only be her.

The clerk at KAL's prestige lounge announced KAL Flight KI017 to Los Angeles just moments after she left. Will hung up the telephone. His message had been brief because the call was expected. It would only have been a surprise if the call had not been made.

But Mi was gone. Looking at his watch, he thought it strange she wasn't back by now. Will decided to head down to the main floor, hoping to cut across to the gate and save time. Something felt wrong, though, as Will scanned the terminal. She was nowhere in sight. His heart kicked up a beat. "I'm looking for a lady, dressed in a brown business suit," he said to the KAL clerk.

"Yes, sir," the clerk said, "I believe she went to the ladies' room over there."

"Thank you." Will's heart raced.

The hallway was long and dark, with poorly lit, blinking fluorescent lights. It was empty, save for one person. As Will walked down the hall, he was passed by a man in his early thirties, wearing a black leather coat and bearing a deep scar on his hand. The man looked down. Will made a point to remember his face.

At the end of the hall stood two doors facing each other. One was the men's room. Will glanced quickly into the men's room, expecting nothing, and was unsurprised. When he opened the other door, he saw nothing but a row of gray metal stalls facing a row of white porcelain sinks.

Will stopped and squatted down, looking through the bottom of the stalls. His heart sank when he saw, on the far end, a slumping leg. He ran to the stall.

Mi Yong sat against the side wall, staring straight ahead, her eyes fixed, her blouse soaked in blood. A large gaping wound ran across her throat.

They say you don't feel the razor when it

cuts across the neck, only the pressure of a hand. You feel dizzy, then cold, then simply tired as life drains away.

Will slammed his fist against the wall. He knew that reporting the murder would be useless. The police would detain him, then discover there was no Gunnery Sergeant Donald Ruskell in the Marine Corps. Meanwhile, the killer would be gone and Krowl might be warned. He reached into her pocket and pulled out her passport and ticket. He checked again to make sure there was nothing on her that would help a quick identification. He knew that she would approve.

Will kissed her on the cheek and gently closed her eyes. He had to flee before anyone else saw him in the restroom. He backed out, leaving the stall door slightly open, so she'd be found soon.

Fortunately, Will made it down the hallway before anyone else turned the corner. His heart pounding, he walked across the terminal, looking at the international gates of each flight, hoping for any opportunity.

At none of the gates did he find what he was looking for. He kept moving, past flights to Tokyo, to Singapore, to Los Angeles. Still no man, no scar.

I   I   I

Rei knew the police would cover all exits from the airport once her body was found. His original plan was to leave the airport, then take a taxi to the remote farmhouse that hid the secret tunnel to the North. Her death was well worth a plan change. Killing Mi settled an old score, and it would bring great praise from his superiors.

The smartest plan change, he decided, would take him somewhere least expected. "I need one ticket to Los Angeles."

"Sir," said the woman at the check-in counter, "this isn't usually done when the flight's boarding."

"I'm sorry, but traffic held me up." He held out a blue American passport, knowing it would eliminate any dispute over visas. He also held up a gold American Express card.

"If you have a seat in first class," Rei said, "it would be appreciated."

"Yes, sir, I think KAL 017 does have a seat in first."

"Thank you."

"It'll cost $5,128.61." She shuddered to give him the amount, and gave him a slight bow as she did.

"Yes, that's fine. My expense account can handle it." He returned the bow.

"Thank you, Mr. Nagota. You can board at your leisure."

"Thank you," he said, smiling.

Will saw only the shape of the man and his black leather jacket as he passed through the boarding gate, but recognized him instantly.

L.A., he thought. *Perfect.*

Pyongyang's troops were moving across the city. Armed guards were on each corner with no one walking the streets. The city, like the country, had become an armed camp ready to explode.

Kim Jong-un was surrounded by his most

loyal guards as he entered the Nuclear and Chemical Defense Bureau. Now was the most dangerous time. He had to move fast. His father had told him that it was critical that he got to this one man first.

"Choe Hak-son, will you follow me?"

The old man was respected by the military. The answer was critical. Likewise, it meant that the wrong answer was death for either the young man in the room or the old advisor.

"You are the one."

"Yes."

Kim Jong-un had thought that he'd have some time before this day came.

"There is an order that must be given and must be executed now." Kim Jong-un had that same cocky style of his father. "Jang Song-thaek."

He didn't need to say more. The uncle was a threat.

In less than an hour, men from the Ministry of State Security showed up at the Politburo and dragged the old man out from the meeting hall. It was very public which was intended. At the same time agents showed up at the North Korean embassy in Havana with orders that Jang's son-in-law was to immediately return to Pyongyang with his wife and children. Jang's son, the ambassador to Malaysia was also recalled under armed guard.

They and their families were shot within an hour of returning to the city. The granddaughters and grandsons cried for mercy but their pleas fell on death ears.

Jang had a special fate. He was fed to a pack of captive, wild dogs.

46

"Holy Jesus!" said the normally soft-spoken Tom Pope. The others on the morning shift at the SIOC operations center turned his way.

As a frequent visitor to the FBI's operation center, Tom was cleared to use computer terminal six—a joint, highly classified Department of Defense and Department of Justice computer that received and monitored classified e-mails. Many of the e-mails were random communications on global events. A few were directed to specific recipients. If the subject matter was critical, the computer flashed an attention-getter as soon as the user logged on.

Tom Pope logged onto his e-mail account at 0600. He often began his typical fourteen-hour days by swinging past the operations center and reviewing critical e-mails. Immediately, an alarm on his computer beeped; as he scanned the e-mail text, he was already dialing the home telephone number of Dave Creighton.

"Hey, this is Tom."

"Yeah? What happened?" said Creighton.

"I'm at the SIOC and just received this e-mail info'd to me."

"What part of the world?"

"The resident agent in Seoul," said Tom. The FBI had agents stationed in certain spots around the world. For the FBI, Seoul was not considered one of the more critical assignments. In the criminal-justice system, Seoul was similar to Japan, in that crime was well-contained by both the local culture and aggressive police departments. There was the occasional drug trafficker, particularly dangerous in this anti-drug society, but he was rare. And Seoul was not known for terrorists.

"What's he got?"

"Let me just read it to you:

"Inchon International Airport discovered

body of mid-twenties Asian-American female, murdered by a sharp object severing the arteries in her neck. Estimated time of death was fourteen-hundred local time. Fingerprints fail to identify subject. A witness noted a mid-thirties Asian male wearing a black leather jacket seen walking in the vicinity of the crime. Only other noticeable feature was a scar on one hand.'"

The world was starting to tumble in its orbit.

"He sounds like a match to Boston," said Creighton.

"I'm e-mailing an urgent reply and I'll attach the Boston sketch," said Tom.

"Good idea. Call the Aviation Department." September 11th had brought many changes, including millions of dollars to the Bureau to enlarge its aviation department from half a dozen airplanes to well over eighty. The pilots were all FBI agents, and many of the airplanes were used for surveillance of suspects. Electronics allowed the aircraft to, among other things, eavesdrop on possible terrorist cell phone calls.

The FBI air force also provided executive transportation when critically needed. It was available twenty-four seven to those on a very short list. Dave Creighton was on that list.

"Tell them it's Creighton-approved, Whiskey Tango Authorization Ten," said Creighton. "Call me for confirmation, and it's an international trip to Seoul."

"Okay."

"They'll probably recommend the Falcon 7X."

The Falcon 7X was the newest addition to the FBI fleet.

"They'll want to take two crews and probably need to stop in Alaska or somewhere on the west coast for refueling and a change-out of crew members," said Creighton. "Who do you need to take with you?"

"My team," said Tom.

"Okay. She can carry you five easily, and even with the backup crew, you'll have plenty of room."

"I'll check with you from Andrews."

Tom was impressed with the Aviation Department's reply. It didn't hurt that he mentioned authorization Whiskey Tango 10 and Creighton's name. The aircraft would be ready for departure before he could even get to Andrews.

It didn't take long to gather his team of five agents. All were at work in the other end of the building, and each had to scramble to their homes to grab a bag. No one knew how long they might be overseas.

Debra Pope looked up as Tom banged through the front door. He gave her his sheepish grin.

"Where to this time?" said Debra.

"Korea."

"What?" As he frantically packed a bag, she leaned against the door to their bedroom. "How long?"

"No idea. Best guess is probably five days."

The phone rang. "I'll get it," she said, running down the stairs as Tom finished packing his hanging bag. He'd learned a long time ago that packing for five days was the only thing that worked. More than that was too bulky, and with less, he always ran short.

"It's the Bureau," said Debra, handing Tom the wireless handset.

"Hey, this is Pope," said Tom.

The conversation was brief.

"Thanks." He hung up.

"What's up, Tom?" She hated to ask the question, because she already knew the answer.

"I can't say much."

"Oh."

"But, it's a change. No Korea—California."

| | | |

Tom followed protocol and stayed off his cell. At Andrews, the Department of Justice hangar would have a landline, and he could call Creighton and give him a secure update.

As he pulled into the gated parking at the hangar, Tom saw the white three-engine jet just beyond. A man in his mid-thirties wearing a black baseball cap walked around the glistening aircraft, peering into the engine's cowlings. Even across the parking lot, Tom could see a bright white "FBI" monogrammed on the man's cap.

"Change of plans, guys," said Tom.

Tom's team waited in the hangar's lobby, bags stacked near the door.

"I need to talk to Creighton first," said Tom, heading into the hangar's office. "I need HQ, please, on a secure line," he said.

Another man, who was wearing a black FBI hat and a black FBI-imprinted sweater, pointed toward a different office. The desk placard read, "Walter Hudgins, Aviation Director." Tom dialed Creighton's private number directly. "Boss," he said, "this is Tom out at Andrews."

"Yeah, what's up?" said Creighton.

"The SIOC called me half an hour ago. They got a confirmation by the KAL clerk on the photo. The man seen heading toward that hallway was the one in Boston. Another KAL clerk confirmed he was on a flight leaving

Narita, Japan, and going to Seoul just an hour earlier."

"Narita?" Creighton liked how, at the end of an investigation, all the pieces would fall into place.

"Yeah," said Tom, "and we know something else. He's not in Korea or headed to Korea. He was last seen boarding a KAL flight to L.A."

"Why L.A.?"

"I don't know, but my guess is Seoul got too hot or too hard. That new airport, Inchon, was built in a harbor and basically has just one access route."

"It's just after eight here. What time does his flight get into Los Angeles?" said Creighton.

"It's supposed to get in at nine."

"So if you take off now, you might get there before he does."

"It'll be close."

"Do you want local help?" said Creighton.

"Right now, I'd like to keep it small and low-key—just us."

"Okay, get going."

The Falcon spun out of the hangar and taxied to Andrews's main runway. Tom soon felt the three engines surge as they pushed him back into the seat during the 40,000-foot climb. Many of the Bureau's aircraft were gray-paneled, office-type accommodations. The Falcon 7X, though, was the director's international transport for his many long flights, so it was outfitted in a far more opulent manner. Seated in the plush leather seats amidst light wood trimmings, Tom felt like a squatter occupying another man's house.

"Fellas," he said, "how we looking for arrival time?" Tom had wandered up to the cockpit after the aircraft had leveled off. It was an azure blue day—clear, with only a wisp of high-altitude clouds.

"We're probably going to get there about 0845, local time," said the pilot. "The winds are fighting us today."

Tom looked down at his watch. It was half past eight on the east coast. He could call for help, but was afraid it might pose too high a risk if the assassin spotted local agents. And if they were this close, he didn't want the guy flagged off by some misguided agent.

"If it looks later than that, let me know."

While the Korean Airlines Boeing 747 flew across the Pacific, throughout the night and into the day, Will could not sleep.

I want him.

Will hadn't wanted someone to die so badly in years. He stared at the constantly moving map in his lounge seat in the jumbo aircraft's bubble. The winds had been favorable as they crossed the water to the east. A tailwind of well over one-hundred fifty knots pushed the aircraft to a ground speed of more than seven-hundred fifty miles per hour.

Will didn't care much about the speed as he heard the engines' throttle change on the final descent into LAX. The jetliner banked several times, and on the third or fourth turn, Will saw the coastline. Los Angeles was covered by a low layer of smog. He could see approaching aircraft, all traveling from east to west in a long straight line, heading down into the cloud cover until they disappeared one at a time.

The man in the black leather coat sat at the far end of the first class cabin, closer to the nose and farthest away from both the door and stairway of the business-class bubble downstairs. Will had checked on him twice during the night, once watching him drink champagne. Surprise remained Will's advantage. If the man knew of his connection to Mi, Will had no sense of it.

As the airplane crossed over Los Angeles and turned back to the west for landing, Will considered what to do.

"Ladies and gentlemen," said the attendant, "we're landing in Los Angeles at 8:15 a.m. local time, well ahead of schedule, due to a tailwind. Please fasten your seat belts and bring your tray tables and seats to an upright position."

Will looked at his watch, the Soviet-made

one he had worn in North Korea. He had changed its time through half a dozen time zones. It had been a long week.

"Miss, what gate will we be going to?" said Will, stopping the flight attendant.

"International A-26," she said.

"And where is Delta?"

"I believe they're in Concourse B."

The flight attendant was a thin wisp of a Korean woman—beautiful, too—who bowed every time he spoke to her.

"If we got in early, I was hoping to catch a different connecting flight," said Will. "Official business," he added, indicating the Marine uniform. "I appreciate the airplane being early, but my original connection is not for several hours."

"Yes, sir?"

"Would it be possible for me to move down to the door after landing so I might have a chance to make that earlier connection?"

American carriers would not likely be so hospitable, but Korean Air took great pride in its reputation for excellent customer service.

"Of course, sir," she said. "As soon as we touch down, you can come down to one of our crew chairs near the door."

"Thank you."

Shortly thereafter, Will felt the float as the behemoth aircraft raised its nose as the wheels settled to the ground. In his mind, he could see the pilot pulling back on the yoke as the tandem wheels came down onto the tarmac.

The engines went into a high-pitched whine as they reversed their thrust. As soon as the aircraft's forward momentum slowed, Will unbuckled his seat belt and headed down the short flight of stairs from the bubble to the main deck. There, the attendant waited near the door, signaling him to an open, adjoining crew seat.

Will sat down, straightening his Marine uniform, and inspected his enlisted cover. His highly-shined Corfam shoes glistened in the daylight. The flight attendant gave him an awkward smile as the 747 taxied across connecting runways, finally reaching its gate.

"I'll open the door and get you going," said the flight attendant.

He smiled at her again, *"Kamsa hamnida,"* he said in thanks.

"Ch'onmaneyo."

It would have been different if Mi were here, Will thought. The seat next to him, through the night, had been very, very empty. It was hers. The thought only steeled his will.

The giant door swung open just as the aircraft came to its final stop, and Will, glancing over his shoulder, saw the passengers in both first class, behind him, and coach, to his side, begin to bunch up in their surge to the exit after their ten-hour flight.

Will bolted, leading the crowd out of the jetway.

"Welcome to Los Angeles, Gunny," a KAL attendant said, greeting him at the end of the hall. "U.S. Customs is to your left."

"Thanks," said Will. He looked behind him and saw that the black-jacketed man was heading for U.S. Customs as well. There was only one way out and Will was tracking his target.

Will moved down the hallway to a massive open room with lines of desks and Immigration officers. One line was marked for U.S. citizens.

"Yes, sir. Welcome back," said the Immigration officer as Will approached.

"Thanks."

"Are you on a passport?"

"No, I'm returning on orders from a military conference in Korea," said Will.

"SsangYong already?" The customs officer was a plump red-headed woman with an healthy dose of freckles.

"You bet," said Will.

"Anything to declare?"

"No, ma'am."

"Okay, thanks." She passed him through.

Will began to walk away, but then stopped. "Miss?" he said.

"Yes, sir?"

"There was a man on the flight—I hate to say this about anyone."

"That's okay. You can't be too careful. If you're concerned, we are too."

"He's about ten back in this line, black leather jacket, gold ring."

She glanced, trying not to be obvious. In a fake gesture, she seemed to be counting the people through the line, as if assessing how much work was left in the day. "Yeah?" she whispered

"He may be carrying some drugs."

"Thanks."

Instead of going to Baggage Claim, Will crossed to an escalator, outside Customs, that headed up to the main terminal. He didn't have much time. As he rode up the escalator, Will watched a mother and her young child ride down. Will looked at his watch, an unneeded reminder.

At the top of the escalator, he crossed over quickly and purchased, at a small tourist shop, an L.A. Dodgers jacket and hat, and a copy of the *Los Angeles Times*. The headline "North Korea's Leader Dead" covered much of the front page. The loss of the missile was on page ten.

"That will be five-fifty."

Will smiled at the young Hispanic clerk, and she gave him a shy grin back.

"Hey," he said, "could I ask a small favor?"

"I don't know," said the clerk.

"I have to make several telephone calls," said Will, "and it would be a big help."

"For?"

"For me to give you this ten and you give me that five dollar roll of nickels." The cash register had several rolls of coins.

"Oh, no problem," she said.

"Thank you."

Will walked quickly from the L.A. international terminal to a restroom just above the escalator. His heart was beating rapidly again, as if he were back in North Korea. In one of the back stalls, he pulled off his Marine sweater and cover and put on the oversized Dodgers jacket. He absentmindedly bent the bill of the cap, pulling it down over his eyes, and then bundled up the sweater.

As he headed out, Will spotted the door to the maintenance closet, tried the handle, and opened it. He stashed his sweater and Marine cover behind a box of paper towels.

At the top of the escalators, he found a bank of chairs. He began reading the *Times*, waiting.

| | | |

Rei reached the Immigrations desk a few minutes after Will. From the eyes of the Immigration officer, he sensed that something was wrong.

"Your passport, please," she said.

He handed her the blue and gold U.S. citizen passport.

"Mr. Nagota of San Francisco?"

"Yes." His English was perfect.

"Do you have anything to declare?" she said.

"No, not this time."

"Why did you return to Los Angeles if you're from San Francisco?"

"It was a more convenient flight."

"I thought KAL had several flights to San Francisco that left the same time as this one."

"I wasn't aware of that." Rei, nervous, twisted the ring around on his finger. Another Immigration officer arrived, this one with the body of a football linebacker, his hand on a holstered Glock 40-mm pistol.

"Mr. Nagota, I must ask you to accompany this officer. It's nothing unusual. We're just required to make random inquiries with occasional U.S. citizens."

"No problem," said Rei.

"Follow me, sir." The larger officer walked ahead, slightly to Rei's side, and kept his weapon holstered but available. They passed Baggage Claim on their way to an office marked "IMMIGRATION." Rei walked in silence, smiling. As he passed a pile of bags on a cart, Rei deliberately caught his foot and stumbled to the ground.

"Get up now, sir." The officer didn't fall for it. He kept his distance as Rei stood up and brushed off his clothes.

"I'm sorry," said Rei.

"No problem. Let's go."

Rei turned his back to the officer, but then swung around, catching the man's hand with the ring's point.

"Damn it," said the officer. As he reached for his pistol, his body seized in a spasm, and he fell to his knees.

Rei backed away. "Help! This man is sick!" he screamed.

The crowd, along with several other officers, turned toward the fallen man. Rei backed out, turned, and headed up a hallway to the escalator. He tried not to show the smile on his face, intentionally staring downward as he hid his ring hand in his jacket pocket. With his other hand, he held onto the escalator rail. He glanced about quickly, smiling at another man descending.

What a silly jacket, Rei thought, observing the man's blue and white jacket and matching hat.

Will turned his left shoulder toward the man riding up, then braced his left foot on the lower step, his right foot above.

The swing of his fist, reinforced by the roll of nickels, caught Rei squarely on the nose and crushed his nasal and cheek bones. Lifted off his feet by the force of impact, Rei fell down the stairs in a heap. The blood from the subdural hematoma pooled almost immediately beneath his skull, pressuring the sensitive brain. He looked like a Raggedy Andy doll as he landed at the base of the escalator, one leg bent behind the other.

Will couldn't tell whether Rei was conscious when he stepped over his body and rode the escalator back up. He didn't expect it to matter.

I I I

Airport security found their suspect near death, bleeding profusely from his nose and left ear.

Meanwhile, Tom Pope thought he and his team would arrive early enough to catch Rei—until they learned KAL Flight 17 had arrived nearly an hour ahead of schedule.

Rei had already been transported to the

UCLA Hospital Head Trauma Unit, where he was diagnosed with a massive brain injury. With tubes inserted into his throat, he lived for only two more weeks. Neither the FBI nor the LAPD identified any suspects in his death. Tom Pople couldn't ask any questions of, or get any answers from, the dying man. From the beginning, he had been comatose; then he was dead. All Tom knew was that his search for the killer was over.

"Admiral."

Krowl, working in his Pentagon office, looked out over the leafless trees standing between him and the Potomac River. It was another frigid day during another cold Washington winter. Frost outlined the edges of the glass panes.

"Yes?" Krowl watched two bundled-up joggers fighting the wind as they made their way down the popular bike path. Clouds of breath appeared in the cold. Krowl, feeling his protruding stomach, had given up running a long time ago.

"Mr. Feldman of Justice is here," said Krowl's secretary.

Krowl considered the appointment a major inconvenience. Some low-level assistant attorney general had called about a matter well below his paygrade.

"Tell Commander Sawyer to join us," said Krowl.

Whatever Justice wanted, Sawyer could handle it. It was probably nothing more than gathering environmental data for some JCS exercise. *We probably killed too many birds somewhere.* Gunnery ranges always had neighbors that complained.

A man entered the room. "Admiral, I'm Isa Feldman." Little gray hairs accented the sides of Feldman's face, which was dominated by a bold nose. A sweater and an old herringbone blazer covered his white shirt and tie. A tobacco-shop smell permeated his clothes.

"Mr. Feldman, this is my aide, Commander Sawyer," said Krowl as Sawyer entered.

"Hey, Commander. Never spent time in the military, but I appreciate all you guys," Feldman said in a thick New York accent. He had a broad smile of yellow-stained teeth. He looked little like the toughest and brightest litigator in the Justice Department's civil division.

"What brings you to this side of the river, Mr. Feldman?" Krowl rocked back in his chair as he directed Feldman to take a seat.

"Well, it's just bizarre."

"Yes?"

"You see, we got this claim against the government filed down in Georgia," said Feldman. "It's in the U.S. Court of Claims under the RFJ program."

Krowl continued to rock in his chair, showing little more than casual interest in the conversation. Sawyer had brought his notepad, foreseeing some data-gathering task one of the young lieutenants could handle.

"Should this go through DOD's legal office?" said Krowl.

"Oh, Admiral, normally it would. And I've already talked to Jim Sizemore about this. That's not the problem."

"Okay." Krowl kept rocking.

"It's that the allegation by this Matthews

guy—he's the attorney for the plaintiff—mentions you by name."

"Oh, really?"

"Yeah, yeah. Some nut, I'm guessing."

"So why is this my concern?" asked Krowl.

"Well, the allegation is that you acted as an agent for the old U.S. of A. in making a contract with a man," said Feldman. "He says you told him a guy was on the RFJ list, and that if he photographed this guy, he would qualify for the reward."

"That's not likely."

"Oh, I thought not."

Krowl continued to rock, but now at a somewhat faster speed.

"Anyway," said Feldman, "we prepared a Motion for Summary Judgment, and the old judge down there set it in for a hearing next week."

"Great. Anything else? I do have a busy schedule." Krowl's tone clearly changed.

"Well, yes, sir. I think we might need you at that hearing, and Jim Sizemore agrees."

"Is that really necessary? The Joint Chief

of Staff's office doesn't have time for frivolous local lawsuits."

"Well, normally we could do this by affidavit, but the attorney on the other side has already requested that you be there," said Feldman. "I'm thinking we can nip this all in the bud by going down there this once, proving there's nothing to it, and shutting the whole thing down right away."

"Come on, Feldman. I really don't—"

"Well," the lawyer interrupted. "Here's the thing. If you don't appear voluntarily, they have a subpoena for you."

Krowl stopped rocking and leaned forward. "What a waste of time."

"Admiral, we agree. In fact, we're going to ask this judge to sanction the plaintiff and his attorney for bringing this frivolous action."

"What's that mean?"

"The plaintiff and his lawyer will have to pay money out of their own pockets."

"Good," said Krowl.

"But I do need you and the other witness in Albany, Georgia, next Wednesday."

"The *other* witness?"

"Yes, sir, someone with the Central Intelligence Agency named James Scott," said Feldman.

"Scott?"

"Yes, sir. Had to bring him back from overseas. Apparently, he was recently reassigned out of the U.S."

Krowl paused. "One second here. Who's the son-of-a-bitch who filed this suit?"

"The plaintiff is a W. N. Parker."

49

"All rise."

The deputy of the United States Court of Claims looked sternly over the courtroom as Judge Richard O'Mara took his seat.

"We have a motion in the case of *W. N. Parker versus the United States of America.* Madam Clerk, please call the case for motion."

"Yes, sir, *W. N. Parker versus the United States of America*, a case for breach of contract," said the clerk. "Mr. Matthews for the plaintiff and Mr. Feldman for Justice."

"I'm Gary Matthews, Your Honor," said Matthews.

"And I'm Isa Feldman."

"It's my understanding," said the judge, "that Justice has a Motion for Summary Judgment."

"And," added Feldman, "an assessment of costs and fees for this baseless and frivolous claim. I also have with me Admiral Julius Krowl of the staff of the JCS and Mr. James Scott of the CIA."

Krowl was decked out in full military honors, with a chest full of medals and gold leaf on the sleeves of his Navy blue jacket. With his gold-rimmed glasses and cocky air, Krowl contrasted sharply with the unassuming Feldman, and also with James Scott, dressed in a dark, conservative pin-striped suit and striped burgundy tie. Scott had a pad and pencil and doodled nervously on the pad's edges, looking distinctly out of place and uncomfortable in the courtroom environment.

"Aren't they potential witnesses?" the judge asked of Krowl and Scott.

"Yes, sir, they are," said Feldman.

"Mr. Matthews, do you want to invoke sequestration?"

"No, Your Honor." Sequestration required witnesses to wait outside the courtroom so as not to hear another witness' testimony and potentially change theirs. It was highly unusual for Gary Matthews not to take advantage of the rule. "I think it may be to everyone's benefit for them to hear the testimony."

"And where is the plaintiff, Mr. Parker?" asked Feldman.

"If need be, I'm sure he'll be here," said Matthews.

"Are you sure you *have* a plaintiff?" Feldman asked.

"Why would you believe otherwise?"

"Your Honor, we believe this to be an action filed by an unstable man, previously in the military, but who, according to Admiral Krowl, was last known to be outside the United States and probably dead." Feldman was barely taller than the mahogany podium that separated the plaintiff's table from the defense table.

Gary Matthews sat alone with a single blue manila folder before him. With his gray-vested suit, salt and pepper hair, dark blue tie, and starched white shirt, he radiated confidence and professionalism. "Judge," he said, "this is a summary judgment motion in which the defense is requesting that the Court dismiss this claim. They have the burden to prove it's baseless and you're required to believe every word of our allegations."

Matthews was correct and O'Mara knew it. The judge also knew Matthews' reputation— he did not bring frivolous lawsuits. "I'll hear the motion, but the plaintiff will need to be available for any further matters on the lawsuit," said O'Mara.

Isa Feldman didn't expect any more from the judge at this point. He was simply establishing the groundwork.

"Mr. Feldman, it's your motion," said O'Mara.

"Yes, Your Honor. In brief, the United States Government never entered into a contract with Mr. Parker to do anything. Admiral Krowl, one of our military's most distinguished leaders, did meet with Mr. Parker, very briefly, in Vienna, Georgia, not long ago to ask him some questions regarding a matter of national security. Mr. Scott attended that meeting. No promises were made," said Feldman. "Now Mr. Parker has brought this preposterous claim that he was assigned to locate a man on the RFJ list. He wasn't, and the list did not even include the man in question. Admiral Krowl will testify under oath that a matter of national security was discussed, but no more, and Mr. Scott will corroborate that testimony. And without Parker, their testimony will go unchallenged. Even with Parker's testimony, theirs will be more credible."

"Mr. Matthews," said O'Mara.

"Judge, Admiral Krowl sought out my client, then represented to him that a reward existed to locate this certain person of interest," said Matthews. "My client agreed. An offer was made and accepted, consideration exchanged, and terms performed—that's the precise definition of a contract."

"Very well. Mr. Feldman, who would you like to call?"

"Only one witness at this time—Admiral Julius Krowl."

Krowl stood up straight and swaggered to the witness stand. The courtroom was empty, except for those in front of the bar—Matthews at one table, and Scott and Feldman at the other. A court reporter sat below the witness stand and a U.S. marshal sat across from her on the other side of the judge, who peered down from his mahogany bench. The gold seal of the United States of America hung directly above the judge, and above the seal, in large gold letters, were the Latin words "Lex et Justitia"—Law and Justice.

"Admiral, do you swear to tell the truth, the whole truth, and nothing but the truth, so help you God?" said the marshal.

"Yes," said Krowl.

"Please tell the Court your name," said Feldman.

"Julius Krowl."

"Your occupation for the record."

"I'm a rear admiral in the U.S. Navy, and I serve on the staff of the chairman of the Joint

Chiefs of Staff as the J-3A." Krowl had leaned into the microphone, and his voice thundered through the courtroom.

"Admiral, you can lean back a little," said O'Mara. "Go on, Mr. Feldman."

"Admiral," said Feldman, "do you know a W. N. Parker?"

"Very casually," said Krowl.

"Did you meet with him?"

"Yes."

"Why?"

"We believed he had a friend from the past currently involved with a belligerent government." Krowl smiled as he spoke those words, liking the way they sounded. It made Will Parker appear sinister.

"Did you enter into a contract with Mr. Parker to do anything?"

"Absolutely not."

"Offer him a 'proposal,' as is alleged in this complaint?"

"Never."

Scott stared at Krowl's mouth as he spoke each word. Krowl, avoiding Scott's eyes, looked instead at the judge, then Feldman, then Matthews.

"Did you offer him any monies?" said Feldman.

"No."

"Did you commit the United States government to pay him some twenty-five million dollars?"

"Never," said Krowl.

"You've read the complaint. Is there a word of truth in any of its allegations?"

"No."

"Thank you. He's your witness."

Matthews rose from his seat. "Admiral, I'm Gary Matthews."

"I know who you are."

"You are the J-3A of the Joint Chiefs of Staff?"

"Yes."

"In that position," said Matthews, "surely you have the authority to commit the Department of Defense and the United States government."

"Yes, I do," said Krowl.

"Judge," said Feldman, incensed by the cross-examination, "we will stipulate that the admiral had authority to act as an agent, but that's moot because there was no contract."

O'Mara leaned forward on the bench. "Admiral, the plaintiff's complaint refers to a mission in the DPRK. This would be North Korea?"

"Yes, Judge, and we'll be asking the FBI to investigate this further," said Krowl. "We know Parker did indeed travel to North Korea, but not on our orders. Of course, such travel would be illegal."

"Anything else from this witness?" said O'Mara.

"No, Judge," said Matthews.

"Anything else, Mr. Feldman?"

"No, Your Honor, except possibly the cross of Mr. Parker, should he appear."

"Mr. Matthews, this sounds convincing," said O'Mara. "Do you have any testimony?"

Gary Matthews glanced down at his folder, apparently preoccupied. Krowl came down from the witness stand, his lips curved in a grin.

"Mr. Matthews?" said O'Mara.

"Yes, sir."

"Anything else?"

"Well, yes, I do have a witness," said Matthews. "A Miss Clark Ashby."

Scott and Krowl looked at one other, equally perplexed. Feldman bent over to the admiral. "Who is she?" Feldman asked.

"No idea," the admiral said.

A shapely redhead entered the courtroom, dressed in a black business suit with a high-collared white blouse.

"Please state your name," said the marshal.

"Clark Ashby." She sat down in the witness chair, placing a leather briefcase to the side.

"Ms. Ashby, do you swear to tell the truth, the whole truth, and nothing but the truth, so help you God?" said the marshal.

"I do."

Scott, covering his mouth, leaned over to Krowl. "Who is this woman?" he asked.

"*I* don't know." Krowl didn't appear shaken. "But she can't know anything."

"Please state your occupation," said Matthews.

"Court reporter as certified by the State of Georgia and the United States government."

"Did you have occasion to be in the Vienna Courthouse in October when Admiral Krowl and Mr. Scott visited?" said Matthews.

"Yes, but I didn't know their names then," said Clark.

"These two men here?"

"Yes, those are the two."

"Did you see them leave the courtroom with Mr. William Parker?"

"Oh yes, they left with him at the break in a trial we had."

"Did you stay in that courtroom?"

"Yes." As she spoke, Clark absentmindedly opened her briefcase. She pulled from it a small, square black object.

"Oh, God," said Scott, collapsing back into his chair.

"Scott, cool it." Krowl grabbed him by the arm.

"Feldman, stop this now," said Scott.

"What?" Isa Feldman looked bewildered.

"This is a matter of national security. Stop it now!"

"Your Honor, may we have a short break?" Feldman said, standing up, flummoxed by Scott's outburst.

"Why now, Mr. Feldman?" the judge asked.

Feldman, confused, replied, "I'm told this may be a matter of national security."

"Okay, ten minutes." The judge, the court reporter, and the marshal left the courtroom, leaving only Clark, Matthews, and the Defense.

"It's all over," Scott told Krowl.

"Oh, control yourself."

"Do you remember the trial down there?"

"Yes."

"And our meeting in his office?" Scott, standing now, leaned directly into the admiral's face. "He bloody well recorded it."

The courtroom fell silent as Krowl let the thought sink in. He recalled the recording device that Parker had used so dramatically in the drug trial. It made sense that, during their meeting with Parker, he'd had the recorder on.

"Oh, God," said Krowl, turning an ashen white.

"She heard everything," said Scott. It sounded like a statement, but in fact, Scott was looking for confirmation or denial from Matthews and Clark.

"Everything," said Matthews in a quiet, assured voice, "and it was all recorded as well."

"Mr. Matthews, we need to talk to Parker," said Scott.

"Why?"

"To stop this."

"Let's go into the jury room."

Scott led the way into a side room with a long government-style metal table surrounded by gray steel chairs. A few old, torn magazines were piled up at one end. At the other, out several windows, the roof of a red brick building, where pigeons roosted on the ledges, was visible. Krowl and Feldman, but not Matthews, followed him in.

Krowl sat down, his glasses in one hand, his other hand covering his face. He was an ugly man, only much uglier now, broken by his own ruthlessness.

Feldman took the seat across from Krowl. "What's going on?"

"Parker's complaint is all true," said Scott, still standing. "I'm calling the Agency, and the director will have the money wired to Parker now."

As Scott spoke, Matthews stepped through the door, followed by Will Parker.

"Colonel." Scott had the look of a guilty man who'd witnessed too much and let things go too far. "Tell us what you want."

Will took a seat directly across from Julius Krowl.

"I want Krowl retired today."

"Done." Scott now dominated his side's conversation.

"As an O-4." A reduction stripped Krowl

of all honors of flag rank. It was the lowest officer rank for eligible retirement. For an Academy man known as a fast-moving flag officer, it would mean utter humiliation.

"No," Krowl protested.

"If not," Scott said to Krowl, "you're probably looking at charges of attempted murder, conspiracy to commit murder, misuse of government equipment, fraud, and perjury—probably good for several life sentences served in Leavenworth." Then Scott turned back to Will. "What else do you want?" asked Scott.

"That's it."

"Okay," said Scott, moving away from Krowl. "Here are my terms. We'll wire you the money within the next hour. This claim is dismissed with prejudice, then sealed forever. And you give me every copy of that tape."

"Done," said Will. Matthews nodded.

As Krowl remained slumped in the chair, his hands covering his face, Scott followed Will out of the courtroom, catching up to him on the stairs. "Colonel?" he said.

Will looked at Scott from the landing just below. "I thought I told you not to call me that."

"Why did you really do it? Take the mission?"

"Did you do your research, Mr. Scott?"

"I don't know. What do you mean?"

"Did you know the flight that William and Debra Parker were on?"

Scott recognized the names of Parker's parents. "One coming back from Europe."

"Yeah," said Will. "Pan Am Flight 103."

Scott's eyes widened. Will Parker had been one of America's first victims of terrorism.

"This war has been going on for a long time, Mr. Scott. For me, it's been personal."

Scott nodded. "And many believe North Korea provided the bomb that took down that jet."

As Will Parker walked away, Scott called out again, "Mr. Parker?" Will turned. "How did you know to record it?"

Will smiled tightly, turned away, and walked down the stairs to the waiting Clark Ashby.

| | | EPILOGUE | | |

The Central Intelligence Agency reported a firing of a multi-stage Taepo Dong-3X or Unhar 3 missile from the newly-discovered complex near the DMZ. The launch occurred shortly after the reported death of one of North Korea's leading scientists, Doctor Peter Nampo. The missile failed to reach a geo-synchronized orbit of the earth, likely, according to the world's scientists, because the payload's weight unduly affected the rocket's trajectory. The rocket disappeared from radar and was presumed destroyed upon re-entry.

In the weeks following the failed launch, Chinese sources reported an upheaval in the government of Pyongyang. Besides the death of Jang, a vice prime minister, several generals were absent from prominent activities, including the annual parade in honor of Kim Jong-un. Deeper intelligence sources revealed the homes of these leaders in the secret inner city of Pyongyang had been vacated and their children missing from school. No other intelligence reports reflected the military leaders' whereabouts.

Meanwhile, Kim Jong-un promised the world that he would arm a multi-stage missle with a miniaturized two-stage H-bomb by 2020. The bomb would be able to reach Los Angeles. Famine still had a grip on the country, and more than one-fourth of its children suffered from severe malnutrition. Despite these concerns, North Korea had not complied with requests to acknowledge the existence of secret underground research facilities near Kosan and in three other locations. North Korea remained committed to the development of a multistage intercontinental missile, despite Western overtures aimed at prompting a dialogue with North Korea.

In the country of Somalia, a U.S. Delta Force attacked a suspected terrorist camp, finding a mobile rocket launcher equipped with an intercontinental missile. It bore no markings. The payload was missing, as were many of the terrorists believed to be connected with the remote desert site. The nature and extent of the planned operation remains a secret.

On December 21, 2011, at oh-eight-hundred five, the United States launched its third series GPS IIR-10 satellite, Number SUN47. The satellite became the latest of twenty-nine making up a worldwide GPS system, on which both the military and corporate America increasingly rely.

The Trident submarine U.S.S. *Florida* returned to its homeport in Bangor, Washington, several weeks after an incident off the coast of North Korea. Its mainsail showed some slight damage attributed to a brush with an ASDS during a training mission. The repair in dock took only a few days. The world paid little attention.

A stranger in civilian clothing was seen at Pier 10A greeting the crew and a Marine team onboard.

ABOUT THE AUTHOR

Anderson Harp served 30 years in the U.S. Marine Corps, rising through the ranks to become a Colonel. He headed the instructor group that prepared Marines for operations in high altitude, mountainous and Arctic environments and trained in the Arctic Circle. He has served as the Officer in Charge of Crisis Action Team for Marine Forces Central Command. His decorations include the Defense Meritorious Service Medal, Meritorious Service Medal and Navy Commendation Medal. As an officer in the Marine Corps Reserve, he was mobilized for Operation Enduring Freedom and served with MarCent's Crisis Action Team. Anderson Harp lives with his family in Columbus, Georgia.

ACKNOWLEDGMENTS

A continued thank you to those that have helped make Will Parker real and interesting.

To the late Bill Steber, always a Marine, and other supportive Marines to include Bob Harriss, Tom Ragsdale, Joe Sawyer, Bill Todd, Bill Buckley, Pat Rogers, Ken Icenhour and Senator Seth Harp I wanted to say a thank you.

I greatly appreciate the input, advice and counsel of the many members of the Marine Corps Reserve Association formerly known as the Marine Corps Officers Reserve Association.

Likewise, to the late Dale Oliver and Gary Christy, I appreciated their encouragement and advice.

To Lee and Bonnie Green, and their good counsel and friend, Jeff Casurella, I appreciate the reminder that good citizens rise to the call of duty and particularly appreciate their steadfast loyalty when I was called to duty for the invasion of Afghanistan.

Also, to the author Andrew Peterson, who has been counsel on writing and the faculty and fellow students of the MFA program at Queens University of Charlotte.

And thank you to the reader, whose interest has given great support to the writing of Will Parker stories. Your emails and comments are read and appreciated.